P9-DHO-972

Place at the Table
508851 EN Fiction
Faruqi, Saadia
4.4
10

A Place at the Table

A Place at the Table

Saadia Faruqi
& Laura Shovan

CLARION BOOKS
Houghton Mifflin Harcourt
Boston New York

Clarion Books
3 Park Avenue, New York, New York 10016

Copyright © 2020 by Saadia Faruqi & Laura Shovan

All rights reserved. For information about permission to reproduce
selections from this book, write to trade.permissions@hmhco.com or
to Permissions, Houghton Mifflin Harcourt Publishing Company,
3 Park Avenue, 19th Floor, New York, New York 10016.

Clarion Books is an imprint of
Houghton Mifflin Harcourt Publishing Company.

hmhbooks.com

The text was set in Adobe Garamond Pro.
Art by Anoosha Syed
Chapter ornaments by Kaitlin Yang
Book design by Sharismar Rodriguez

Library of Congress Cataloging-in-Publication Data

Names: Faruqi, Saadia, author. | Shovan, Laura, author.
Title: A place at the table / Saadia Faruqi & Laura Shovan.
Description: New York : Clarion Books, [2020] | Audience: Ages 10 to 12. | Audience:
Grades 4–6. | Summary: Sixth-graders Sara, a Pakistani American, and Elizabeth,
a Jewish girl, connect in an after school cooking club and bond over food and
their mothers' struggles to become United States citizens.
Identifiers: LCCN 2019029395 (print) | LCCN 2019029396 (ebook) |
ISBN 9780358116684 (hardcover) | ISBN 9780358118923 (ebook)
Subjects: CYAC: Cooking—Fiction. | Muslims—United States—Fiction. |
Jews—United States—Fiction. | Pakistani Americans—Fiction. | British Americans—
Fiction. | Family life—Fiction. | Middle schools—Fiction. | Schools—Fiction.
Classification: LCC PZ7.1.F373 Pl 2020 (print) | LCC PZ7.1.F373 (ebook) |
DDC [Fic]—dc23
LC record available at https://lccn.loc.gov/2019029395
LC ebook record available at https://lccn.loc.gov/2019029396

Manufactured in the United States of America
DOC 10 9 8 7 6 5 4 3 2 1
4500793925

*For Nasir, who's the reason
I became an immigrant*

—S.F.

For my mother, Pauline

—L.S.

A Place at the Table

1

Sara

COOKING IS PAINFUL. Sitting at the back of an afterschool cooking club I didn't sign up for is even worse. And listening to a bunch of whiny white kids complain about the cooking club is actually excruciating.

Especially because my mom is the teacher.

I look at the clock on the wall. Three thirty p.m. This is going to be a long afternoon.

"Now, class, please settle down and join me at the table," Mama calls politely, her hijab slightly askew, sweat shining on her forehead.

I cringe. I can't help it. Her Pakistani accent is thick, even though she's lived in the United States for almost three decades.

The kids in Mama's class giggle and look at their phones, their bored fingers swiping the screens. They're a small group, twelve middle-schoolers. There are only two boys, even though the flyer Mama spent so much time on specifically said everyone was welcome. A few are veterans, seventh- and eighth-graders who did cooking club with the original teacher,

Chef Elaine. From the way they keep throwing suspicious looks at Mama, it's clear they don't think anyone can replace their teacher, especially not some foreign lady in a hijab.

I stifle a sigh. Everyone stands in pairs in Poplar Springs Middle School's kitchen classroom, where I'll be taking FACS —Family and Consumer Science—later this year. I hang back from the group, near the giant metal appliances. There's an open kitchen with neatly stacked pots and pans where the FACS teacher, Mrs. Kluckowski, does demonstrations. But there are also six cooking stations for kids, each with its own stovetop, oven, and sink. A metal island on wheels stands in the middle of the room. Mama waves and points, finally convincing everyone to gather around. Supplies for the club's first recipe are piled on the island: a brown bag labeled ZEBRA BASMATI RICE, a bucket full of onions and potatoes, a bunch of wilting cilantro, and a few bright tomatoes.

Thank God I'm not part of this stupid club, I think as I stretch out my legs on the floor and lean against the wall. It's an inconspicuous spot at the back of the kitchen, near the metal refrigerator. I make a small pile of my things on the floor: backpack, sketchbook, a can of still-cold Coke. It's not as if I'm trying to disappear, but I won't exactly be upset if these junior chefs don't notice me. Like that would ever happen.

Poplar Springs is a small suburb in central Maryland, halfway between Baltimore and Washington, D.C. Some residents can trace their families back generations; others are transient, moving every time they get a new job. There are a handful of

2

brown people. Most of the Muslim kids go to an Islamic school called Iqra Academy, thirty minutes away. Not all, though; there are two eighth-grade girls I know from the mosque. I sometimes see them laughing in the hallways, but they just nod at me. There's also Ahsan Kapadia in sixth grade, but we don't share any classes. Like me, he's quiet and keeps to himself. Like me, he was at Iqra until middle school.

I sigh again as I think about my school. At least, it *was* my school until this fall. My best friend, Rabia, who I've known since preschool, doesn't understand why I left. To be honest, neither do I. It was one of those decisions eleven-year-old girls don't get to make on their own.

Like which afterschool clubs to be present at, apparently.

I've already gotten narrow-eyed looks from the other kids. I think a couple of them are sixth-graders too, new to Poplar Springs Middle, like me. I feel their questions hanging in the air like heavy steam. I bet they're dying to ask who I am, if the lady in the headscarf is my mom or my aunt. As if all Muslims know each other.

Then there's Mrs. Kluckowski, short and barrel-chested, wearing a brown blouse and a plaid skirt that reaches almost down to her puffy ankles. Frizzy hair frames her frowning face. She stands near me at the back of the room, writing in a small notebook. Finally, she gives Mama a stern look and walks away.

No worries. I'm a master at ignoring people. You have to be when your parents get dirty looks at the mall and somebody shouts, "Go back home!" a couple of times a year. You definitely have to be when not even one of your close friends from elementary school is in this new, very large middle school. I think of Baba's favorite quote from that eighties show he loves, *The A-Team:* "Pity the fools." And if that doesn't work, ignore them.

Unfortunately, ignoring is difficult right now. "Class, let's get started," Mama practically shouts. Her accent is more pronounced, with the *T*'s and *R*'s harder, so I can tell she's getting annoyed. She holds up a wooden spatula. "Can anyone tell me the correct name for this utensil?"

"What's she saying?" A tiny girl with freckles and a thin, dark ponytail whispers so loud that everyone starts giggling again.

I feel a frown digging into my forehead. These girls really are the height of disrespect. If Rabia were here, she'd walk right up to them, hands on hips, long braid swishing like a whip from under her hijab, and tell them to knock it off. I feel a little sorry for Mama. She's chewing her lip, ruining that pink lipstick she put on at the last minute. She looks as if she's about to drop the spatula and run away.

I'm not about to rescue her. Mama literally dragged me to this detestable cooking club because she thinks I'm not old enough to stay home alone.

"I'm in sixth grade, Mama," I'd protested. "I'm old enough to stay alone for an hour without burning the house down."

To be honest, I'd wanted to shout at her, but thought better of it. It would've been rude, and Pakistani parents like mine don't care much for their kids' impolite American ways.

4

"We never talked back to our parents, not even once!" Baba likes to say in his proudest voice.

I don't think that's anything to brag about, but clearly he does, so I always try to be respectful. Yet how have I been rewarded? Here I am, sitting on the graying floor of this freezing metal kitchen, listening to a bunch of complaints from girls who don't know how to boil an egg.

Okay, I'm guessing about the egg-boiling part. I don't care how many classes they took with Chef Elaine—most of them don't look like junior chefs, with their polished nails and confused faces as Mama tries to explain the different types of utensils. Mama told me last week that the old teacher left suddenly and took the binder of club recipes with her. When Mama took over, she had to come up with lessons from scratch.

"Spatula!" Mama says grimly. "It's a spatula!"

"We know," one girl scoffs. She's wearing a tight white T-shirt with a smiling cupcake emoji on it and the words SWEET STEPHANIE's in sparkly silver font. I recognize her. She has her own cupcake business. I've seen her in the cafeteria, handing out samples when the teachers aren't looking. She probably knows how to make eggs ten different ways. If anyone in this awful class has an ounce of cooking experience, it's her.

She's never offered me a sample. Good thing I don't like cupcakes.

I grit my teeth and look away from Stephanie's superior smile, away from Mama's flustered face. At least I've got my

5

drawings. Thank you, past me, for packing my sketchbook and pencils at the last minute.

I insert my earphones and press PLAY on my iPod. Selena Gomez always puts me in a good mood. I pull a red pencil from my case. The garden I'm drawing has only one red rose, right in the center, and I want it to be perfect.

I hear Mama over Selena Gomez's melodious voice. "The first thing I'll be teaching you to cook is rice with potatoes. In my language, we call it *tahari*. It's very simple and quick."

"Tahari? I thought he was a fashion designer," Stephanie blurts out.

More laughter.

"I hope it's plain rice," the freckled girl with the too-loud whisper says. "Like, not spicy?"

Mama tries to smile, but it's causing her quite a bit of effort. "It won't be too spicy, but you did sign up for a South Asian cuisine class," she says, very sweetly.

"I can't eat spicy food. It makes me . . ." The girl sticks out her tongue, panting like a dog. Stephanie laughs. Is this a cooking class or a comedy club?

Time for some intervention.

I lean forward and stare the loud girl down until her eyelids flicker. Then I notice the girl next to her elbowing her in the side. She's in sixth grade too. I recognize her from language arts class. Elizabeth something.

She has wavy brown hair with bangs so long, they threaten

6

to cover her glasses. Elizabeth and her friend are a total mismatch. For one, the loud girl is way shorter than Elizabeth. Her name-brand jeans and fleece are the preferred uniform of Poplar Springs students, and if she weren't so outspoken, she'd blend in with everyone else. I have to admit, I prefer Elizabeth's style. She wears brown corduroys and a Harry Potter T-shirt. It's black, with gold letters that read WHEN IN DOUBT, GO TO THE LIBRARY. — HERMIONE GRANGER. She must be a little bit brave to wear something so book-nerdy.

Mama sighs very obviously, her cheeks puffing. "The good thing about spice is that you can adjust it to your taste," she says, patting her hijab in a gesture I recognize as nervousness. "Now, first thing is to soak the rice in water. Does anybody know why we do that?"

I can answer that. I've been watching Mama cook since I was tall enough to stand by myself in the kitchen. I knew the names of all the spices on Mama's spice rack before I could read: salt, paprika, turmeric, cumin, coriander, mint. The list is as long as it is colorful.

When I was old enough to go to kindergarten, Mama had time to open her own catering business. Suddenly our kitchen went from one pot on the stove to three or sometimes four huge cauldrons of steaming food cooking all hours of the day. Biryani and chicken korma on the stove. Samosas in the fryer. Dahi bara in the fridge. It's like living in a restaurant, only I never get to leave. That's why I hate cooking. I have to scrub my hair for hours to get the smell of the spices out.

Mama is still looking around expectantly. The students all gaze back in silence, a few of them frowning as if she, their teacher, has no right to ask questions. Really, does nobody know why rice must be soaked before cooking?

I jab the PAUSE button on my iPod. Time to speak up, if only to save Mama some face. "If we soak the rice, it becomes softer and cooks faster," I call out loudly.

They all turn to look at me, mouths open—especially Stephanie, who thinks tahari rice is a fashion trend, and the loud one with the dark hair.

"Who is that?" the girl says to Elizabeth. I stare right back.

"Shhh, Maddy! Listen," Elizabeth whispers.

Mama raps a hand on the metal island to get everyone's attention. The clang from her wedding ring makes a few of them jump.

"Thank you, Sara," Mama says. "Everyone, this is my daughter, Sara. She will be spending our club time doing her homework. Quietly."

I nod and try to cover my sketchbook with my arms. Great. Now everyone knows my mother dragged me along, and that I was doing everything but homework.

Mama throws me a *Sorry* look and continues. "Let's measure two cups of rice in this bowl."

8

As the kids gather around my mother, I start up my music again. Before I can look down at my drawing, I notice Elizabeth watching me. Not in a mean way. More like she's curious. I hate people staring at me as if I've got a horn growing out of my forehead. I have to resist the urge to cross my eyes or make a face at her. It's not like we've ever officially met, even though we share Ms. Saintima's language arts class. Sometimes I see her in the halls, but Poplar Springs is so different from Iqra Academy, like a big, noisy circus where all the performers know each other except me. I don't talk to anyone most days. I keep my head down and rush from one class to another.

I suddenly miss Rabia like a craving for that mint chutney Mama used to make when I was little. I haven't seen her since school started.

I notice that the edge of my tunic sleeve is wrinkled, and I smooth it carefully. My eyes shift down to my drawing. The garden seems ugly now. Whose idea was it to draw a single rose in the center of all these white lilies?

Oh, yeah. Mine.

I feel someone's gaze on me. I sneak a peek, looking up at the kids gathered around the cooking island. Elizabeth again. She raises her right hand to her glasses, and I notice she's wearing bracelets, her only jewelry. One has a Star of David charm. It glints in the fluorescent kitchen lights like it wants to be noticed. When she sees me looking back at her, she smiles a little.

Ugh. The last thing I want to be is friendly right now, stuck in this hot kitchen with a bunch of rude kids making Mama nervous. I glare at Elizabeth until her smile slips and she looks away.

Good. Message sent and received.

2

Elizabeth

IF YOU BELIEVE in stereotypes, British cooks fall into two categories. Terrible ones who boil everything until it's as gray and soggy as English weather, and the ones who bake perfectly iced cakes and adorable meat-filled pastries for BBC cooking shows.

My mother is British, but she probably thinks a Victoria sponge is a cleaning product, not an airy cake filled with jam. Mom is a great believer in instant mashed potatoes, frozen dinners, and Hot Pockets. She does cook when Dad is home, but canned tuna, frozen peas, and mayonnaise tossed over noodles is not my idea of delicious.

When Poplar Springs Middle announced that an afterschool cooking club was starting, I signed up immediately. Mom doesn't like cooking? Fine. I'll do it. All I need is someone to teach me. My brothers still tease me about the Stilton scrambled eggs I made, and that was weeks ago. How was I supposed to know Stilton is England's stinkiest cheese?

When it's finally the first day of cooking club, I bounce into the FACS room with my best friend, Maddy Montgomery.

Maddy leads me to the station next to Stephanie Tolleson. She tosses her ponytail and says, "This is going to be amazing. I get to be with my new best friend"—she waves at Stephanie—"and my old best friend. That's you, Elizabeth." Maddy nudges me and smiles.

Great.

When I first told Maddy there was a South Asian cooking club, she crinkled her freckled nose and said, "No. Thank. You." Maddy is not an adventurous eater. Then she found out Stephanie was in the club and it was all, "I cannot *wait* to be in the kitchen with you and Steph. Since she has her own business, Steph wants to learn as much about cooking as possible."

Puh-leeze. Maddy's only known Stephanie since this summer. When I was at sleepaway camp, which I am never doing again, they met at the Club, where Maddy does swim team.

I'm not so sure about this "new best friend, old best friend" deal. One best friend should be enough for a person. It's enough for me.

Maddy drifts over to the next kitchen station. She's gushing with Stephanie and some seventh-grade boy about all the fun they had on swim team this summer. Nobody tries to include me in the conversation, so I focus on what our teacher is saying. Something about potatoes. Mrs. Hameed walks over and puts a mound of them on our counter.

Maddy says, "See you later," to Stephanie, as if our station

12

is on the other side of town instead of two steps away. Ugh. This was supposed to be *our* thing, BFF time.

"I'll chop," Maddy offers.

"Large chunks," Mrs. Hameed instructs. "The pieces should be slightly bigger than the end of your thumb."

"Ew," Maddy says as Mrs. Hameed walks away. "Now I'm going to picture big hunks of thumb in our rice." She hacks at the potato I've just peeled.

I push my charm bracelets up my arms so they don't dangle as I peel. Then I sneak a glance at Mrs. Hameed. She's wearing a green headscarf decorated with white teardrops, and makeup that shows off her dark eyes. My mother doesn't do makeup, except for special occasions.

Some kids near our station start grumbling about making food with names they can't pronounce.

"Chef Elaine was so much better," Stephanie says in a low voice.

"What's wrong with mac and cheese, or chocolate chip cookies? American food," Maddy adds.

The red-haired boy from swim team grins and says, "Right?"

Mrs. Hameed ignores the chatter and goes on teaching without getting frazzled. When grouchy Mrs. Kluckowski comes in with her notepad, Mrs. Hameed nods politely and acts as if our FACS teacher is invisible.

I like her style. If she can ignore the complaining, so can I.

13

I'm not here to gossip. Yes, I want to spend time with Maddy. The only class we have together this semester is PE. But mainly, I'm here to learn. If I pay attention and work hard, maybe I can take over making dinner at home. I already know how to bake challah and some other breads, but my older brother says he needs meat to put meat on his bones. He is pretty skinny for a fifteen-year-old. Dad says David hasn't gotten his man-muscles yet. Gross.

What if I add chicken to this rice and potato dish? I can tell David and my younger brother, Justin, to think of it as a breadless Hot Pocket. They consider those things a miracle of culinary brilliance.

I'm so busy planning my own version of tahari rice that I don't notice Maddy's terrible knife skills. The potato is a mess of jagged bits on her cutting board. It's never going to cook evenly.

"Let's switch places," I suggest. "I'll chop; you peel."

Maddy shrugs. She catches sight of that girl in the corner, huddled over her sketchbook. "Who sits on the floor in the school kitchen?" Maddy snorts. "Her jeans are going to smell like onions and disinfectant."

The girl has long black hair clipped back with a silver barrette. She's wearing jeans and a blue-gray tunic with bell sleeves. I know her from language arts class. Ms. Saintima calls her *Sarah*, the American way, but her mom pronounced it "Sah-rah." I like the way her name makes a little rhyme. It's weird

14

that she's never corrected our teacher. Ms. Saintima would be cool with it. Plus, it's October. We've been in school for weeks.

Maddy catches me staring and nudges my arm. "You know her?"

"We have a class together, but she hardly ever talks."

Maddy snorts again. "I wouldn't talk either if I had an accent like that."

Was she even paying attention before? Probably not. She was too busy talking to Stephanie. "Mads," I say, "she sounds exactly like us." I don't know why I'm sticking up for Sarah. *Sara.* Whatever. I don't even know her.

"Her mom is, like, impossible to understand." Maddy makes sure Mrs. Hameed isn't nearby. "My brain has to work overtime when she talks."

"You'll get used to it," I say. Maybe having a mom with a foreign accent makes paying attention to Mrs. Hameed easier for me.

Mrs. Hameed calls us to a giant soup pot on the teacher's stove. The moment she tosses cumin seeds into the hot oil, I know this club is where I'm supposed to be. I breathe in, close my eyes, and inhale the warm, nutty aroma. When I open them again, Maddy is chitchatting with Stephanie. Loudly. I catch Sara scowling at them.

Most of the kids in sixth grade have friends from elementary school, but I don't think Sara does. She sits alone at lunch and hangs her head down in class, barely speaking, even to

15

teachers. Did she move here from far away? That might explain it, but it's no excuse for being unfriendly.

Mrs. Hameed reaches up to the wood-framed mirror hanging from the ceiling. She tilts it so we can see chilies, tomatoes, and onions glistening in the pot below. When she asks for a volunteer to stir, no one raises a hand. But all of those rich colors and flavors are calling to me. I step forward and take the wooden spoon.

Mrs. Hameed directs one of the eighth-graders to pour in the soaked rice with its water. "Carefully," she explains as I stir. "The rice is fragile."

Rice is fragile? No one ever told me that. At my house, rice boils in a plastic bag or gets heated in the microwave.

When Mrs. Hameed is pleased with the mixture, she puts the whole pot into the oven so it can finish cooking. "Time to set the tables," she calls.

I spot a package of napkins on the counter, but Sara's in my way. She's still on the floor, absorbed in her sketchbook.

"Excuse me," I say.

Nothing.

"I need to reach the napkins."

Typical. Sara must be the least friendly kid in our grade. I poke her shoulder. Hard.

As she looks up and scowls, her hair falls away from her face.

"Oh, you're wearing earphones," I stammer.

16

She glares at me, as if I've accused her of stealing. "Is class over?"

"No. The rice is in the oven."

Sara leans back and relaxes a little. I want to grab the napkins and rush back to Maddy, but my mouth keeps moving. It does that sometimes.

"I didn't know that was a thing. Cooking something on the stove and then sticking the entire pot in the oven."

Her eyes narrow as if to say, *Why are you still talking to me?* Finally, Sara mutters, "Good food takes time and patience."

I laugh without meaning to. "Tell that to my mom. Does your mother have a cooking club for grownups? Because I will sign my mom up so fast."

"One cooking class is more than enough." She shakes her head and returns to her sketchbook.

I'm trying to be nice, but if she's more interested in her artwork than in me, fine. I'm reaching for the napkins when Sara speaks again.

"All we do at my house is cook." Her voice is quiet. "My mom has a catering company."

"But you'd rather draw." I lean over to peek at her sketch.

Sara snaps her book closed, but not before I see a swirling garden created in black ink, one red flower in the center. It's beautiful. If I could draw like that, I'd study animation when I grow up. But my hands are big and clumsy. I'm better at kneading dough than drawing.

17

Sara slides her sketchbook into her backpack without saying another word.

Conversation over, I think. I head to the table, where Maddy is already sitting next to Stephanie.

Stephanie's all right, I guess. People like her because she's always sharing samples of the cupcakes she bakes. But she'd rather watch *America's Got Talent* than *Doctor Who.*

Maddy and I used to argue for hours about which actor was the best Doctor Who, a time-traveling do-gooder who clashes with monsters, saves Earth from aliens, and witnesses historical events like the destruction of Pompeii. How cool is that? Not cool enough for Maddy, now that she's friends with Stephanie Tolleson.

Maddy's complaints about Mrs. Hameed's accent and the spicy food are annoying, but I put up with her because she's my best friend. We've been together since third grade, when we both showed up for the school Halloween parade wearing the Eleventh Doctor's tweed jacket and red fez hat. I laugh to myself, picturing Sweet Stephanie in a fez and nerdy bow tie. That is so not her look.

When it's finally time to eat, everyone gets a ladleful of bright yellow rice and potatoes in a plastic bowl. I chew slowly, savoring the flavors. They're so delicious that the noise in the room fades away for a second. How can such simple ingredients make my tongue feel like it's dancing with warmth and smoke?

18

No one has taken the time to teach me about food before. Not even my grandmother. She taught me to make challah, but Bubbe says the kitchen in her New York apartment is too cramped for showing me more complicated recipes.

But tahari rice is easy. I bet I can make this at home. No Stilton cheese necessary.

I take another bite and shoot Maddy a huge grin. And that's when she spits her rice into a napkin. "My tongue is on fire," she tells everyone at the table.

Sara drops her plastic fork with a clatter. All eyes turn to the end of the table, where she's sitting by herself. She treats everyone to a lethal scowl.

This is why she has no friends.

I don't know what Sara's problem is, and I don't have time to care. I'm too worried about Maddy. Since we started middle school, sometimes she feels like a new person. Spitting out her rice was rude, but I know she's showing off for Stephanie. I ignore her and enjoy my food.

The door opens before we finish eating. A few parents wander into the room. Stephanie tries to hand some of them her brochure.

"I cater birthdays and bat mitzvahs," she says. Her smile matches the grinning emoji-faced cupcake on her Sweet Stephanie's T-shirt.

I walk over to Mrs. Hameed and tell her, "I can't wait to try this recipe at home!" I feel like I should curtsy or something, which is ridiculous. It's not like Mrs. Hameed is the Queen.

19

She's a regular mom who happens to be our cooking teacher. I blush, totally embarrassed that I even thought about curtsying to Mrs. Hameed.

I'm taking a printout of the recipe when Maddy's dad comes in. He's driving me home today. Mr. Montgomery doesn't like it when we make him wait. I rush to the door in time to hear him grumble to Maddy, "That Arab lady is your teacher?"

I know that Mrs. Hameed is not an Arab. This is a South Asian cooking club, after all. The Hameeds are from Pakistan, not the Middle East. But I'm not about to say that to Mr. Montgomery.

3

Sara

ON SATURDAY, I wake up to the smell of steaming-hot parathas and eggs, the way I've done every morning since I can remember. Mama and Baba are at the kitchen table, eating and watching a morning talk show. Some blond reporter with a toothy smile is praising the qualities of an L.L.Bean jacket versus the Sears brand.

I quietly say, *"Salaam,"* and get a bowl from the cabinet.

"Paratha khaa lo. I just cooked it," Mama tells me, her eyes glued to the television. She waves to the freshly cooked paratha in the foil.

So what else is new? I almost say, but it's too much effort to talk just yet. Who invented mornings, anyway? I fill my bowl with chocolate cereal and pour milk over it before anybody objects. "No, thanks," I say in English, and settle next to Baba, who's got a plateful of fried eggs sprinkled with pepper. "You can give my paratha to the twins."

Baba looks up from his plate, eyebrows threatening to touch his hairline. "Eggs are good for you, jaanoo," he tells me in Urdu. He's big and bulky, all wrapped up in a tattered jacket even though the central heating is on full blast.

"Er, no, actually, too many eggs could increase your cholesterol, Baba." Again, I reply in English. He grumbles under his breath. It's a game with us: the older generation speaking one language, the kids responding in another. But Mama and Baba always give up in the end.

He switches to English. "What are you talking about? See how strong and healthy I am?" Baba flexes his biceps.

"That's not muscle, Baba!" I groan. "That's fat. F-A-T!"

Mama scoffs. She has a not-so-secret habit of eavesdropping on other people's conversations.

She reprimands me, her tiny frame rigid with indignation. "Our parents used to eat paratha and eggs every day in the villages of Pakistan, and they lived to be ninety."

I wave a spoon dripping with milk. "They lived a different lifestyle, Mama—you know that. They worked on farms and walked everywhere, so they got plenty of exercise."

"Hmph," Mama mutters, sipping hot tea. I make a face at her. Mama and I are often at loggerheads about the weirdest things, like how people in villages lived a hundred years ago. Still, I secretly enjoy our little arguments. She's very knowledgeable but doesn't like to rub it in.

Baba puts up his hand like a police sergeant. "Please stop, you two. I have ulcers from listening to you all the time."

I don't tell him that spicy food will irritate his ulcers. I jab a spoon in my cereal, which has absorbed so much milk that

22

the pieces look like bloated life jackets bobbing in a speckled ocean. Ew.

Baba goes back to his eggs. I look around and catch sight of the papers from the cooking club last night, lying on the kitchen counter with a bunch of unopened mail. A slim booklet with an American flag on the front sticks out from underneath, jogging my memory. "Why are you watching that blond airhead again, huh, Mama? Don't you have your citizenship test to study for?"

Mama makes an impatient sound deep in her throat and whispers, "Later."

"Kya?" Baba abandons his egg halfway to his mouth. His grayish-black goatee quivers on his chin. "You told me you were almost done with your studying."

Mama gives me an exasperated look. I am instantly ashamed, but in my defense, I didn't realize she hadn't been studying for that thing at all.

"I'm doing it, okay?" she tells Baba, touching his shoulder in a comforting gesture. "It takes time. If I had someone to help me, it would go faster."

Both of them turn to look at me. Uh-oh.

I pretend to focus on my soggy cereal. "Maybe I'll have a paratha after all," I say weakly, trying to make them happy.

Too late.

"You will help your mama study," Baba commands. He gets up from the table and wipes his mouth, then turns to Mama. "It's ridiculous that you've been studying for months and

23

haven't finished yet. Sara is going to help you, and that's the end of it."

Baba doesn't usually talk so firmly. In his job as a pharmacy technician, he speaks little and works way too hard. Both Mama and I glare at him.

"But . . . it's not fair," I splutter. "I'm already staying back with her in that stupid cooking class! Why do I have to be part of this, too?"

Mama's hand freezes. I see her teacup tremble slightly, and I wish I could take the words back.

Baba frowns. "Don't you want your mother to be a citizen of this great country? Do you want her to float around between two cultures forever?"

I groan. My father is always so dramatic. When he puts it like that, the choice is clear. "Okay, fine. I'll do it," I say with gritted teeth.

Mama relaxes. "Thank you, jaanoo. That will be such a big help." She smiles at me.

I bite my lip, then reluctantly smile back. "Anything for family, right?"

Later that afternoon, I sit on my bed and stare at my laptop, wondering if I should send Rabia a message on Google Hangouts. It's past two o'clock, so she must be watching *America's Got Talent* videos. We used to watch together on weekends, with the Hangouts bar open in the corner of our screens, commenting on all the contestants,

24

laughing, even though we could only see tiny squares of each other.

Rabia's family spent the summer with her grandparents in Pakistan, so we haven't watched *AGT* since fifth grade ended and I left Iqra. I drag the laptop onto my thighs and ping Rabia before I lose my courage. It's dumb, really. What am I afraid of? She's still the same girl I've always known.

The computer rings and rings. I count five beeps before she answers.

"Sara!" Her face is grainy and dark, so I know she's in her room with the curtains drawn, probably listening to music really low.

"Hey, Rabia. How's it going?" I try to act casual, as if I don't think about her every day when I walk into school without a friend.

"I'm fine. I have to get started on a project about solar ovens, but it is so boring!" She tosses her hair back in classic Rabia style. "How about you?" Her face looms across the screen, the same wide sparkling eyes, her curly hair longer than I remember it.

I'm suddenly tongue-tied. "We did solar ovens in science last week."

She laughs. "Yeah, you're in public school now," she teases. "All high and mighty, doing lessons before us private-school kids."

I relax. "I'm pretty sure it's supposed to work the other way around."

25

She laughs again. "So how is it, your new school?"

"Do you want the good, the bad, or the ugly?"

"Definitely the good."

"Hmm." I glance out my window. The neighbor's cat is climbing awkwardly on a high branch, its claws gripping the wood as if it's petrified. I know how that cat feels, but I search for the positive anyway. "The teachers are nice, especially my art teacher. We're starting a new project on Monday, and I'm dying to know what it is."

Rabia rolls her eyes, but her smile is gentle. "You and your art obsession."

I shrug. "I prefer to call it my passion."

"Not sure your parents would agree."

The cat is stuck on the branch now, swiveling its head from side to side in slow-motion panic. "We'll see." Call me an optimist, but I'll never give up hope that my family will take my art—and me—seriously.

"Sara!" Mama calls from downstairs. Ugh.

"Gotta go," I tell Rabia. "Remember our trip to the mall is coming up soon." I breathe anxiously. "You're still going, aren't you?"

"Are you kidding? It's our tradition. I wouldn't miss it!"

"Sara! *Jaldi aao!*" Mama calls again, louder, and I shut the laptop.

Downstairs, the family has gathered for packing duty. Baba has work today, but everyone else is at their positions in the kitchen. Mama's catering business is a family affair. We all

26

have to pitch in whether we like it or not. My twin brothers, Rafey and Tariq, are only eight years old, but they pack food like quick-fingered professionals. I'm a bit on the messy side, so I ladle and try not to spill too much.

Mama points to the butter chicken in a gigantic pot on the stove. "Four containers, please," she tells me. I pick up four plastic takeout containers from the counter and start ladling. It's still warm, and I don't want the curry splashing on my white T-shirt. It's got an American flag on the front, with white flowers where the stars should be. It's almost worn out with so many washings, but it's my favorite comfy shirt.

The flag reminds me of our conversation at breakfast. "I'm sorry I said anything about your citizenship test to Baba," I offer.

She smiles. Her face is warm and flushed, but the little creases in the corners of her eyes always make me smile back. "It's okay. I was probably annoying you with all that talk of ancient village people."

I giggle, and the twins look at us curiously. "Anyway," I say. "When's your test?"

Rafey says, "You have a test, Mama?" He's the leader of the duo, always asking demanding questions.

Tariq adds, "We had a math test on Friday. It was really easy. Fractions are stupid!" He grins as if it's a joke. Everything is a joke to Tariq.

The twins moved to our local elementary school this year, but they seem to be loving it. They're math geniuses. At least

27

Baba thinks so. The teachers treat them like little princes. Disgusting.

Mama looks up from the lettuce she's cutting. "Don't say *stupid*, please. It's not a nice word."

I've seen that prim, frowning expression before. She had it painted on her face in cooking class yesterday. I'd never seen Mama that way before, all reserved and almost strict. A teacher, not my mama. It was strange, and I'm not sure I liked it.

A little thump in my chest makes me swallow. I'm feeling angsty again, just like in the morning. "Kids say much worse words than *stupid*, Mama. This is America. You should get used to it."

She stops and puts her knife down. "Sara, I've lived in this country longer than you've been alive. Please don't act like I don't know anything."

The twins gaze at us with their mouths slightly open. Not a good look when half your baby teeth are missing.

"I want you two—you three—to always act kind and respectful. Just because your friends are using bad words doesn't mean you should. Right?"

"Right, Mama," the twins chorus. "We love you, Mama." Rafey hugs her quickly. Tariq hates hugs, but he grins to let her know his feelings.

I stick my tongue out at them. Sucking up, as usual.

We get back to the work at hand, all of us practiced in our assigned tasks. Customers usually come in the evening to pick up their orders, so we have to make sure everything is ready by four o'clock at the latest. Once the butter chicken containers are packed, Tariq sticks labels on them so we're sure we're sending the correct orders home with each customer.

"Time to watch cartoons!" howls Rafey. He runs off toward the television, with his trusty twin sidekick behind him.

Mama takes out a pot of biryani from the fridge and hands me white Styrofoam boxes to fill. I breathe in the smell of fragrant rice and succulent lamb.

"Good?" Mama asks, smiling at me.

Biryani is one of the few Pakistani dishes I actually like. I nod, relieved she doesn't seem really mad. "I'm sure it'll be great. You make good food."

"Seems like some of your classmates don't agree."

It takes me a moment to realize she is talking about the cooking club. "Oh, them! Don't worry about them, Mama. They're idiots."

Mama throws me a warning look but doesn't scold. Apparently, *idiot* isn't as bad a word as *stupid*.

"They didn't like the food, I think?" she murmurs, her mouth turning downward.

"Not everyone!" I reach over and hug her. "That girl Elizabeth seemed to really like it. She said her own mom doesn't cook much." I think of the way Elizabeth closed her eyes and breathed in a long sigh when the tahari was handed out.

Mama hugs me back, places a little kiss on the top of my head, and I know all is forgiven—for now. No doubt we'll be at loggerheads again pretty soon.

29

"Do you know Elizabeth?" she asks.

"Not really."

"I hope she can bring the others to her side," Mama says, her face grim. "I can't afford to lose this class."

I freeze, my hand trembling with the weight of a spoon full of biryani. Mama and Baba rarely talk finances in front of me. "What do you mean?"

Mama shakes her head and forces a smile. "Nothing, jaanoo. Forget I said anything."

I slap the spoon down on the table, and little grains of rice fly around me. "I'm not a little kid anymore. I want to know."

She takes a deep breath. "I know you're not a little kid, but Baba and I never want to burden you with our problems."

I can't believe what she's saying. "It's not your problem, Mama! It's our problem. We all help with the business."

"Don't worry, it'll be fine. *Sub theek hai.*" Her face smooths and she turns back to the biryani. Her long hair falls forward, shielding her face and hiding her feelings. This conversation is over.

Back in my room at night, I replay Mama's words over and over in my mind. *I can't afford to lose this class.* She'll never admit it, but she needs my help. It's clear to me: no matter how boring I find Mama's cooking club, I'll try to win over that girl Elizabeth and make sure the club is a success. How hard can it be?

4

Elizabeth

THE FRONT DOOR SLAMS, waking me up. That's David, leaving for the high school bus. He's a sophomore and, like Dad, isn't home much. The robotics team and theater crew keep him late after school. When David is home, he's holed up in the garage tinkering with engine parts or tweaking his team's robot.

Not that I blame him. Things have been pretty bad since Mom came back from England.

I hurry downstairs. There was a full box of Cheerios yesterday, but David eats huge soup bowls of cereal for breakfast. I'd make myself toast if the toaster weren't in the garage, along with the remains of several other small appliances my brother offered to fix.

Unless I want scrambled egg Hot Pockets this morning, I have to get to the cereal before Justin does.

"Hi, Mom." I shake the box. "We're low on Os."

Mom sits in a corner of the family room, legs buried under the gray blanket she's knitting. Our schnauzer, Robin Hood, nestles at her feet. The only thing Robin has in common with the legendary hero of Nottingham is that he's an expert thief. Of peanut butter and jelly sandwiches.

The yarn Mom is knitting pools in her lap like strands of overcooked spaghetti. "It wouldn't hurt to say 'Good morning' before you start whinging, Elizabeth," she scolds. Her short brown hair is brushed, which is a good sign. But her eyelids are puffy. She's still in her bathrobe, which she calls a *dressing gown*.

"Good morning, Mother dear," I say with an extra dose of sweetness. Sometimes my sarcasm makes Mom laugh. Other times, it pushes her buttons. That's when she gets angry and says that all she wants is some peace and quiet.

Mom spent the whole summer in England, taking care of my grandmother. David and I got shipped off to sleepaway camp. We couldn't stay home with Dad, because he was traveling for work. Even Robin Hood was sent away. He spent the summer in New York with Bubbe. Robin is Bubbe's BFF: best furry friend. But don't tell her Persian cat, Claude. He gets jealous.

Justin's lucky he's only nine. He got to go with Mom and spend time with our cousins, my aunt Louise's kids, all summer.

No one even told me Nan died until I got home from camp, which I was totally not okay with. Dad's excuse was that they wanted me to enjoy my summer. Ha! The JCC performing-arts camp is where my parents met when they were college students. They are super romantic about it—how they spent the summer putting on theater productions in the woods—so I'm kind of not allowed to say how much I hated it.

I come over and sit on the arm of the sofa. Mom puts down her needles and slips an arm around my back. After Mom came home from England, a big box covered in British stamps arrived on our doorstep. I was hoping there'd be some keepsakes inside, something of Nan's that I could hold on to. But the only thing in there was a bunch of Nan's unused yarn, cushioning some commemorative plates. British people love those things: a plate for the Queen's birthday, a plate with the prince's wedding portrait on it. They're not for eating. Mom hung ours up in the hallway with the rest of our family photos, which makes it seem like Elizabeth II is my honorary grandmother.

Our family is together again, but I think spending the summer on opposite sides of the ocean stretched us thin. Mom is sad about losing Nan, and probably she misses Aunt Louise. She might be pining for England, like always. Maybe all three are knitted together, like the woolly blanket she's working on.

Mom sips her tea. "We have other food in the house besides cereal, Elizabeth," she says, and goes back to knitting.

I'm glad I don't have to ask her to make my lunch today. I made tahari rice this weekend, carefully copying Mrs. Hameed's recipe. There's no way the garbage-pails-on-legs that are my brothers have eaten it. If food isn't wrapped in plastic or cardboard, they won't touch it. Thank goodness we don't keep kosher. If we did, my brothers would probably starve. Ninety percent of Hot Pockets have bacon in them.

Sometimes I wish we did, though. Keep kosher, light candles on Friday nights, follow rules and traditions. Even though Mom converted to Judaism when my parents got married, we're not very observant.

Watching Mom knit makes my eyes heavy. It's so cozy and warm sitting next to her that I ease back into sleep.

"Wake up." She nudges my arm. "No more lollygagging. You'll be late for school. And make sure Justin is awake, would you?"

I run upstairs and shout "School!" into my brothers' bedroom. I refuse to go in there ever since David set up a motion-detecting alarm in the doorway.

I head to my room to get dressed. As soon as I open my drawer, I spot a problem.

"Mom!" I yell loud enough for her to hear me through the floor. "I need clean underwear!" I head back downstairs, almost tripping over Robin Hood. Robin barks at me, then races ahead to the family room and barks at Mom.

"Mom, please tell me you did laundry this weekend."

She scrunches her eyes closed, as if I've given her a headache. "You're old enough to do your own laundry."

"But I was cooking this weekend. Besides, you never taught me like you said you would."

"It's my fault, is it?" Mom stands up. Yarn tumbles from

34

her lap. She's tall, but softer-looking than usual, with rounded, puffy cheeks.

Mom steps over the yarn and heads to the laundry room. "I'll check the dryer," she says.

Her phone rings. I call out to Mom, trying my best not to shout. "Should I answer your phone?"

Mom calls back from the laundry room. "Only if it's Aunt Louise. I'll ring her back in a bit." I look at the screen, pick the phone up off the floor and answer. "Hi, Aunt Louise."

"How's your mum today, Els?" Auntie asks. My family nickname is my initials, ELS, for Elizabeth Leah Shainmark.

"Not so good. All she wants to do is knit and listen to audiobooks, and nobody did the laundry." I don't tell her that I was too distracted with cooking to check that I had clean clothes.

Aunt Louise sighs. Even though she's three thousand miles away, the sadness in her voice flows into me, making my eyes prickle. She's the older, more sparkly sister, but there's no happiness in her words when she says, "Your mum is doing her best to take care of herself. Things are hard for her right now." She pauses. "You know the English saying 'Keep Calm and Carry On'?"

"It's on Mom's favorite teacup."

"That's what she's struggling with. The carrying-on part. Is she there?"

"She said she'll call you back." I say goodbye to Aunt Louise, pick up the knitting, and place it carefully on the sofa.

35

When I finally get to the laundry room, Mom has the place pulled apart.

"This was all I could find," she says, handing me a fistful of cloth.

I hold it up.

"Mom," I say, tears threatening again. There are some things I am not willing to do, even to help Mom stay calm. Wearing my little brother's underwear is one of them. "These are Justin's underpants. BOYS' underpants. I have PE today. There is no way." My voice is tight. There are some kids who like wearing boy-style shorts. I am not one of them.

She hands me laundry detergent. "Wash your dirty pants in the sink."

I know she means underwear. "They won't dry in time."

Mom's blue eyes are dull, tired. "Those are your choices, Elizabeth."

"It was Aunt Louise on the phone," I mumble. Mom pushes past me into the family room, picks up her phone, and heads upstairs. "Hi, Louise," I hear her say. "Sorry about that. Teenagers." She says the word with the fakest laugh ever. Also, she knows I'm only eleven.

I trudge upstairs, hoping I can find a pair of underwear to wash.

Then, as she's closing the door to her room, Mom says something that makes me freeze. She tells Aunt Louise, "I wish I could be there" and ". . . coming home for good."

Robin waits for me at the top of the stairs, stubby tail wagging, but I don't move.

Mom wants to go back to England for good? Will she take us with her? What about Dad? My mother said this was the year she'd get her U.S. citizenship. I was so excited. Because how can we be a family if we don't all belong to the same country? But then Nan got sick and Mom didn't have time to study. I haven't seen her reading the *Learn About the United States* booklet in months.

I only have a few minutes until the bus comes. I've got to get dressed and pack my backpack. If I wear Justin's underwear, I might have time to find Mom's study book.

I race back downstairs, sweating from all the running around. The booklet isn't in the mail pile or with the old newspapers. I stop and throw my homework folder, container of tahari rice, and water bottle into my backpack. I'm running out of time.

One last place to search. The coffee table is covered in Mom's knitting projects, but I bet her magazines are underneath. There, buried under issues of *O* and *Royalty Monthly,* I find the booklet with its bright American flag waving on the cover. I put the study book in the kitchen, right next to Mom's teakettle. She'll get the message: I want her to stay here, on this side of the Atlantic, with us.

Then I'm upstairs, rushing to pull a pair of jeans over Justin's underwear. The leg holes are too tight—he is nine, after

37

all—and there's that gross extra pouch in the front, which I don't even want to think about. Thank goodness my jeans are thick. I grab my favorite *Doctor Who* sweatshirt, which used to be Mom's. She watched *Doctor Who* on TV when she was a kid. Except she says "telly" instead of "TV," which I think is one of her most adorable Briticisms.

It's not that I want Mom to give up everything about being English. Of course not. But I want to know she's here, that she belongs to our family one hundred percent. That she's not going to fade into her sadness or go back to Nottingham for good.

The sweatshirt comes down to the middle of my thighs. I roll up the sleeves and put on the charm bracelets that each of my grandmothers got me for my tenth birthday. I quickly touch my favorite charms: Star of David on my left wrist, then Union Jack flag, teacup, and blue police box on my right. The last charm is my favorite because it's Doctor Who's time machine.

At school, I'm so wiggly that Ms. Saintima asks if I have ants in my pants. My friend Micah laughs, along with everyone else. Sara from cooking club glares as if she's saying, *How dare you distract me from my studies?*

I shrug. My brain is too frazzled to care what that stuck-up girl Sara thinks. Time to focus. I need to come up with a plan for PE or everyone will know I wore boys' underwear to school.

By the time Maddy and I meet in the hallway, I feel like I'm going to barf. The bell is about to ring. In moments, I'll be changing in the locker room and Justin's snowy white undies

38

—I hope they're snowy white . . . did I check?—will be on display for the world. Or at least for the girls in my gym class.

Maddy pulls me into a corner and unzips her backpack. "I need to show you something," she hisses. A flowery smell whaps me in the face. She points to little pillows wrapped in purple-and-pink plastic.

"You got your period?" I whisper.

"No. My stupid mother made me bring pads." She blows the hair off her freckled forehead and then, in a quick motion, pulls her dark hair into a ponytail. She used to wear it in a cute bob because we hated how every girl in our grade had long straight hair. But she started growing her hair out this summer while I was away.

Maddy says, "My mom got her period in sixth grade. She's convinced it's going to happen to me, like, any minute."

I sag against the wall and catch my breath. "Cover them with something," I suggest. "If they fall out by accident, everyone will see."

"Good thinking." She shoves a pencil case on top of the pads. As Micah comes bounding up to us, Maddy yanks the zipper closed, hiding all evidence of feminine products.

Micah Rosen-Perez is my Hebrew-school buddy. This is the first time we've gone to actual school together. He has curly brown hair pulled back into a ponytail. He wears cargo shorts no matter how cold it gets outside. And he's a percussionist. Micah's drumsticks are always either in his hands or in his pocket.

39

Maybe the scent of flowers has gone to my head, because an idea sprouts there. "That's it!" I gasp and give Maddy a hug. "You're the best."

"What the heck, Els?" Maddy pushes me away and glances around the hallway to see if anyone noticed how immature I am.

"Group hug?" Micah asks.

"You wish," I say, walking down the hallway as fast as I can without getting yelled at. "Tell Mr. Graff I went to the nurse," I tell Maddy.

"You okay?"

I turn around and put a hand on my stomach. "Girl stuff."

"TMI," Micah calls back.

I congratulate myself on my brilliance. A couple of weeks ago, Angela Lee got her first period during PE. "I'm having a female issue," she informed Mr. Graff. "Can I go see the nurse? She has an extra set of clothes."

Mr. Graff wrote Angela a pass without a word.

I have never been so glad to be a girl. I'll have to fib when I tell the nurse I got my period and that I need to borrow fresh clothes, but it's worth it to keep the secret of the underpants safe.

5

Sara

ART IS USUALLY my favorite class, but Mrs. Newman is watching me intensely. What's her problem? I look at my pad and pretend to sketch, but my drawing of the garden is complete. I don't want to ruin it by adding even one more stroke of pencil.

She moves on to another student. The colorful bangles on her arms—there must be twenty at least—jingle like noisy bells.

"People, take your time," Mrs. Newman trills. "There's no need to hurry. Slow and steady hands make good drawings!"

I'm sure she's talking about me. A few students giggle, but most are busy with their own work. The new project Mrs. Newman assigned is not as interesting as I'd hoped. More like super boring. Make a flyer for a local business? Come on! That isn't really art.

Is it?

There's a familiar calm in the room, but the jingle-jangle

of Mrs. Newman's bracelets always gives me a slight headache. I raise my hand.

"Yes, Sarah?"

She's pronounced my name wrong again. Baba says Americans have a hard time understanding foreign concepts, which always makes me want to shout, *I'm not a foreign concept!* But all I can do is grimace and stay quiet, because it's no use.

"Can I go to the bathroom, please?" I beg with a little wiggle, as if I'm holding in my pee with great effort.

Mrs. Newman frowns, but even her disappointment is pretty. Brown curls wave about her face as she shoos me to the door. "Don't take too long, or I'll need to assign some extra art homework just for you!" she teases.

I hide a smile. She hasn't figured out that I don't mind extra work, especially in art. Anything to keep me from packing curry dinners at home. I rush to the door before she changes her mind. Freedom!

The bathrooms are down the hall. I don't really need to go, so I drink long sips from the water fountain and read the flyers jumbled together on the bulletin board. Maybe they'll give me inspiration for the art assignment. Jazz band is holding auditions on Friday. Debate club is searching for members. Whoever made these flyers has zero imagination.

The nurse's door across from me bangs open. A tall girl wearing glasses and a too-big sweatshirt slinks out. Elizabeth. She looks startled to see me.

42

"Hi," she says. There's a sheepish look on her face.

I look her up and down. She's wearing ratty gray sweatpants with POPLAR SPRINGS printed in green down one leg. That's strange. She usually dresses in jeans or corduroys.

I debate for a second. People don't typically say hi to me in the hallways. But she talked to me in cooking club last week, so I mumble a quick hello.

"You're Sara, right? I loved your mom's class!" She leans forward, like she's sharing a secret. "Do you know what we're making on Friday?"

My eyes must be popping out of my head. First, she's used the absolute correct pronunciation of *Sara,* which is almost a miracle. Second, she seems genuinely excited about Mama's cooking, which is . . . also a miracle. I have to admire this level of enthusiasm, even if I can't understand it.

"I'm not sure," I reply, keeping my face straight so she doesn't think I'm being friendly. Then I remember that Mama needs her to be happy about the cooking club. I add weakly, "I think something with chicken."

She says "Awesome" with a smile so dazzling, it could power the entire school during a blackout. Wow, this girl is really interested in food.

There's an awkward silence as we size each other up. I don't really want to talk to her, but she stands there expectantly. "You're Elizabeth, right?" I finally ask, even though I know her name.

She nods. "We have language arts together."

"Oh, yeah." I look back at the nurse's office. "What happened?"

"What? Oh . . . nothing. I'm fine. I needed to . . . um . . ." Elizabeth's cheeks go bright pink. I resist the urge to lean closer. White people blushing is such a scientifically curious phenomenon. How must it feel to have your entire face turn red? When I'm embarrassed or nervous, I just go hot, but at least I can hide my feelings. Blushing is like having your secret emotions exposed to the world.

"I told the nurse I got my period so I could get out of PE." Her words come out in a rush. She widens her eyes and presses her lips together. "I can't believe I told you that."

"Oh, okay," I say, trying to act mature, but inside I'm amazed at how open she is. When I got my first period over the summer, Mama was so hush-hush about the whole thing, as if I should keep it super secret.

"What about you? How'd you get out of class?" Elizabeth asks.

"I got my period too," I say boldly. We stare at each other for a shocked second. "Just kidding—Mrs. Newman's bracelets were driving me nuts." We burst out laughing.

Together, at the same time.

I catch my breath. I can't believe it. I'm actually laughing at a joke with another sixth-grader. I never thought I'd do that with anyone other than Rabia.

44

The bell rings, and the warm feeling leaves me with a whoosh. A rush of students surrounds us, and the laughter dies in my throat.

"There you are, Els!" A loud, tinny voice attacks us from behind. Maddy, of course. Her words could wake the dead with their harsh, judgmental tone.

Elizabeth greets her friends. Maddy ignores me, but a boy from language arts class—Micah, I think—smiles at me. I stay focused on the bulletin board, as if it's the most interesting thing in the world. Actually, some of the announcements are quite cool, even if the designs are boring. For instance, there's an international festival coming up in December. Students are encouraged to explore their cultural backgrounds and create displays.

I begin to walk away, to create a little distance between me and Elizabeth's friends. I'm already thinking about the festival. Is this for real? What cultural background do the white kids in school have? Do they even know where their ancestors came from?

"Maddy, calm down," I hear Elizabeth behind me, and I jog a few more steps ahead, letting other kids swirl around me.

"She is so uncool. Why were you even talking to her?" Maddy's voice jars me.

"Hey, Mads. Ease up. I've got enough cool to spread around." Micah grins, putting an arm around both girls' shoulders. I like his dark, curly ponytail and how laid-back he is.

Elizabeth lowers her voice, but I hear her loud and clear. "I was just asking about cooking club. It's not like we're friends or anything."

My lips tighten. So much for thinking we hit it off.

Maddy says, "Her mom's not even American. My dad says they should only hire PLU at this school."

"What the heck is PLU?" Micah asks.

Maddy tosses her ponytail. "Oh, you know. 'People like us.'"

I stare straight ahead. It's not the first time I've heard something like this. Three years ago, our family went to a carnival in D.C. A group of men in baseball caps in line behind us had grumbled, "There should be a separate line for immigrants," and "It's not right Americans gotta wait longer because of these people."

And last year when Rafey was sick with pneumonia, and Mama and I took him to the urgent care clinic, a white doctor told us he only treated Americans. PLU. We'd had to leave and go to the emergency room to get poor Rafey treated. Mama sat frozen as she drove to the hospital, but as I sat in the back, comforting Rafey, I couldn't stop the tears falling down my cheeks.

Not anymore. I'm older. Stronger. *Just ignore,* I tell myself. *I-G-N-O-R-E.*

"My mom's not a citizen either," Elizabeth says to Maddy, so quietly I can hardly hear her. The crowd of students thins, laughing and talking on their way to the next class. I stand

46

frozen in the middle of the hallway, unable to breathe. *Calm down, Sara,* I tell myself. *This mean talk is pretty normal. You should be used to it by now.*

I think of the way Mrs. Kluckowski spoke to Mama outside the FACS room before the rest of the class showed up, all snide and superior. I remember the time the clerk at the grocery store snarled, "Stupid Arabs!" at Baba as he struggled to find change in his wallet. I think of all the times since I came to this school when a teacher has scoffed at me or a student has glared. The message is clear: *You're different. You're not wanted.*

I blink to clear my eyes of tears, flip my hair over my shoulders, and walk back to the art room to get my backpack. Hopefully Mrs. Newman will have forgotten all about me.

At home, the twins play with Legos as I do math homework at the kitchen table. "Guys, keep it down!" I yell, not for the first time. "I'm doing complicated stuff here."

Tariq drops a handful of Lego bricks so they clatter on the floor. "Sorry, can't hear ya!"

I resist the urge to kick him under the table. He's a big crybaby and will go running to Mama, so I smile sweetly instead. "Of course you can't hear me. You have donkey ears instead of human ones."

Rafey's mouth drops open. "She called you a *gadha!*"

Mama chooses that exact moment to enter the kitchen carrying an armful of paperwork. "Sara! *Bhai ko sorry kaho!*"

47

"He should apologize for making so much noise when I'm doing my homework."

"You can do homework in your room," protests Tariq, shuffling the Legos so they click and rattle.

"Stop it!" I cover my ears with my hands. Juvenile, I know.

Mama dumps her papers on the table with a thump. "Everyone, quiet!" she says, in English this time, loud and clear. We all gulp and quiet down. "Boys, go into your room to play. I'll call you when dinner's ready."

My brothers make faces at me as they put their toys in the box and leave. I glare back at them.

Mama sits next to me at the table. "*Kya hua,* jaanoo? Having a bad day?" she asks gently.

I shake my head. "Nothing more than usual," I mumble, going back to my worksheet. There's no need to tell her about Maddy and the mean things she said. And even though Elizabeth and I laughed together for a minute in the hallway, she still acted like she didn't care when Maddy showed up.

Middle school stinks. I'd better get used to it.

"Are you sure?"

"Yes, Mama." I clear my throat and scribble on my worksheet to show her I'm extremely busy.

She stares at me for a few seconds, then shrugs. "I'm here if you want to talk," she tells me, but her tone is distracted. I look up. She's focused on the papers in front of her, a frown on her face. They're bills, lots of them.

"What's all this?" I ask, pushing away my homework. Some of the bills have big red letters on them, the amounts underlined in black. I crane my neck to read.

"*Kuch nahi,*" she replies quickly, putting her hands over the words.

"That doesn't look like 'nothing,'" I protest. "That looks like several thousand dollars you owe some bank."

Mama pushes me away. "Go back to your homework, Sara. Bills aren't your concern. Your baba and I are going to deal with this. We never want you to worry about money, okay?"

"Ugh. I'm not a baby anymore. I'm part of this family, and I deserve to know what's going on!" I can be very stubborn when I want to be.

She rubs a hand on my cheek. "Of course you're not a baby. You're my big girl."

I want to stomp my foot, but that's probably babyish. This is so frustrating. Mama and Baba think I'm old enough to go to a big public school. They think I can help out with the family business, prepping pounds of veggies, mixing all the spices, packing hundreds of foil trays before a big party. I do all those things for the family, but I can't be trusted with a bunch of bills?

"What do you owe that bank for?" I demand. I narrow my eyes into slits and my lips into a thin, straight line. Maybe Mama will figure out I'm serious.

She sighs. "My catering business," she says. Her long black

49

hair falls forward, covering her face. "I took out a loan last year to grow the business. Get more supplies. Advertise in the paper. That sort of thing."

"How much?"

"Enough that we couldn't pay the fees for your private school this year," she whispers. "Baba didn't want you to know."

This is huge. This is unbelievable. Here I'd been assuming they'd made me switch schools because Poplar Springs was so much closer. Here I'd been acting like a martyr all these weeks.

Mama looks so small sitting there with the papers spread around her. Her signature smile is completely gone.

"How will you pay it back?" I finally ask.

She looks up at me and squares her thin shoulders. "I'll think of something," she replies, smiling bravely. "You just worry about that long division. It won't solve itself, you know."

6

Elizabeth

ON THURSDAY, I open my lunch and take out a PB&J on stale wheat bread. The food situation at my house has to change. I wish Doctor Who would swoop in, park his TARDIS at our front door, and introduce my mom to culinary delights from across time and space.

"What's wrong, Els?" Micah asks, drumming the cafeteria table with a plastic knife and fork.

Maddy says, "You're glaring at your sandwich like it just broke up with you."

"My advice?" Micah says. "Stuff the whole thing in your mouth and chew real hard. That'll teach it a lesson." He demonstrates by shoving today's cafeteria lunch into his mouth. Tuna salad on a bun with lettuce and a soggy slice of tomato. His lips barely close over it.

Everyone laughs—Micah, Maddy, and the band kids who take up the other half of our table. But I am not amused.

"You don't understand. If I'm forced to eat another chicken

finger, another PB&J, if I even smell another Hot Pocket, I am going to barf." I put down my sandwich and sigh. "The only thing keeping my taste buds alive is that tomorrow is Friday."

Micah closes his eyes and puts a hand over his heart. "God bless Pizza Day."

"No." I shove his arm. "I'm talking about cooking club. I hope we're making parathas. I watched this amazing Pakistani chef make them on YouTube."

Salma Aunty's Desi Kitchen is my current YouTube obsession. Every night when my homework is done, I ask Mom if she's in the mood for a *Doctor Who* rerun. If she says no—lately, she always says no—I go online and watch Salma aunty. I like her big smiley cheeks and the way her pink hijab matches her manicure.

I had to look up the word *desi*. It means "South Asians living abroad."

My favorite episode is parathas. Salma aunty chatters happily as she rolls her dough out like pizza, but instead of tomato sauce, she tops it with special butter called *ghee*. Then she dusts the dough with flour and does this complicated folding, squishing thing before rolling it into flat circles and frying the parathas. They look drool-worthy, like flaky pancakes.

"You watched Indian cooking on YouTube?" Maddy's hair is pulled back so tight, her eyebrows practically jump up her forehead.

I push my bangs away from my glasses. "Pakistani, not Indian," I say. "There's a difference."

52

"What difference? They're all a bunch of foreigners." Maddy tosses her ponytail and dips a spoon in her yogurt, like what she's saying is no big deal.

"My mom is a 'foreigner,'" I say.

"Your mom doesn't count. She's English," Maddy retorts.

My shoulders crunch together. Maddy doesn't know what it's like when your mom is from another country. Mom may speak the language, but it's been hard for her to make friends, and drive on the opposite side of the road. Plus, people always ask her where she got her beautiful accent.

"And Puerto Rico?" Micah asks. "Is that on your list or off?" Micah has stopped drumming the table. He's holding his plastic utensils in two tight fists. He tells me, "Cookie says Americans like to forget that Puerto Rico is part of the U.S."

Cookie is his abuela. She got her nickname because she's such an amazing baker.

"Whatever. We were talking about cooking," Maddy says. She puts her spoon down and busies herself tightening her ponytail, as if she's bored with this conversation. But I know better. Maddy only fusses with her hair when she's worried about something. "I'm dropping out of the club," she announces.

I stop chewing my sandwich. "Why? I thought you were excited. 'I get to be with my two best friends.' Remember?" A whine slips into my voice.

Maddy says, "I could deal if the food was edible. And my parents don't like it that the teacher hardly speaks English."

"What about Stephanie?" I ask.

53

Maddy twirls her dark hair around one finger. "She wants me to stick with it too. But she has other friends in the class. It's not like we're partners or anything."

I shudder at that thought.

"Your mom can pick you up on Friday, right?" Maddy asks.

I shrug, because this is sixth grade and I am not going to yell at Maddy or, worse, cry in the middle of the cafeteria.

"Sure, I'll tell my mom," I mutter. "And I'll find another partner. No big deal."

Maddy must hear the sarcasm in my voice, because her freckled nose crinkles and her mouth twists into a smirk. "You should ask that kid Sarah to be your partner. If you can get her to talk."

Micah throws me a sympathetic glance.

"Hey," I say, grabbing his muscular arm. "You like to eat."

"Sorry, Els. Ms. Khouri's advanced percussion group is on Fridays. Got to practice if I'm going to be a rock legend." Micah tosses his curls. A couple of strands come loose from his ponytail and tumble to his forehead.

"You've got the rock-star hair down," Maddy says.

What am I going to do? Even if Mom remembers to pick me up tomorrow, I have no cooking partner. Do I even know any of the other kids? I was so worried about Maddy and Stephanie last week, I hardly talked to anyone else. I'm not about to ask some eighth-grader if she can be my kitchen big sister.

The next day, I slide into the FACS room, put my backpack on the sewing tables, and sit down. The other kids won't notice me back here. Everyone is gathered around Stephanie, who's wearing a Sweet Stephanie's apron with a grinning pink cupcake on the front. She's peeking into the grocery bags Mrs. Hameed brought.

Sara's mom tries to greet the kids, but Mrs. Kluck talks over her. Everyone knows—because she makes such a big deal about it—that Mrs. Kluck has been at Poplar Springs Middle since it opened. She acts like the FACS room is a kingdom and she's wearing the crown. At last, Mrs. Kluck sits at her desk and pretends to grade papers.

Mrs. Hameed adjusts the blue fabric of her hijab and pulls papers out of a binder. She holds up a flag-covered booklet in one hand and frowns at Sara before stuffing it into her purse. It looks exactly like *Learn About the United States,* my mom's citizenship study guide.

"Maddy?" Mrs. Hameed calls, taking attendance. "Madison Montgomery?"

Someone pokes my arm. Sara. Why is she sitting next to me?

"Where's your friend with the sensitive taste buds?" she says in a mocking whisper.

I should stand up for Maddy. She is my best friend. But she's not here. *She bailed on you, remember?* I tell myself.

"She's not coming," Stephanie calls out.

55

Mrs. Hameed checks the attendance list. "Maddy, Jordan, and Ethan are absent, correct?" Her face crumples, squished like the paratha dough I saw on YouTube.

Three people didn't come this week? No wonder Mrs. Hameed looks so miserable.

From her desk, Mrs. Kluck clicks her tongue.

Mrs. Hameed straightens her spine and lifts her shoulders, reminding me of the way Nan always told me and my brothers to stop slumping like lazy Americans and use our good British posture.

"Let's see. Jordan and Ethan were working together. And Maddy . . ." Mrs. Hameed consults her class list. Then her attention lands on me. "Elizabeth, not to worry. We will find you a partner."

Sara's hand shoots into the air. "I'll be Elizabeth's partner."

I spin to face her, my mouth open.

"Don't get excited," Sara whispers. "I'm just trying to get Mrs. Kluckowski off my mama's back."

I should thank Sara for saving me from social isolation, or at least from being stuck with a pair of older kids who don't want me in their kitchen. But all I can think about is what Maddy will say when she finds out who I'm cooking with.

56

7

Sara

IT WAS A MISTAKE to raise my hand so quickly. All nine of Mama's remaining students turn to stare at me. I want to hide under the table, but it's too late.

I tell Elizabeth, my heart thumping, "It doesn't mean we're friends or anything. Just kitchen partners." It's best to be clear about these things.

Let's face it: I've always been a coward, preferring to hide behind my sketchbook or iPod. But Elizabeth looked so hurt when Stephanie said Maddy wasn't coming. I remember the very loud, very disrespectful remarks Maddy made in the first cooking class. Why anyone would miss her is beyond me.

Mama smiles gratefully at me and scribbles something in her notepad. "All right, then, Elizabeth and Sara will partner up, and we can get back to our delicious food!"

I try not to groan at her tone. Mama is trying too hard, which is probably a result of Mrs. Kluckowski sitting at the back of the room, arms folded over her chest like a cranky army sergeant. I nod toward her. "What's she doing here again?"

Elizabeth pushes her glasses up her nose and leans closer to me. "My older brother says everyone calls her Mrs. Kluck, but no one's brave enough to say it to her face." She lets out a snort of laughter. "She's kind of terrifying."

I want to giggle at the nickname too, but stop myself. Mama and Baba would be furious if I ever shortened a teacher's name, even a teacher as grumpy as this one. The sour expression on Mrs. Kluck's face makes it look like she swallowed a whole spoonful of achar.

FACS is a stupid name for a class. When I got my course schedule, Mama explained it's a new, fancy name for home economics.

"What's that?" I'd asked, puzzled.

"Oh, something we old people used to study in school," she mocked. I made a face at her weak attempt at a joke.

Now, of course, Mama doesn't look like she's ever joked in her life. With a very calm and collected look, she explains that we are making a simple chicken curry that could be eaten with rice or naan, or even by itself. "As I explained in our last class, onions form the base of most Pakistani curries," she intones like a college professor.

"Why's your mom speaking like that?" Elizabeth whispers. "She loves talking about food."

I'm surprised that Elizabeth has picked up on it. "How do you know she's not always this serious?" I whisper back.

"Your mom is friendly. Last week she kept a smile on her face, even when kids were giving her a hard time."

58

Mama is definitely like that. Always smiling. The thought of the big stack of bills on the kitchen table rises in my mind. Another person would have been crying at the idea of debt, or at least getting angry or stressed out. But not her. "That's my mama," I say proudly.

Elizabeth tilts her head toward Mrs. Kluck. "I bet it's because of her. What do you think they were talking about before class started?"

I look at her, uncertain. Does she want to be my friend? Sometimes she gives me signals, like asking me what we're cooking in Mama's class. But then she tells Maddy we're not friends.

The idea of making a new friend—a white girl at that—is scary and exciting, like standing in front of a roller coaster, not knowing whether I should get on or stay back. All my friends in elementary school were Pakistani and Indian. People like me. People who understand what it's like to be different.

Elizabeth is still looking at me with her eyebrows wiggling. Thankfully, I don't have to answer her. "Elizabeth," Mama calls out, and Elizabeth jumps. "Will you and Sara be in charge of these spices, please?"

Soon, everyone is busy. Some girls are measuring turmeric and coriander; others are chopping onions and tomatoes. I help Elizabeth grind spices, then hang back as the rest of the group gathers to watch Mama.

"When the oil is hot, we fry the onions in the pot," Mama

tells us. "And once the onions are soft, we'll add the tomatoes and spices to make a curry base."

I look around. I could cook this curry in my sleep, but some of the girls can't take their eyes off the bubbling pot in the mirror above the cooking area. Could Mama actually be winning the class over? *They're starting to like Mama's food,* a little voice inside me whispers, almost disbelievingly, and it's oddly comforting.

When I was nine years old, our neighbor Mrs. Miles told everyone she was moving away because she couldn't stand the smell of curry at all hours of the day. I was so confused. She had always been nice to us, waving from her porch and letting the twins play with her little white dog. Did the smell of curry bother her that much? To me it always felt like home and weekday evenings.

Later, I found out the truth. Mrs. Miles's son made her move to a retirement community. But her comment still cut, reminding me of the thorns I drew in my garden sketches. Raw, and doubly painful because they're attached to flowers. Barbed comments hurt more when they come from a neighbor or a friend.

Mama calls a girl in the front to turn the onion mixture into a thick paste using a potato masher. "You can also use a blender to do this," she tells us. "But I'm old-fashioned. There's nothing like a good mashing to bring the curry base together."

Everyone *ooh*s but I can hear a loud sniff from behind me.

60

Mrs. Kluck. I spin around to glare at her, and she glares right back. Yikes.

Mama puts the chicken pieces into the pot and asks Stephanie to stir. For once, Stephanie's air of confidence dips. "I'm more of a baker," she says, taking over the spatula as if she's never held one before.

Elizabeth takes a deep breath next to me, half closing her eyes. "This must be what heaven smells like," she murmurs.

"I hope not," I say, low enough that only Elizabeth can hear. "A heaven full of spicy flavors that stick to your clothes and make you sneeze? No, thanks!"

Elizabeth laughs, and I laugh back. Mama looks at us. The corners of her mouth turn up.

Elizabeth whispers, "Mrs. Kluck can't deal with the fact that your mother is teaching us to cook real recipes. My brother told me that all she ever makes in FACS is boring stuff. Strawberry jam and chocolate chip cookies. I could make those with my eyes closed."

I nod in sympathy, even though the thought of strawberry jam on some toasted bread isn't too bad.

Mrs. Kluckowski coughs loudly from the back, and I straighten immediately. I have to be the perfect cooking student. I don't want Mama to get in trouble because of me. I raise my hand. "Should we start on the rice while the chicken is cooking?"

Mama sends me a grateful look. "That's an excellent idea,

Sara," she says. "Let's see how much you all remember from last week."

Without Maddy here, I notice that the other girls are more relaxed, less rude. Even Stephanie is peering into the chicken pot with a look of curiosity. The others seem genuinely interested in what Mama's teaching them. My stomach rumbles, and I suddenly have a craving for chicken curry. I'll die before I admit it to anyone, but it's my favorite food. When the chicken and rice are ready, Mama ladles it onto plates. I'm the first to dig in.

Elizabeth is right beside me, using prepackaged naan Mama heated on the stove to soak up the curry. She watches as I take a big bite. "Didn't you say you don't like your mom's cooking?" she asks, smirking.

"Beggars can't be choosers," I mumble.

"Admit it: you secretly love this dish."

I swallow a mouthful and wipe curry from my chin. "Shhh! Don't tell my mother!"

After we clean up, Mama's students walk out the door, clutching their food boxes. Stephanie's white apron has splotches of curry on it, making the giant pink cupcake on the front look like it has orange swirls. I notice her website URL is on there too. I want to hate her, but I have to admire her guts. She's annoyingly focused on her business, always selling.

Mama should learn from her. The thought pops into my head like a lightning bolt, and I shake my head to clear it. What am I thinking? My dear, sweet mama learning from someone as obnoxious as Stephanie Tolleson? Never.

Still, I consider the happy-faced cupcake on Stephanie's apron for a long time. I'm suddenly thinking of my art assignment, how I have to make a flyer for a local business. Mama's stacks of packaged food containers pop into my mind. They don't have any labels on them, other than the customer's name. No website address like Stephanie's apron. Nothing to tell the buyer who made all that food they're enjoying.

"Earth to Sara!" Elizabeth waves a hand in front of my face. I blink. The room is almost empty. She's the only person left, except for Mrs. Kluck—who sits at her desk pretending not to watch Mama's every move. Does she think we're going to sabotage her kitchen?

Elizabeth is too busy chattering to notice. Maybe she thinks if she keeps talking, I won't realize no one's here to pick her up. "I'm so full, I can't eat another bite," she says. She picks up her container of chicken curry and inhales. "Can you believe we made something this delicious? We're a good team. I know my way around measuring spoons and utensils. And you're an expert on spices. Even with the chili powder, it wasn't that spicy. You're like a younger version of Salma aunty."

I wrinkle my eyebrows. "Who?"

"She's a YouTube chef. I'm addicted to her videos. She has so much fun cooking, but she likes eating even more. I bet if Maddy watched Salma aunty, she'd appreciate Pakistani food."

63

"Yeah, right," I say, rolling my eyes. I seriously doubt that Maddy would ever like anything Mama cooked.

I lift chairs up on the tables while Mama stands at the sink, washing pans.

Mrs. Kluck—I decide to use the nickname, although I would never say it in front of Mama—bustles into the kitchen to make a pot of coffee. As she passes by, she warns us, "Be sure you clean underneath there. Don't leave food on the floor for the janitors. It's not their job to clean up after clubs." She says the word "clubs" as if she really means "diseases."

"I'll help you, Sara," Elizabeth says. She asks Mrs. Kluck where to find a broom and dustpan. Our teacher motions toward the back closet like a queen waving to a lowly servant.

"Thank you," I whisper to Elizabeth. As I put more chairs up on the worktables, she sweeps underneath. Despite Mrs. Kluck's complaining, all that's there is a bit of onion skin and a few gum wrappers.

"Don't mind her," Elizabeth whispers. "She's been here so long, she acts like the FACS room is her royal palace."

I watch Mrs. Kluck pour herself a mug of coffee. She doesn't offer any to Mama, even though they're standing barely three feet apart.

Elizabeth's broom knocks Mama's tote bag with a loud thump, and I jump. "Whoops," Elizabeth says as papers tumble to the floor.

Did I imagine it, or did Mrs. Kluck chuckle?

"What is her problem?" I mutter, leaning down to pick up

64

the papers. Elizabeth squats, helping me gather them. Underneath the pile is that citizenship booklet. I brush a bit of coriander off the flag on the cover. Elizabeth's eyes meet mine.

"We have this book at home," she says.

"You—what?" I gape at her.

"My mom's from England. She never got her citizenship. She said this was the year she'd do it." Elizabeth lifts her shoulders and drops them again. "Stuff got in the way. She hasn't studied in a long time." She pushes her glasses up, and I pretend not to notice her eyes filling with tears. "It's no big deal," she says, but I can tell it is a very big deal.

I nod so hard, my hair flies up. "I didn't know you were British," I say. "You don't have an accent."

Her laugh is short and as bitter as dark coffee. "I'm only half British. When we visit England, everyone calls us Yanks. But Americans hear my mom's accent and assume I was born in England. Sometimes I feel like I don't belong in either place."

I can't help but stare at her. When we stand up, Elizabeth hands me the papers. "I'll shut up now," she says.

"Don't feel bad." I take a deep breath. Before I can talk myself out of it, I admit, "It's nice to know I'm not the only one feeling weird around people."

"Maddy says I talk too much," she confides.

Maddy has a lot of opinions. All of them negative. I bite my lip before I say that out loud.

Elizabeth seems to know what I'm thinking. "Maddy isn't that bad. We've been friends a long time, but she's only in one

65

of my classes this year, so I hardly ever see her. I hope she comes back to cooking class."

"I feel like we're doing fine without her," I say boldly.

Mama walks up to us before Elizabeth can respond. "Ready, Sara?" Mama says, wiping her hands on a dish towel. "Elizabeth, hasn't anybody picked you up yet?"

Elizabeth checks the clock. "My mom should be here soon." She gives Mama an apologetic smile. "I'm not allowed to have a phone yet. I'm asking for one for my bat mitzvah."

I grimace and give Mama the side-eye. "Your mom's not the only one who's old-school."

Elizabeth is still talking to Mama. "Are you getting your citizenship soon? My mom is too. Or—she's supposed to. I hope."

At her desk, Mrs. Kluck chokes on the coffee she's been sipping. I jump in: "Elizabeth's mom is an immigrant too, Mama. From England."

"I see," Mama says. "You two have lots in common, then. How long—?"

Before Mama can finish her question, there's a knock on the classroom door. This must be Elizabeth's mother. The two look exactly alike, if you take away Elizabeth's glasses. Her mom has a short, less unruly version of Elizabeth's hair and sky-blue eyes instead of Elizabeth's brown.

"Sorry I'm late," she says. She has a soft, lilting accent. I imagine a lonely queen in a cliff-top castle, looking out at her subjects below. "I should wear a chauffeur's cap for all the time I spend shuttling you and your brothers around." She smiles.

"It's all right, Mom. I helped clean up."

Mama gives Mrs. Shainmark a friendly nod. "Elizabeth's been a big help," Mama says, and there goes Elizabeth, blushing again.

We all say goodbye to each other, even to Mrs. Kluckowski, and leave. Elizabeth waves to me, and without thinking about it, I wave back.

8

Elizabeth

THE SECOND MOM AND I pull into the driveway, Justin bolts out the front door. Robin Hood is at his heels, jumping and barking. I hold the pizza Mom and I picked up after cooking club out of Robin's reach.

Justin skips around Mom. "I have a big surprise!"

The door flies open again.

"Daddy!" I screech.

Mom jogs up the steps and into our father's arms. Dad is so tall and broad-shouldered, he fills the doorway. David stands behind him, like Dad's skinny shadow.

"I caught an early flight. Couldn't wait to see my family," Dad explains, taking the pizza from me. He's a sustainable-building consultant. Sometimes he goes away for two weeks at a time, visiting green-building sites in other cities. He says he's trying to cut back on travel, at least until Mom feels better, but I have seen zero evidence of that. "I hope you ordered mushrooms," Dad says.

"Ew," Justin says. "You're the only one who eats fungus."

"There's a fungus among us," Dad jokes, kissing the top of Justin's head.

"Worst dad joke ever," David says, but he's grinning.

We set the table. It's Friday night, so I go to the cabinet where we keep the brass Shabbat candlesticks.

Mom puts a hand on my arm. "I'm not up to it tonight, Elizabeth."

"Can we at least say the Hamotzi?" I ask. It's a prayer we say over challah, thanking God for the bread we eat. Pizza is bread, so we could pray over that.

"Not tonight, Elizabeth." Dad's voice is firm. "Tomorrow we'll go to services as a family. Then I'm taking the three of you out. Mom needs a break."

I wonder if Dad has noticed the darkness under Mom's eyes and how slow she is to smile.

"I have robotics," David says. "First tournament's coming up soon."

Justin raises his hand. "Soccer practice."

"I'll go to services," I cut in quickly. I'm supposed to meet Maddy at Bean Heaven for a Halloween-costume planning session. But that can wait.

The next day, Dad and I get up early for services. The synagogue is a modern building. Dad helped install solar panels on the roof, so he's super proud of it. Huge windows overlook trees and a pond.

When the congregation sings my favorite prayer, Ma Tovu,

Dad rocks back and forth on his loafers. The melody is sad, but hearing it fills me with hope. I love the line about the temple being a place of glory. I look out the windows. The autumn leaves are more beautiful than stained glass.

Dad closes his eyes, nodding with the beat as we sing. I slip my hand into his. He squeezes back. It was worth getting up early on a Saturday to spend time with him.

Micah is here too. That's another thing I like about services. Micah usually comes with his family. It's hilarious to see him in khaki pants, a button-down shirt, and loafers instead of cargo shorts and high-tops. His curls are slicked into a neater-than-usual ponytail.

After services, everyone gathers in the lobby. We eat challah and the cookies the Rosen-Perez family brought for hospitality.

"Shalom, Elisheva. Shalom, Michah."

Micah chokes on his Manischewitz grape juice and covers his mouth so it doesn't spray all over Mrs. Gruver, our Hebrew-school principal. She has appeared out of nowhere and planted her manicured hands on each of our shoulders.

"Shalom, Mrs. Gruver," we both say.

I'd like to tell Mrs. Gruver that both our names are from the Torah and she doesn't need to prove a point by using Israeli pronunciation. Also, I want to tell her that my first name is supposed to be *Elizabeth,* like QEII. My name is British and Jewish, like me.

"Where is your mother, Elisheva?" Mrs. Gruver asks, craning her neck so it stretches from her lace-trimmed collar. When she's satisfied that my mother is ditching services, she adds, "I haven't seen her in months."

I decide not to tell her that's probably because my grandmother died. If Mrs. Gruver's such a great principal, she should know that already.

"Don't forget, Elisheva, it's your family's turn for Oneg Shabbat in a few weeks. Cookies and juice. We're counting on you," Mrs. Gruver says as she leaves us to prey on another poor, defenseless Hebrew-school student.

I give Micah a shove. "Why didn't you warn me she was right behind me, *Michah*?" I say his name with a hard "ch" rolling in my throat, Mrs. Gruver–style.

"What was I supposed to do, *Elisheva*, pull my ear?" He pulls his ear so hard, he messes up his hair. "We need a secret sign. The Gruver Approacheth."

I laugh. This is what makes Micah such a good friend. When we joke around, no one's feelings get hurt. Not that Mrs. Gruver doesn't have feelings. I'm sure she does. She just takes being principal way too seriously.

That afternoon, we pile into the car for our hike. Robin Hood is so excited when David puts his leash on, he can't stop barking.

"Are you sure bringing Robin is a good idea?" I ask.

"He needs the exercise," Dad says.

David leans between the front seats to scratch Robin's head. "Next to Mom, you're the laziest Shainmark," he tells our dog.

71

Aunt Louise's words pop into my head. "Mom's not lazy," I argue. "She's doing her best to take care of herself."

David says, "She's supposed to be taking care of *us.*"

Dad interrupts us. "Not today! It's Mom's day off. Today we are fending for ourselves."

At the park, Robin Hood races from tree to tree, his gray mustache quivering as he sniffs. When David and Justin stop to pick up after our dog, I follow Dad's long strides along the wooded path.

"Heard from any of your summer-camp friends?" Dad asks.

"What summer-camp friends?"

"I thought you liked it there."

"That's David, Dad. I hated it."

This was David's third summer at camp, so he had actual friends. But I'd never spent more than one night away from my family before. For me, performing-arts camp was six weeks stuck in a cabin with a bunch of eleven-year-old divas. And every single one of them wanted the lead role in *Annie.* If I never hear the song "Tomorrow" again, it will be too soon.

I've tried to tell my parents how homesick I was this summer, how much I longed to curl up with Mom and Justin, eating the Walker's salt-and-vinegar crisps Mom gets at the British-goods store, watching Doctor Who save Earth from aliens once again. But Mom and Dad have been too busy, or too sad, to listen.

I wish I were still little. Then Dad could swing me onto his shoulders and I'd ride there, reaching up to touch the branches.

"I'm glad you're home," I say quietly, and he hugs me with one arm.

Later, when we get home from our hike, David disappears into the garage. As usual, Justin follows him. "Can I help with your robot?" he asks.

Mom is dressed and busy folding laundry. That's a relief. "Guess what?" she asks Dad.

"The Spice Girls are getting back together?" he teases. The Spice Girls are Mom's favorite British pop group.

She shoves an armful of laundry at him. "I guess you could say that." Mom pretends to hold a microphone to her mouth. She sings, "All you need is positivity." She grins, then explains, "Louise is planning a girls' weekend for us. It's just what I need."

Dad nods, but rubs the back of his neck as if it's sore. "I'll check my travel schedule. If it's only a weekend, we'll make it work." He puts a hand on my shoulder. "Elizabeth can practice her new cooking skills."

Mom says, "I'll need an extra day or two for travel. She found a great deal on a hotel in London."

"London? Nicole, we're down to one income. You know we can't afford—"

Mom argues, "It's only five days. You can manage, Els. Can't you?"

My heart flip-flops. "Can I go with you?" I ask.

A few days ago, Mom was talking to Aunt Louise about going home for good. If she goes to London, I'm going too. Someone has to make sure she comes back.

73

"Stay out of this, Elizabeth," Dad warns. "Nicole, I need to speak with you."

Mom follows him upstairs. I plug some headphones into the family laptop, select the angel food cake episode of *The Great British Baking Show*, and turn up the sound so I can't hear them arguing.

The next morning, Dad leaves for another business trip. As soon as he's out the door, Mom is crying on the phone to Aunt Louise.

All week, I try to persuade Maddy to stay in cooking club. I can't take another person leaving me. Not now, with Dad away and Mom wishing she weren't here. But Maddy won't listen.

"I just want to make normal food," she says, finally arriving at our table after spending half of lunch talking to Stephanie. "Steph is going to make some suggestions to Sarah's mom."

Micah says, "I wish she'd make some suggestions to the school cooks." He holds up today's lunch. The rubbery sandwich sags like a sad frown.

"Maddy, her name is SAH-ra," I enunciate. "The first part sounds like *car*."

Maddy's ponytail swishes back and forth. "Too confusing."

She's being ridiculous. We've been classmates with Roozbeh, Hye-Jun, and Megha since forever. Sara's name is not that difficult.

I'm totally shocked when Maddy shows up to our third

class. Good thing Sara's not here yet. By the time she arrives, Maddy and I will be set up and Sara can go back to her artwork.

I wave to Maddy, but she walks over to Stephanie's station. Steph hands her a pink gift bag with polka-dot tissue paper inside. Next thing I know, Maddy is putting on a white apron with the bright pink SWEET STEPHANIE'S logo plastered on the front. She notices me watching and mouths *Sorry.*

What is happening?

I barely notice when Sara walks in with her mom.

"Hi, Elizabeth. Guess what we're making today," Sara teases.

I can't speak. My brain is stuck on Maddy and Stephanie and their matching aprons.

"Are you all right?" Sara waves a hand in front of my face. I swat it away like it's a pesky fly.

Finally, Maddy comes over. I glare at the too-cute cupcake on her apron and cross my arms at her. "Why didn't you tell me you were coming to class?" I demand.

"I knew you'd be mad." Maddy's green eyes are shiny, like she might cry. She pulls me away from my station. Away from Sara. "You have a new friend," she says, her voice low and insistent. "Why can't I?" Her cheeks flush pink underneath her freckles. "Stephanie's nice, Els. Like, she's a really good person. Her business—"

"I don't care about her business. Cooking club was my idea.

75

We were supposed to do it together." The words bubble out of my mouth and deflate, like dough that's been left to rise too long.

Maddy motions to Sara, who's chopping herbs at our station. "You already have a kitchen partner."

I set my mouth in a hard line. "Okay, I guess." I stomp back to my own station.

"Oh, good. You're here," Sara says. "You're going to love today's recipe. Garlic naan. It's like pita without the pocket."

"I know what naan is," I snap.

"Sorry!"

I wash my trembling hands and sprinkle flour on the wooden board at our counter.

A cloud of flour wafts over from Maddy and Stephanie's area, followed by a burst of laughter. They're both covered in a layer of white dust. Mrs. Kluck is there in a flash, scolding them about respecting her kitchen equipment.

"Let 'em have it, Mrs. Kluck," I mutter.

When we're done kneading flour, water, and yogurt into a smooth ball, Mrs. Hameed gives each team sliced garlic, spices, and fresh coriander. We flatten out the dough with rolling pins and press these flavorings into it. The green leaves remind me of Sara's artwork. If I'm stuck with her, I might as well make conversation. "Did you finish your art assignment? The one with the red flower?"

She shakes her head no. Sara rolls the dough halfheartedly. It's misshapen and uneven, nothing like Mrs. Hameed's example. She says, "I was excited about taking art this semester. But we have to stick to the assignments. No 'doing your own thing.'" She stops rolling and makes air quotes with her fingers. "Mrs. Newman is making us work on a business flyer next. I never knew art could be boring."

"Girls!" Mrs. Hameed makes us both jump. "Less chatting, more rolling. Your dough must be thinner."

"Here. Let me do that," I offer, taking the rolling pin.

Finally, Mrs. Hameed calls us to the demonstration kitchen. "Unfortunately, there is no tandoor oven in your classroom. Still, there is a way to make traditional naan." She spreads water on some rolled-out dough.

I strain my neck to see what's happening.

Sara nudges me. "Calm down. It's just bread."

"Just bread? Bread is my life." Bread is my favorite thing to bake. It makes people happy. The smell of a freshly baked loaf can coax my brother out of the garage and a good mood out of my mom.

Mrs. Hameed slaps the dough water-side down on a griddle, where it cooks like a pancake. The dough bubbles, but the top is still pale. Then Mrs. Hameed flips the entire griddle over, bread and all. I'm sure the naan is going to drop onto the flames, but she explains that the water seals it to the metal. "Now I simply cook the naan over the fire." Mrs. Hameed moves the dough over the blue flames of the stove. The bubbles brown and crisp.

When she's done, we spread butter over our naan. It melts

77

and pools over the hot bubbles of bread. As Sara and I eat, I watch Maddy and Stephanie. They are having way too much fun together. If my stomach weren't so full, it would be tangled up like a mess of yarn.

"Attention, everyone," Mrs. Hameed says as we pack up our extra dough. "I have an announcement. Poplar Springs Middle has an international festival coming up soon. We have been invited to showcase our cooking club." Her smile is sunbeam-bright.

Mrs. Kluck harrumphs in the back of the room.

Stephanie's hand goes up. "Is it a contest? Is there a cash prize?" She's so excited, she bounces on her toes.

Sara's mom explains that we're supposed to come up with special recipes for the festival. Yes, there will be a contest element, "but they have not said anything about prizes," Mrs. Hameed says. "Please see me when you've decided on your team."

Sara looks at me. "So. You and me?"

Her face is so hopeful, but out of habit I say, "I need to ask Maddy first."

Sara points to the demonstration kitchen. Maddy and Stephanie are standing together, talking to Mrs. Hameed. Their arms are linked, as if they're the ones who've been best friends for years.

"I think Maddy already has a partner," Sara says.

9

Sara

"I'll be Batman. You be Robin!" Rafey shouts.

"I'm always Robin. It's not fair!" Tariq shouts back.

Ugh. Why are Saturday mornings so noisy? For once I'd like to sleep in and wake up at noon. Of course, now that I'm awake, I hear Baba's voice in my head saying, *Nonsense! No daughter of mine is going to sleep the morning away,* in his Mr. T voice.

The twins gallop past my bedroom door, screeching. I put my pillow over my head, but it doesn't help. They're not the only ones being loud. Mama is banging spoons against pots in the kitchen. Morning is usually her favorite time of day, when she can sip her chai and plan the afternoon's cooking. Something's up.

I drag myself out of bed and put in my headphones. Selena Gomez croons in my ears as I pull out my sketchbook. The idea for my art assignment takes shape. My hand flows over the paper in broad strokes, a familiar feeling in my stomach as inspiration takes hold. Bubbly, like I drank a lot of Coke. I don't know how long I sketch. Papers are crumpled and thrown away. Different color combinations tested and discarded. I'm not sure I have anything good, but it's a start.

It's after ten o'clock when I go down to the kitchen, my stomach grumbling. "You're awake!" Mama says, her tone harsh. I stare at her. Or, rather, around her.

The kitchen is a mess. Papers are stacked on the table where paratha and eggs usually wait for me. Pots and pans are strewn about, filled with partially cooked food. The onions in one pan are still white and stiff, and the ground beef in another is pink, half cooked. I wrinkle my nose and hold my breath. Spices have spilled from the counter onto the floor. That turmeric is going to leave a stain. Without thinking, I get a paper towel and cleaning spray from under the sink.

"Mama, what in the world is going on?"

"The test! Your father gave me another lecture about how important it is." She gestures at the citizenship booklet, sitting on the stack of papers—right on top of all her bills.

I pull the booklet toward me. "All right, let's go," I tell her, mimicking that stern teacher voice she does so well at cooking club.

Mama frowns. "What—now? I'm busy."

"Doing what?"

She waves in the general direction of the stoves. "Cooking. What else? That's the only thing in my life, isn't it? Cooking for you kids, then cooking for other people's kids. And now teaching cooking to a bunch of schoolkids. I never thought

80

this would be my life when I was in college." I can't believe what she's saying. Mama's frustration rarely gets the best of her positive attitude.

"College is overrated," I say tartly, hands on my hips. It's a dumb thing to say, because I totally don't believe it, but I'm going for comedy here.

She doesn't get the joke. "*Kya?* I should have stayed uneducated? Is that what you're saying?"

Her outburst is so uncharacteristic, I can't help but laugh. "Mama, you're losing it!" I gasp.

"Don't be disrespectful," she says. But the corners of her lips turn upward.

There's that smile. Finally, like the sun peeking out from behind gray clouds.

My stomach grumbles again. "How about this? I'll get some breakfast while you finish all this cooking. We'll meet in the living room in one hour to study. Got it?"

Mama gives me a quick, tight hug. "*Shukriya,*" she says. "You're a good daughter."

One hour later, we're in the living room, where Mama is pacing and wringing her hands. It's obvious that she's studied almost *nothing* for the citizenship test. "Who signs bills that become laws?" I ask.

"Easy, the governor. I saw him just last week on the news, talking about a new law for small business."

"National laws, Mama! Not state laws!"

She bites her lip. "Let's see. The Supreme Court?"

81

"Mama! We learned this in elementary school. The president signs bills into laws! The president!"

She runs her fingers through her untidy hair, making me wonder if she's brushed it since the night before. Her *shalwar kameez* is wrinkled, with smudges of turmeric dotting the hem. "Did you forget that I didn't grow up here?" she asks.

"How could I?" I flip some pages. "How many members does the House of Representatives have?"

She stops to think. "Fourteen. No, sixteen!"

I stare at her. "Mama, that's not even close. It's in the hundreds."

She continues her pacing and almost collides with the coffee table. "Oh. Okay. One hundred?"

"NO! That's the Senate. The House has four hundred and thirty-five!"

She turns to look at me, perplexed. "That many? Isn't that too much?"

I flip more pages, trying to hold on to my sanity. "Forget it. Who wrote the Constitution?"

She wrings her hands. "How am I supposed to know that?"

I make a frustrated sound. "By reading this booklet!" I yell. "Mama, you're impossible!"

For once she doesn't lecture me about yelling at an adult.

On Sunday, Baba takes us to the mosque. Actually, he takes Rafey and Tariq to Sunday school at the mosque, but I tag along by begging in my nicest voice.

"I thought you were going to help your mama study," he

grumbles. He's wearing a bright yellow T-shirt that's tight across his belly, and jeans that are baggier than they need to be.

"I did help. We practiced for a long time yesterday." There was more arguing than practicing, but he doesn't need to know that. "Please?"

"*Theek hai, chalo,*" he agrees. I hide my delight. I miss the mosque, Iqra Academy, and all my friends so much, it hurts. I'm dying to see everyone, hug everyone, put my face down on the prayer-hall rugs and breathe in that musty smell mixed with the perfume of all those who prayed there before me.

Baba looks at me with narrowed eyes, but he hugs me as we get in the car and asks, "You okay?"

I nod and shrug like it's no big deal.

The mosque is about thirty minutes away, closer to the mall, where buildings are taller and farms are fewer. It's really just a big warehouse that a bunch of families bought and refurbished a long time ago. It's painted dull brown on the outside, but the inside is really nice. There's one huge hall laid with light-green carpet for praying, a long and narrow dining room laid out with rows of tables and plastic chairs, and another smaller hall for Sunday school. Rafey and Tariq are met at the door by a small, thin woman with graying hair, her smile as warm as honeyed paratha.

"Nasreen aunty, *salaam alaikum!* You look so pretty!" I say. It's true. She's wearing a crisp white *shalwar kameez* with tiny orange flowers on the dupatta.

"*Walaikum salaam,* Sara. How nice to see you!" She hugs

83

me tightly. "Ever since you left for middle school, you've just disappeared."

I hug her back. She smells like chai and ginger, sort of like Mama. "I'm sorry. I'll try to come more often."

"You better!" Nasreen aunty was my teacher for math, English, and social studies at Iqra for three years. She's also Mama's best friend and Rabia's mom. I look around eagerly. "Where's Rabia?"

She points to a table in the corner. "Sulking in the back somewhere. I told her to teach the little kids their alphabet, but she said she needed a break from all the Arabic. Maybe you can talk some sense into her."

I doubt it. Rabia can be very stubborn. But I head over to where she's sitting. When she sees me, she throws her arms wide enough to hug a bear.

"Rabia!" I squeal.

She's the same Rabia I've known since forever. Brown skin like mine, dressed in jeans and a long red tunic, a black gem-studded hijab on her head. She could be my twin. Plus the hijab, of course.

We hug, then laugh, then hug again. Seeing each other on grainy Google Hangouts is not the same as being face-to-face, close enough to smile together.

"You totally forgot all about me, you meanie!" she cries, and the tone of her voice makes me think that she's been missing me. A lot.

"It's the fault of those terrible middle school teachers and

84

their homework," I say. "And the students are awful, all white and superior."

She pauses, her eyes scrunched up as if she can't figure out whether I'm joking or not. "Wait, is it true? Are they really awful to you?"

I shrug. "Nah, it's okay. Most of them just ignore me. Except Elizabeth."

"Who's Elizabeth?"

"No one. Maybe my friend." I stop, thinking. "I'm not sure yet."

Rabia slaps me lightly on the arm. "You'd better not make new friends and forget all about me!" she warns, and I heave a sigh of relief that she's still my best friend.

We put our jackets on and sneak out to the empty playground. Rabia sits on the swings, lifting her face to the sun with half-closed eyes. "It's been weird since you left," she admits.

"Really?" I know exactly what it's like to sit alone in class, watching other people with their friends. "Sorry, I guess."

She shrugs. "It's getting better. Although we all miss you. The other day in art class, we were watching a documentary about French impressionism and one of the girls said you'd have known all the names of the painters."

I smile a little because I probably would have. I sit on the other swing and take out my sketchbook. It's been a long time since I just sketched.

"Anything interesting?" Rabia asks.

I turn the page to show her my sketch from this morning.

85

It's a rectangle with a henna-inspired border and a cooking pot in the middle with steam rising from it. HAMEED'S KITCHEN, it says on the bottom in Arabic-style script. "What do you think?"

She opens her eyes wide. "I didn't know your mom had a name for her catering business!"

I slap the sketchbook shut. "She doesn't. I made it up," I mutter. "It's stupid."

She tries to move my hands. "No, it's not! I really like that design on the border. Have you shown Aunty yet?"

I stand up. Baba's waving to me from the front of the building. "I have to go," I tell her, relieved.

She pouts at me as I leave. "I want to see that when you're done with it, young lady!" she calls.

"I'll think about it," I tease, and she sticks her tongue out.

At school on Monday, every time I pass Elizabeth in the hallway, she's giggling with Maddy. I'm surprised she's forgiven that girl for choosing someone else as her cooking showcase partner.

Finally, I gather up courage and wave, but they don't notice. Her friend Micah sees me, though, and waves back at me madly, like he's trying to hail a taxi. He's funny.

Spending time with Rabia has somehow made me even lonelier. The bright lights of the school hallways feel garish after the mosque's warm yellow bulbs. And the mass of students with their loud laughter seems rude after my Muslim

86

friends' kind smiles. Someone in a red hoodie and blue jeans torn at the knees almost bumps into me. "Sorry," he mutters, and I recognize Ahsan Kapadia from elementary school at Iqra.

"Hi," I start to say, but Ahsan has already disappeared around the corner with a bunch of other boys. I guess I'm the only one who didn't get the "How to Make Friends in a New School" memo.

On Tuesday, as soon as the last bell rings, I head to the water fountain. I need to wake myself up with a few splashes of water on my face. I nearly fell asleep during social studies. Kids stream out of their classrooms and hurry noisily past me. I take a big gulp of water and look up at the bulletin board. There's the International Festival flyer again. The bright yellow paper catches my eye. There's some fine print at the bottom. I lean forward, trying to read it, wondering if I can sue the school if I go permanently cross-eyed. I can just imagine the headline in the town newspaper: "Girl Loses Eyesight After Reading Recipe Competition Rules."

"What's so interesting?"

I turn around so fast, my hip bangs into the water fountain. Ouch. Elizabeth is standing next to me, laughing.

I throw a mock-angry look at her. "And what are you doing outside the nurse's office again? Having another period scare?" I ask.

She blushes. Again. She moves closer to me to let other kids pass. "How was your weekend?" she asks.

I shrug. "My mom drove me nuts with her citizenship test. She doesn't know even the basic facts, like each state has two senators."

Elizabeth throws up her hands in exasperation. "My mom won't even pick up her study book. Does she think she can walk into that test and pass just because she speaks English?" She pauses. "Not that your mom doesn't speak English. That's not—I meant, because my mom grew up speaking English."

I smile again to show her I understand.

She looks down at her hands, where she's playing with the charms of her bracelets. "I'm not even sure my mom wants to be American anymore. She doesn't get how important it is."

How important it is to me, Elizabeth doesn't say, but I know how she feels.

An idea drops like a ton of bricks on my head. I reach out and grasp her hand. "Don't you see? This is perfect!"

She wrinkles her eyebrows. "What's perfect? I feel like it's the actual definition of imperfect."

The end-of-school rush of kids is getting thinner. I pull Elizabeth with me toward the front doors. "We both have the same problem. Moms who need to study for the citizenship test. Moms who are driving us nuts. Moms who have already met once."

Elizabeth's eyes open wide, and her mouth stretches into an O as she figures out what I'm hinting at. "They could practice for the test together. Study buddies!" she exclaims, as if it's all her idea.

I roll my eyes. "Bingo."

"Sara, you're a genius."

Finally, someone who understands me. "I know."

10

Elizabeth

HALLOWEEN IS NEXT WEEK, but Maddy and I still haven't picked our costumes.

"What about *Alice in Wonderland*?" I suggest at lunch. "There's a ton of characters to choose from. The Mad Hatter. The Cheshire Cat." Micah leans close to me, tilts his head, and does his best impression of a grinning cat. I push him away. "I'll go as Alice. You'd make a great Red Queen, Mads."

It's a mean thing to say. The Red Queen is bossy, impatient, and orders people's heads chopped off unless they do what she wants. Actually, she's a lot like Mrs. Kluck. Maddy isn't as bad as that. She's been spending more and more time with Stephanie, even at lunch. I miss her, but I don't know how to tell her, and my suggestion comes out as a veiled insult.

If Maddy caught my burn, she ignores it. "You only want to go as Alice because she's British," she says. "Anyway, I've been meaning to tell you. Steph is baking for a charity event on Halloween. She wants me to help serve cupcakes." Maddy smiles like this is the best news ever.

My mouth is too dry to speak. I touch my Star of David, then each of my British charms, which usually calms me down. But I can't stop shaking my head.

"Is she making you wear a cupcake costume?" Micah teases Maddy.

"Don't give Steph any ideas," Maddy says. "The uniform is jeans and a Sweet Stephanie's apron."

"That's no fun," he says. "But at least you get to eat cupcakes." Micah raps his drumsticks on the table. "Band room. See ya later."

Now that Maddy and I are alone, I take a sip of water and choke out, "You can't skip trick-or-treating. We have to come up with costumes, carve pumpkins together, trade candy with Justin. Those are, like, friendship traditions."

Maddy leans back, arms across her chest. "I told Steph you wouldn't understand."

I don't care that I'm pouting. "That's not fair."

Stephanie interrupts us. "What's not fair?" She's been walking around the lunchroom with a tray of chocolate milk containers—lined up to hide the mini cupcake samples she is definitely not supposed to be giving out right now.

"Elizabeth doesn't want me to volunteer at your charity event," Maddy says.

"That's not what I said," I protest.

"It's for a really good cause," Stephanie says in her snottiest tone.

Maddy nods, her dark ponytail bouncing up and down.

Lately she's been wearing her ponytail higher up, exactly like Stephanie.

Maddy leans toward me and says, "It's a Halloween party for sick kids. Kids who can't trick-or-treat."

Now I feel like the worst person ever.

"Maybe I'll ask Sara to go with me," I say, secretly hoping Maddy will be jealous.

"Great idea!" Steph says. She gives me a knowing look. "Sara could use a friend."

"To show her American holidays and stuff," Maddy adds.

Steph gives her head a small shake and raises one blond eyebrow at Maddy. They're not supposed to be having secret, wordless conversations. Maddy is *my* best friend.

How could she do this to me? Maddy knows how much I love Halloween. I'd ask Micah to go trick-or-treating, but he always helps his family host a giant haunted house. Every year, they buy a new decoration for their lawn. Not cheap cardboard gravestones, but full-on motorized zombies that creep across the driveway by themselves. He told me it freaks out the little kids in their neighborhood.

"That's settled, then!" Stephanie flounces away.

I wish Micah were still here. I'd tell him, "If Halloween doesn't work out this year, at least I have Purim," and he'd know exactly what I meant.

Micah and I agree that Purim is the best Jewish festival. Every spring, our synagogue celebrates the story of Esther. There's a special book that tells what happened when an evil man named Haman tried to kill off all the Jews in Persia—even the Persian queen, a young Jewish woman named Esther.

Everyone dresses up as Queen Esther, her husband the king, or Haman. Lots of kids reuse their superhero and princess costumes from Halloween. I always go as Esther, tweaking my outfit each year. Last spring, Bubbe helped me bedazzle my purple cape.

Micah's favorite character is Haman. "The villain always has the best part," he says. "Also, the best cookies." We both love hamentaschen, triangle-shaped cookies that are supposed to resemble Haman's hat.

During Purim, our congregation gathers at the synagogue to listen to the Megillah, the scroll that tells Esther's story. We boo and spin noisemakers whenever Haman's name is mentioned. Micah is a goof, shaking his fist at everyone. Last spring, he tried to convince *me* to go as Haman. I still have the sheet of stick-on furry mustaches he gave me.

What does Halloween have that Purim doesn't? Endless costume options, running around in the dark, and bags full of candy, that's what. I make up my mind. At cooking club, I'm going to ask Sara if she wants to go trick-or-treating with me.

On Friday afternoon, our recipe is tarka daal – spicy lentil soup with a fried onion garnish. While Sara and I put ingredients into our saucepan, I lead into my question. "Sara, do you like costumes? You know—cosplay, theater stuff."

She stops stirring. "Who doesn't? We still have a giant

93

tub of hats and costumes in our basement. My brothers run around in their superhero gear all the time. It is so annoying." She pauses to wipe her eyes on the sleeve of her tie-dye tunic. "Wait. What does this have to do with daal?"

"It doesn't," I admit. "It has to do with Halloween."

She focuses her attention on the chopping block, which is covered in onions, garlic, and cumin seeds. Maddy's probably complaining to Stephanie right now about the spicy smell. I sneak a glance at their station. I swear their high ponies bounce in unison—one dark, the other blond.

"Do you want to go trick-or-treating together?" I ask Sara. "I usually go with Maddy, but she's helping Stephanie with some catering thing. I was thinking of going as Alice in Wonderland."

I stop talking. Sara is banging her wooden spoon against the sides of the pot so hard, some lentils pop out.

"I don't do Halloween," she says. Her voice has a hard edge.

"That stinks. Is it a religious thing?"

She glares at me as if I just tore up her favorite princess costume. "Don't you know anything about Muslims? We cover our hair and fast from sunup to sundown all year long and we're not allowed to do anything fun."

"I guess that means no?"

"You guessed right."

"Sorry I asked," I mumble. I busy myself at the sink, washing the cutting board, so I can avoid talking to her. Sara goes

94

back to stirring our stew. She hardly says a word for the rest of class. It makes me realize how much we usually laugh together, rolling our eyes every time Mrs. Kluck glares at Sara's mother.

Today, whatever friendly feelings I have toward Sara are smothered by her silence, like when you order a delicious salad at a restaurant and it's slathered in a dressing so oily that you can barely eat a bite.

Mrs. Hameed demonstrates how to fry the onions and cumin, then dumps the mixture into the stew. It sizzles impressively, popping like fireworks. The class *oohs* in appreciation, but Sara stands rigid next to me. I ask, "When are we meeting to work on our showcase recipe?"

She replies tartly, "I was going to say Wednesday after school, but you'll be out begging strangers for candy, so forget it."

Why is she being so mean? I try to calm myself down by touching my charms: star, Union Jack, teacup, TARDIS. Then I say, "Your mom expects us to have a recipe. I don't want to let her down."

"Whatever."

Why did I ever agree to partner with Sara Hameed? Maddy's right. Sara thinks she's better than everyone else at this school.

I leave without saying goodbye. I'd rather stand outside in the cold, waiting for my mom in the carpool line, than stand inside getting the silent treatment.

A few days later, on Halloween night, I offer to sit at our

95

door, handing out candy. It's not so bad. I'll get to see all the adorable little kids in their dragon, princess, and superhero outfits. *Dragon Princess Superhero*. Sounds like a great idea for an anime series.

Justin comes into the kitchen, crying. He's dressed in his Spider-Man costume, but the edge of the collar is pulled into his mouth.

"What's wrong?" I put my hands on his shoulders and lean down to examine his face.

"Taemin is sick. He wasn't in school. He's not allowed to trick-or-treat. I can't go without my best friend." I know how he feels. "Halloween is ruined," he sobs.

Good thing he's not wearing a mask. When Justin cries, it's a big, snotty mess.

"Elizabeth can take you," Mom calls out from her knitting spot.

If she's noticed that Maddy's not here to help me put the jack-o'-lanterns on our front step, that I'm not dressed in a costume, she hasn't said anything.

Justin throws his arms around my middle. Robin Hood barks at us, concerned that roughhousing is about to happen.

"Mom, we have to put Robin in your room before kids start ringing the doorbell," I say.

"I'm on it. You deal with Justin." Mom gets up slowly and coaxes Robin upstairs.

"Please come with me, Els," Justin begs. He'll be as tall as

David someday, but for now, he only comes up to my shoulder. "I'll be your best friend forever."

"You already are, you manipulative little beast." With Maddy out of the picture and Sara barely speaking to me, that's probably true. Justin and Micah are the best friends I've got.

I kiss Justin's forehead, the only place on his face that's not covered in tears and goo. I missed him so much this summer. The girls in my cabin played kickball and learned dance routines, but I always sat on the sidelines. How could I play, when missing my family made me feel like there was a tree in my heart that had lost all its leaves?

"You need a costume," Justin says.

I nod. "I have an idea."

I run upstairs and raid my craft drawer. There's the sheet of stick-on mustaches Micah gave me for Purim, looking like a set of hairy lip-caterpillars. I stand in front of the mirror and stick a furry mustache on my upper lip.

Justin pokes his head in my door. "Ready?"

"Still needs something."

"A hat," he suggests.

Justin surveys the row of hats lined up on my closet shelf. He points to the gray-and-pink tweed cap Nan bought me last Christmas in England, right before she was diagnosed with cancer. I press my face to the fabric and inhale, to see if it still smells like her. There's a faint scent of Violet Mints, the

97

lavender-flavored candy Nan loved. It catches me by surprise, even though I was hoping to find it there.

For a moment, it's summer and I'm back with Nan in her garden. She's wearing a cotton dress with flowers on it. We reach beyond the lavender patch into a thick green hedge.

"Quiet," she whispers, parting the small branches. Deep inside the hedge, there's a nest of twigs cupping three speckled eggs.

"Why isn't the bird sitting on her eggs?" I ask.

Nan points to a nearby oak tree. "There she is, a little sparrow. Coming back from stretching her wings, I should think."

I wonder if Justin will have memories like that when he's my age, or if Nan died when he was too young to really know her.

I put the tweed cap on and check myself in the mirror one more time. "It's perfect," I say, combing out my hair with my fingers. I don't even have to change my jeans and sweater. I am a girl, incognito. I think it's my favorite Halloween costume ever.

11

Sara

I HATE HALLOWEEN. When I was little, I'd stand with my face pressed up against the front window, watching the neighborhood kids stride around in their costumes, plastic pumpkins filled with candy clutched in their hands, parents trailing anxiously behind them.

"Sara, stop staring outside!" Mama would scold me. "They'll see you and then they'll come ringing our doorbell, wanting candy."

I never told her that I wished they'd ring our doorbell. I never told her I wished with all my heart to go trick-or-treating with them. Of course not. Halloween is *haram*—forbidden. For one night every year, I wish I was *Sarah* instead of *Sara*.

Elizabeth thinks dressing up in a costume is no big deal. How could she know that Mama and Baba would die of grief if I ever said anything about Halloween? Nasreen aunty had talked about it in Sunday school last year. "We all came to this country for a better future," she'd said earnestly. "We love being American, celebrating holidays like Thanksgiving and July Fourth. But Halloween is a holiday with pagan roots, against the teachings of Islam."

The only person who'd looked unconvinced was Ahsan Kapadia. His family has a huge Halloween display on their front lawn every year, complete with witches and goblins. He left Iqra at the end of that year. I heard Mama and Nasreen aunty talking about it later. "They're not very observant," Nasreen aunty said. "I think Ahsan will be happier in public school."

My dark mood becomes even darker when Mama and Baba begin to argue in Urdu after dinner. "*Kya?* I thought this was already paid," comes Baba's angry voice from the kitchen. I don't usually eavesdrop, but Halloween has put me on edge. All the happy commercials on television showing kids wearing costumes, the noises on the street outside, give a heaviness to the pit of my stomach. Once again, I'm the odd one out, the outsider, not really part of this community where I was born and have lived all my life.

"Don't worry about it—it's my responsibility." Mama's tone is so unlike her. Harsh. Mad.

"Five hundred is not a joke, Hina!" Baba almost shouts. And with a flash, I understand what they're fighting about. Mama's catering-expense bills. The ones she told me not to worry over. Apparently, there's a lot to worry over. Enough

100

to make my normally easygoing parents fight loud enough to wake up the neighbors.

Only the neighbors are too busy trick-or-treating to care.

We pray the evening prayers together as a family, as always. Tariq and Rafey nudge each other and giggle, but I ignore them. I listen to Baba recite the verses from the Quran, his melodious voice washing over me in gentle waves. I close my eyes and breathe deeply again and again. Beside me, Mama is doing the same, and suddenly I want to hug her.

Or maybe I want to be hugged.

By eight thirty, Mama and Baba have gone into their room and shut the door firmly, after reminding me to keep the porch light off in the universal signal of party poopers. Might as well put up a neon sign in our front yard saying: WE ARE DIFFERENT! WE ARE NOT TRUE AMERICANS! NO CANDY OR COSTUMES HERE. MOVE ON TO THE NEXT HOUSE!

Tariq and Rafey are watching the neighborhood kids from their bedroom window upstairs, calling out names and saying things like "Hope that candy rots your teeth, DeShawn!" and "You better share your stash with us tomorrow, Antonio!" They'd better hope Mama and Baba don't hear them.

I envy my brothers. They feel no shame in being Muslim. They're too young to appreciate how different they are from their classmates. If I were in a better mood, I'd ask them the secret to their carefree attitude. The five hundred dollars Mama owes the bank makes it worse, looming over me like a giant spider spinning a web around my family.

I can't help taking a peek out our front window like I used to do when I was younger. Immediately I wish I hadn't. The street lamps are ablaze, and I see Elizabeth crossing the road outside our house, holding a younger boy's hand. He looks about the same age as the twins. Does Elizabeth have a brother too?

She's wearing a hat of some sort . . . and is that a mustache on her face? I bite my lip to keep from smiling.

Elizabeth turns her head toward me, and I quickly drop the curtain. My heart is thudding. I feel like a stalker. Even from behind the curtain, I can hear Elizabeth's brother laughing, her confident voice in reply, and the sounds pull me back to that lonely, hollow feeling I always get on Halloween.

I head back to the kitchen table. I have a lot to do. It's a weeknight, and I have three math worksheets to power through. Plus, my sketch of the business flyer is almost complete. I want to show it to Mrs. Newman tomorrow. I don't like showing anyone my drawings—they're almost like the private part of my thoughts—but Mrs. Newman is different. Her smile makes me feel as if I really have some talent.

I start on math. Fraction multiplications are hard but nothing I can't handle. This was fifth-grade work at Iqra. Of course, the memory of doing math worksheets with Rabia is now stuck in my head. Rabia loved eating chili cheese popcorn with extra butter while she worked. She said it pushed her brain to calculate faster. The smell of those things made me gag, but I loved doing math with someone who understood me. Someone who knew that my favorite subject in the whole world is art. Someone who would never ask me if I'd like to go trick-or-treating.

I reach over to the phone and dial her number.

"Hello? *Salaam?*" It's Nasreen aunty.

"Oh, *salaam alaikum,* Aunty," I say, flustered. "Is Rabia there?"

There's a weird little silence. Then she replies, "Rabia went out for a little while, just around the neighborhood."

Out in the neighborhood? On Halloween? How is that possible? Nasreen aunty is a Muslim-school teacher. She's even stricter than Mama. "What's she doing out tonight?" I ask, my voice shaky. Hot tears begin to pool in my eyes.

"Just for a walk with her father, that's all." Her voice is soothing. "No costume or anything. And you know I don't allow candy."

"Of course not," I echo, but something hard and brittle twists inside my chest as I say goodbye. For a long while I sit at the kitchen table, head in my hands, math worksheets crumpled under my elbows.

Baba wanders into the kitchen and taps me on the head. *"Kya hua, jaanoo?"* he asks. He's wearing a blue-and-white-striped pajama suit, and bunny slippers on his feet. Glasses perch sideways on his forehead.

I sigh. "Nothing happened."

"I'm making tea. Want any?"

I shake my head. "I need to finish my homework. Then I'll go to bed."

He switches on the little kitchen TV and searches for something using the remote. "Channel fifty-three," I tell him helpfully, already knowing what he's looking for.

"*Shukriya.*" The A-Team springs into action, all glossed hair and rippling muscles. Baba smiles and mutes the volume, then begins the familiar ritual of tea making. Put the kettle to boil, take out sugar and one Lipton tea bag from the pantry, milk from the fridge. Find a teacup and mismatched saucer from the cabinet. Sometimes he eats a cracker or biscuit with his tea, but not tonight. He sits beside me at the table and peers at my sketchbook. "Drawing again?" he murmurs.

I pull the book toward me and cover it with the math worksheets. Something about isosceles triangles that I learned the year before at Iqra. Thankfully, he turns to the television screen and lets me work in silence. Mr. T is looking angry as usual, but Baba grins as he watches, as if the big actor is his personal friend. When the commercials come on, he turns back to me. "You know, jaanoo, this Halloween business gets me quite depressed too. Who wouldn't want to go out dressed like a rabbit and beg for candied carrots?" He wiggles his bunny slippers, trying to make me smile.

The image of Baba dressed in a white rabbit suit, front teeth sticking out, crunching a giant carrot swims in front of my eyes. I can't help myself. I giggle.

"That's my girl," he says.

The kettle begins to whistle, and he gets up to pour the boiling water into his teacup. "I have to say, Sara, I expected Rafey and Tariq to be sad tonight. Not you. You're a big girl now. What do you care about these silly holidays?"

Doesn't Baba get it? I'm almost a teenager. Being left out of social situations isn't helping me make friends at middle school.

I put my pencil down with force. Math is winning the battle tonight. "I know you think I'm being childish," I say. Okay, maybe I whine it. "Everything is different in this new school. In life, in general. This girl Elizabeth, she's the closest thing I have to a friend at school. She asked me to go trick-or-treating with her tonight. I mean, aren't we too old for trick-or-treating? But I felt so bad saying no. Like, I'm Muslim, so I can't do anything fun, you know? And even Rabia's going for a walk with Uncle around the neighborhood, and I'm stuck here doing stupid math that I totally know but can't remember for some reason."

My voice wavers and threatens to dissolve into tears again. I wipe my eyes and go back to my worksheet. "Never mind. Forget I said anything," I whisper.

Baba stirs milk and sugar into his tea — one teaspoon of each, measured with slow and steady hands — and gazes thoughtfully at me. I know because I'm peeking at him from the corner of my eye.

"Let me tell you a story," he finally says. "When I was a teenager, there was a new Urdu movie in the cinema, quite

105

scandalous. The whole nation was shocked at the women dancing in sarees and the men singing love songs. It may sound innocent to you, but thirty years ago, it was a big deal. It made the news, I tell you."

I sneak another peek at him. He's sitting back in his chair, eyes half closed, smiling a little. "I was dying to go watch that movie, Sara. But of course my father put his foot down and said, 'No. We're Muslims, and we'll never watch such filth. Imagine the harm it could do to a young child's mind.' I complained and argued, even wept—oh, yes, I did—but he refused to let me go."

I try to imagine Baba as a teenager, with his father standing over him ugly-frowning like a Pakistani Mr. T. Only it's hard to imagine, because I've never seen Dada in real life. He died the year before I was born, and we only have a few grainy pictures of him. Bald like Baba, a thick mustache, and a serious face.

"So that's it? You were a good boy? An obedient son?" I know this is the moral of the story. It's the moral of every story Baba ever tells.

Baba shakes his head. "No, actually, I was quite disobedient. I sneaked out of the house and went with my friends to a midnight showing. I watched the movie, feeling quite brave the whole time."

I lean forward, eyes wide. "Really? You disobeyed your dad? What happened—was it very scandalous? And how did

106

you feel afterward? Did he ever find out?" I pause. "Wait a minute—why are you telling me this? Aren't you afraid I'm going to sneak out and go trick-or-treating?"

He takes a sip of his tea. "I'm telling you because I trust you. You're a good daughter, Sara, much more than I was a good son at your age. You're more responsible and caring. My father never found out that I'd watched the movie, but the guilty feeling of disobeying my father has stayed with me all these years. I have always felt bad about it, a horrible sick feeling in my stomach."

"I know that feeling," I tell him, looking down at the table.

Baba continues, "Your mother and I always try to explain things to you. Why something is bad, why it's better to stay away. We don't just lay down the law and expect you to blindly obey. That was the way things were done in the old days. It's different now. And we trust you'll do what's right."

I look up. "You don't talk to me about everything," I insist. "You don't talk to me about the money Mama owes, or the awful things people say to you in the street sometimes."

He frowns, then reaches over to switch off the television. "I think you should go to sleep, jaanoo," he tells me. "Tomorrow this Halloween business will be over and you'll be happy to be the only child in your school without a stomachache from eating all that candy."

"I'll also be the only one without any friends," I grumble.

With a sigh, Baba gets up and shuffles toward his room,

107

taking his tea with him. At the doorway, he turns and gives me a sad little smile. "This Elizabeth girl sounds okay. I'm glad you're making friends."

He's gone before I realize he never answered my question about Mama's loan. I can help. I *will* help, whether they want me to or not.

12

Elizabeth

It's kind of fun trick-or-treating with Justin. As he dashes from house to house, ringing doorbells, his happiness reminds me of a bubbling pot of delicious lemon curd, cooking on the stovetop. I skip along beside him, not caring who might see me. Who needs friends when I have my younger brother?

When we get home, there's a mountain of giant sneakers by our front door.

"David's mates are here," Mom complains, rubbing her forehead. David always invites more kids than Mom has energy for. "I'm pulling the plug on the game console at nine o'clock. Then they'll bugger off home. Thank goodness."

I chuckle at Mom's British slang.

"Gotta take my costume off." I wiggle my mustache, trying to make her smile. "I'll let Robin out."

The second I open the door to Mom's room, Robin darts downstairs. He barks and sniffs at all the shoes. I let him out in our fenced backyard, where he barks at a few straggling trick-or-treaters. When Robin is sure that the danger is contained, he comes back in, plops down in his bed and falls asleep.

I wish my life were that easy. Bark at people when I'm worried or angry, let them know exactly what I'm thinking, and then — poof! — crash into bed and sleep it off.

I change into my Cybermen pajamas. Aunt Louise sent them to me at summer camp, the only care package I got. "What is that?" the girls in my cabin teased, pointing at the print on my pajama bottoms. Some of them recognized the robot bad guys from *Doctor Who,* but even those girls had never watched the show. It didn't stop them from insisting that I share the Tim-Tam cookies and Jelly Babies that Aunt Louise had tucked into the box.

I wait until I hear David saying goodbye to his friends. By the time I get downstairs, he and Mom are arguing.

"We had a deal. No more video games," Mom says.

"I'm not," David insists. "I'm just going down there to clean up." He thunders down to the basement.

Justin's candy is spread over the kitchen table. As he gorges on sugar, Mom picks over his treats, checking for anything that's open or "out of the question."

"Mom," I ask, "what do you do when you and Aunt Louise have a fight?"

She pops a gummy Life Saver into her mouth. "Are you and Maddy fighting? Is that why you didn't trick-or-treat together?"

I sit at the table and spin a small packet of Starburst.

"Maddy went to some Halloween charity thing with this girl Stephanie. She says we're her two best friends, but she acts like Stephanie is better than me."

It all comes rushing out, how Maddy didn't write to me over the summer, how she's more interested in swim team than *Doctor Who*, how she's transforming into a ponytailed clone of Stephanie Tolleson.

I sigh and unwrap one of Justin's Twix bars, my favorite.

He glares at me. "Rude. Ask first."

"Hmm," Mom says. She stacks David's empty pizza boxes. "Let me guess. Stephanie lives in a big house. She goes to the Montgomerys' church."

"I've never been to her house, but you're right about church." Mom sinks heavily into a chair at the table. "So, about Aunt Louise," I prompt her.

She runs a hand through her short hair. "It's different with a sister. One of us always apologizes. When friends have a falling-out, they don't talk things over. They drop you. My best chum at school did that to me."

Justin pours a mini bag of M&M's into his mouth. Mom swats his arm. "Oi!" she scolds him.

What if Maddy decides she's not my friend, then bottles up all the time we've spent together and puts it away on a shelf to gather dust? The thought makes me feel grimy, as if I'm a dusty old jar, waiting for Maddy to decide I'm useful.

I slump, putting my elbows on the table and my chin in my hands.

Mom asks, "What about your cooking-club partner? You're always laughing together when I pick you up from class."

"I thought we were getting to be friends," I say. "But when I asked her to go trick-or-treating, she got upset."

"A lot of religious people don't celebrate Halloween," Mom says. "Maybe it's a touchy subject for her."

I hadn't thought about it like that. "What should I do?"

Mom stands up. "Why don't you apologize? Do something nice for her. If you were grownups, I'd say, 'Invite her to lunch.'"

Mom slides Justin's haul back into his plastic pumpkin. "Enough sweets for you, young man," she says.

"It's called *candy*, Mom," Justin corrects her.

"I speak *proper* English, unlike some people around here," Mom teases.

David appears, carrying a garbage bag full of pizza crusts and soda cans. "Want to build a safe for your candy, Justin?" he asks. "I saw a cool Lego tutorial online."

Justin jumps up. "Yes! I'm going to lock up all my Twix bars so *someone* doesn't take them." He blinks at me.

"Hey. Don't forget who took you trick-or-treating," I say.

The next morning, Sara walks up to me before homeroom. "I'm sorry I snapped at you about Halloween," she says. She tugs at the sleeve of her tunic. It has lace edging. I wonder if it's itchy.

"I was going to apologize to you," I say.

"You didn't do anything wrong. It's just that I'm not

112

allowed to dress up or go trick-or-treating. And forget about candy." Sara presses her lips together, then lets out a breath. "I get so mad. I hate feeling left out." She squishes her eyes almost closed. Before I can ask if she's okay, Sara says, "That's all. See you in class."

"Wait." I step in front of her before she runs off. "Want to sit at my lunch table today?"

She shakes her head. "Maddy hates me, remember?"

Mrs. Kluck strides down the hallway, seeking out trouble. I can almost hear the ominous *swish-swish* of her pantyhose over the screeches and shouts of the sixth-grade hall. "No loitering at your lockers," she calls over the noise. "Get your things and proceed to homeroom."

I stall, pretending to take a few more books out of my locker. "Maddy's been spending most of lunch at Stephanie's table," I admit. "So, will you? Sit with me. And Micah."

"You mean abandon my corner near the bathrooms?" Sara puts a finger to her cheek, as if she has to give this serious thought. "I don't know. I kind of like sitting by myself." She keeps a straight face, but her sparkling eyes tell me she's joking.

I roll my eyes at her. "Please?"

She's back to fingering her sleeve, and suddenly I think of Justin when he was little. He used to have an old worn-out blankie he'd smooth over and over whenever he was scared or nervous. "What about Maddy?" Sara asks.

"She can sit where she likes," I say, reminding myself that

113

Maddy has ditched me twice since school started. She chose Stephanie for her kitchen partner. And Stephanie again for Halloween.

"It was so different at my old school," Sara says. "We had twelve students in my class, and everybody was friends. Everybody!"

"I thought you went to Bennett Branch Elementary." It's one of the bigger local schools around here, with even more students than we had at Watersville Elementary.

"I went to a private school. My mosque runs it." Sara puts her backpack on the ground as if she has a long story to tell. "It's on the other side of the county. There aren't enough Muslim kids out here to carpool or hire a bus. I guess my parents got tired of driving me every morning."

"I bet you miss your friends." Our school is huge. There are three hundred kids in sixth grade alone.

"I'm getting used to this place. Now that I have a friend here." She looks right at me. I give her my biggest smile.

"So, how about sitting with your friend?"

The hallway seems suddenly silent. Are we friends? Sara seems as uncertain as I am, but I notice she's not pulling at her sleeve anymore.

"Deal," Sara says. "As long as we can focus on our festival recipe."

The homeroom bell chimes. Mrs. Kluck claps her hands hard. "Get moving, sixth-graders!" she calls. Without a word, Sara and I dash to our homerooms.

The next day, I pass Sara a note during language arts: *What are we cooking today?*

I can't wait to get to the school kitchen, where the food is edible. Dad came home last night, and Mom tried to make a special dinner. She cut a recipe out of the *Baltimore Sun,* pasta with walnuts and anchovy sauce. Only we didn't have anchovies in the house, so Mom used canned sardines. The result was noodles covered in Pepto-Bismol–pink gravy. Robin Hood ended up getting most of the pasta in his dog bowl.

Sara checks to make sure Ms. Saintima isn't watching, then opens the paper.

Not telling! she writes back.

Ms. Saintima sits on the edge of her desk. She's wearing red-and-black batik pants and a Harry Potter scarf. Ms. Saintima is my favorite teacher at Poplar Springs. She's young and cool and there's a mile-high stack of fantasy novels on her desk that we're allowed to borrow.

"We've been talking about hero myths," she says. "Ancient heroes like Beowulf and Athena. And modern ones: Superman. Wonder Woman."

Micah high-fives one of his guy friends. They're both into comic books.

"Your homework mission, should you choose to accept it . . ." A few kids groan at Ms. Saintima's *Mission: Impossible* reference. "Write a paragraph about a real-life hero. You have a few minutes to get started now."

115

There's a rush of pens across paper. Everyone tries to zip through the assignment so they won't have homework this weekend.

This topic isn't so easy for me. My mom used to be my hero. When I was little, if I had trouble falling asleep, Mom would lie down with me and tell the story of how she left England. Mom always described herself as brave. She and Dad fell in love as college students, working at the performing-arts camp. Then she left behind her family, friends, even her religion to marry him.

I used to think it was romantic, but now I know coming to America was Mom's one and only adventure. It's like she landed at Ellis Island, where immigrants used to enter the United States, and got permanently stuck there—afraid to make her way to solid American ground. I wish Mom were more like Mrs. Hameed, owning her own business, leading a club at our school.

I want more than anything for Mom to take that citizenship test. Every time Dad is home, she drops hints about how much she wants to go to England. More than once, I've come home from school to find her searching for cheap flights on her phone. Aunt Louise is her only friend. I know what that's like. At summer camp, when the other girls in my cabin were practicing choreography for "It's a Hard Knock Life," I was writing letters to Maddy. I couldn't wait to get home, to see her. Of course Mom wants to go back and be where she can see her sister every day.

Sara is right. What my mom needs is a buddy.

I'm so busy thinking, the bell rings before I write a single word. I'll write my paragraph later. Now that class is over, I dash over to Sara's desk. "You can tell me now. What are we making?"

"Nope," she says. "You have to wait. And stop jumping up and down like that. It could be something disgusting, like tindas."

"Never heard of it," I say as we head to the FACS room.

"It's a vegetable. It's round and green and has no business being in any dish, ever."

"I have supreme faith in your mother's cooking. She can make anything taste delicious. Even those tondas."

"Tindas! You're really kooky, you know that?"

Sara's face has lost that pinched-up, *Don't distract me from my studies* expression. Her smile is like a big hug I didn't know I needed.

"We still have to talk about our festival recipe," I say. "We're the perfect partners. I'm sugar. You're spice."

Sara freezes outside the doorway, her smile gone. "Why am I spice? That's kind of racist."

"How is that racist? I only took sugar because I like to bake." Why is Sara so defensive? It's not like I'm challenging her to a sauté-pan duel. Sara squares her shoulders. I get the feeling I'm supposed to know the answer to this question.

"I don't know how to explain," she says. "It's more of a feeling. My family's from a part of the world that people associate

117

with spices. It's a whole stereotype. Someday I'll tell you about my neighbor Mrs. Miles."

I want to ask what happened. Did her neighbor say something racist to Sara or Mrs. Hameed? Sara's picking nervously at the edge of her tunic. I know she's not ready to tell me that story.

She says, "It's like I can't even cook without someone pointing out—you pointing out—that I'm exotic. I'm different. And you're my friend."

"I was trying to say that we work well together," I protest.

"Then say that."

Sometimes talking with Sara is hard work. What do we have in common, besides the fact that our moms are both immigrants?

That reminds me of Sara's plan. I can picture our moms, sitting at a café table with their *Learn About the United States* books, sipping tea. And that's when a great idea pops into my head.

"Working on the recipe is the perfect excuse to get our moms together," I say. "Operation High Tea."

"I don't know what that is." Sara raises a suspicious eyebrow at me.

I twirl into the FACS room like a big goof. "That's because I just made it up. I'll explain during class."

118

13

Sara

ELIZABETH EXPLAINS HER PLAN to get our mothers together as we roll out spice-infused dough for this week's recipe: samosas. According to Maddy and Stephanie, it looks like someone has dropped birdseed in the dough. Don't they recognize cumin seeds by now?

Mrs. Kluck is on her cell phone about some piece of kitchen equipment that was supposed to arrive this week. "I can't believe this incompetence!" she yells.

Mama practically shouts over her. "Samosas are Pakistani street food, similar to empanadas."

"Yum," somebody calls out.

"You want me to bring my mama to Bean Heaven?" I whisper to Elizabeth. "Who names a tea place 'Bean Heaven,' anyway?"

"It's a coffee shop," Elizabeth says in a low voice while Mama sets out the ingredients for the samosa filling: cooked ground beef, onions, and fresh cilantro. "But they also have traditional British cream tea. Nan used to say it was the most authentic tea she'd had in the United States. It's a whole thing. China teacups. Finger sandwiches and scones with clotted cream."

I can almost see her drooling.

"I bet I can talk my mom into going today, after class," she says. "Can you meet us?"

"Today?" I chew my lip. I don't like doing things without preparing. I need the exact words rehearsed in my mind. I can't just improvise where Mama is concerned. Mama has a brain like a computer. She always knows when something is up.

I cut the onions into slivers while Elizabeth breathes in the cilantro with eyes closed. "Have you ever smelled anything so bright and clean? It's almost lemony."

I fold the onion and cilantro into the keema. "Every day of my life."

Mama teaches us to cut and shape the dough into little fans, fill it with keema and spices, and seal the pastry, forming palm-size dumplings, then carry them into the main kitchen, where she's waiting with a pan full of hot oil. As Mama drops our samosas into the spattering oil, Elizabeth proclaims, "Hey! It's a Pakistani knish!" Everyone stares at her, but a few girls nod.

I raise an eyebrow. "I don't know what a knish is."

"It's Jewish street food—mashed potato in a pocket of fried dough—totally yummy." Elizabeth takes a finished samosa off the plate and bites into it. "Do I detect a scrummy hint of cumin?" She puts on a proper British accent.

"You've been watching too many cooking shows," I tell her, and laugh.

"I think I'm in love," Elizabeth replies. "Can you marry a pastry?"

"Don't eat too many. If we're going to make Operation High Tea work, you need to leave room for tea and scones."

Elizabeth sticks her pinky in the air as if she's holding a delicate teacup. "One always has room for a spot of tea," she says, still in a British accent.

"What sort of name is Bean Heaven for a tea shop?" Mama grumbles, trying to get comfortable on her stool at the coffee bar. She's stacked her folders on the table, and now there's no place for her cup of tea.

I try to act cool, as if the exact same question hadn't crossed my mind. "It refers to coffee beans, Mama," I tell her calmly. "They serve tea and coffee." I'm not allowed to drink coffee, so I order hot chocolate with whipped cream and sprinkles, even though it's warm out for November. The drink is way too sweet, and the sprinkles get caught in my teeth, but I take sips to show Mama everything is fine. It wouldn't do for her to get suspicious. "Mmm, this is nice. Just you and me!"

She frowns. Oops. Too much. I look out the window with desperate eyes. Elizabeth had better get here fast with her mom.

"Yes, it's nice," Mama admits, and relaxes beside me. "Tell me about school?"

I almost drop my cup. "Um, art is going well," I say. "We have this new assignment . . ."

121

"Oh, my gosh, look who's here!" an overly perky voice trills from the coffee shop's counter. It's Elizabeth, finally.

I stand up so quickly, I almost knock over my stool. Elizabeth and her mom stand a few feet away, teacups in hand. I say, "Nice to see you, Mrs. Shainmark. Have you met my mother?" then kick myself because didn't she meet Mama when she picked up Elizabeth last week? Elizabeth watches her mother closely, even as we're talking. Mrs. Shainmark has a faraway look in her eyes.

Thankfully, a Bean Heaven employee with long blond dreadlocks inserts himself into our awkward little tableau with a big plate of scones, jam, and thick cream.

"Elizabeth tells me you're British," Mama says. "How do you like the U.S.?"

Mrs. Shainmark settles herself on a stool and pulls the plate of scones closer. Her short brown hair is the only thing that makes her look different from other moms at Poplar Springs Middle. Her jeans and green sweater are nondescript. For a moment, I'm glad Mama stands out, with her hijab and colorful tunic.

"I've been here more than fifteen years." Elizabeth's mother looks down at her cup of tea. Her mouth settles into a downward curve, as if her whole face feels heavy. But when she looks up again, there's a new light in her eyes. "They say England is gray, but everything about America is too bright. Sometimes I wake up wondering how I'll get through another day of Type-A personalities and firm handshakes."

122

She smiles, a little sadly. "To be honest, I'm just trying to get by."

Elizabeth and I widen our eyes at each other.

"It's not that bad, Mom," she protests weakly.

Mrs. Shainmark takes a scone and passes the plate to Mama, then butters her pastry with the thick cream. "You're right, Els," she says. "I have you and your brothers."

"And Robin Hood," Elizabeth says. "He's our dog," she explains.

Mrs. Shainmark pushes Elizabeth's long bangs to the side, out of her eyes. "Let's ask Mrs. Hameed. What do you think of Americans? Be honest."

"Please call me Hina." Mama smiles again, her eyes crinkling at the corners. "These kids think everything is perfect here. What do they know about emigrating from your home and trying to manage in a new country?"

"Exactly!"

For a few seconds, the conversation stills. Clinking plates and the sound of steaming milk fill the lull. Then Elizabeth jumps in. "Mrs. Hameed is also studying for the citizenship test, Mom."

Mrs. Shainmark stops with a scone halfway to her mouth. "Really? Are you finding it as painful as I am, Henna?"

I grip my hands tightly together and wait to see how Mama reacts to this mispronunciation. But she simply puts a patient hand on Mrs. Shainmark's arm. "It's 'Heena.' And yes, adjusting to this country has been a roller coaster."

123

I relax. It's a relief to know that you can politely correct someone when they say your name wrong.

As our mothers chatter on, Elizabeth and I exchange glances. Who knew Operation High Tea would work so well? We listen for a few minutes; then Elizabeth elbows me in the side and gets up from her stool. "Sara and I need to discuss a class project. We'll be outside," she says, then gulps down her last sip of tea.

I nod emphatically. "Yes. Very important project."

Mama is hardly listening. "The citizenship test is really tough. Even high school students don't know all the facts we're tested on."

"Imagine having to learn a completely different version of history from your childhood. Here, it's not the American War of Independence, but the Revolutionary War," replies Elizabeth's mom, biting into her scone.

We slip our backpacks on and hurry out the door before dissolving into full-fledged laughter.

The weather is perfect for homework. It's been a rainy week, but today is dry. Sunlight twinkles through the trees. We don't usually come to Main Street unless Mama and Baba have friends visiting from out of state. If our mothers cared about history at all, they'd know that this street dates back to the colonial times they're supposed to be learning about. Old brownstone buildings line a winding hill, each one with an antiques shop, a boutique, or a restaurant. Elizabeth and I find an empty bench.

"Phew! That was super weird!" Elizabeth rolls her eyes as she flops down on the bench, making her glasses slide down her nose. "But they hit it off," she says as she pushes her glasses back up.

I sit down next to her and open my binder. There's a bright yellow paper tucked in the cover, the flyer for the International Festival. "I completely forgot about this," I groan.

"What's the big deal? It'll be fun."

"You don't understand — my life is already full of cooking. I have zero motivation to come up with a recipe."

She gives me a cajoling smile. "I'm your motivation! You get to work alongside the great and creative Elizabeth Shainmark!"

"Yeah, okay."

"Plus," she continues, "think of your mom. Mrs. Kluck is already on her back for everything. If we do a good job with the recipe, it will make your mother so happy."

I hadn't thought of that. "It will, I guess. She's been so stressed-out lately."

"See? She needs something to brighten up her day, make her forget the plaid tyrant breathing down her neck."

I think of Mama's pile of bills, and nod. "You've convinced me. Let's do it. But we've lost almost a week, being mad at each other."

"You were mad," Elizabeth points out, poking my arm. "I was just — awkward. I know not everyone celebrates Halloween, but I've never had a friend who didn't dress up and trick-or-treat."

125

"Never? I know I'm not the only Muslim kid in this town."

She thinks for a second. "There was a girl at Watersville Elementary. Her dad was Egyptian." She smiles to herself. "She had the best laugh and always wore bright white Adidas shoes, even with long dresses. Her name was Sariya. We were friends. But I never went to her house or anything. I missed her for a long time after she moved. I know she celebrated Halloween. She dressed up as Wonder Woman one year."

I shrug. "Maybe her family wasn't very religious."

Elizabeth touches her Star of David charm. "I'm probably not the best person to talk to about religion. We only go to synagogue when my dad's home."

The beads of my sleeve catch my attention, and I smooth them out. "I've never had a friend who was Jewish before either."

"Actually, my mom converted. It kind of makes me feel like I'm only half Jewish." She leans close and lowers her voice. "She lights the Hanukkah menorah backwards."

"I thought you just light it," I say.

"To be honest, it's kind of complicated. The first candle goes on the right"—she points to an invisible menorah—"but we light the candles left to right, so each night the newest candle gets lit first."

"That does sound complicated." I shove the flyer into Elizabeth's hand and take out my sketchbook. "So how about a recipe that combines our cultures? Like a mash-up?"

Elizabeth nods so furiously that her glasses slip down her nose again. "Just like a samosa and a knish."

I bend my head down to draw. It's a new sketch, one of Baba and the twins playing Jenga at home. It's not colored yet, and the pencil lines are thin and barely visible. I draw over them, making the sketch darker, firmer.

"That's so realistic," Elizabeth marvels.

I don't even mind that she's watching me.

"Since we're talking about religion, can I ask you a question?"

I stop sketching. Her voice is serious. Bad sign. "What?"

"How come you don't wear a headscarf like your mom?"

Even though I hate the question, I give her credit for asking it. I stare at my drawing, trying to collect my thoughts. "It's not . . . she's never asked me to. It's a personal choice, and she's always told me I can choose to wear it, or not, when I'm older." I pause. This is a topic we often discuss at Sunday school, and sometimes it gets loud because of all the different opinions. "Honestly, I wonder if I'll ever be so brave as to wear it."

Elizabeth looks startled. "Brave? How come?"

"It's the first thing people notice about Mama. They're judging her even before she opens her mouth to speak. I'm not sure I can live like that."

"I think I get it," Elizabeth says. "My mom's really shy. Sometimes it's okay when people ask about her accent. But other times she just wants to buy a gallon of milk without having to explain herself." She nudges me. "I think you're brave."

I put down my pencil and glance back at the window,

where I can see Mama and Mrs. Shainmark laughing over something. They lean toward each other, like they're sharing a secret. I wonder if Elizabeth is someone I will one day share secrets with.

"Thanks," I reply. "Anyway, I know lots of women who never wear the hijab. Even my mama didn't start wearing it until after she got married."

"Will you wear it after you get married?"

I have to laugh. "Married? My parents won't even let me stay home alone. Besides, all the boys in our school are completely ineligible. Either racist or dumb."

She shakes her head. "Micah isn't."

I go back to drawing. "Yeah, he's okay," I mutter. "But he's friends with Maddy, which is weird." I'm looking down, but I hear Elizabeth take in a sharp breath.

"He was my friend first. We go to Hebrew school together. Maddy's only known him a few weeks. Besides, she's not that bad."

"If you're me, she is definitely 'that bad.'"

Elizabeth pulls out a graphic novel and almost literally sticks her nose in it. It's *A Wrinkle in Time.* I want to ask her why she loves time-travel and space-bending stories so much, but I keep drawing. Inside I'm mad at myself for spoiling our good mood. Our mothers walk out of Bean Heaven, chatting on the stone steps of the building. I feel a little bit jealous of how easily they laugh together.

128

14

Elizabeth

School is closed on Election Day because Poplar Springs Middle is a polling station. I could have slept in. That's what David is doing. He stayed up late playing video games. My brother the teenage robot won't power on until lunchtime. Justin, on the other hand, is probably downstairs, still in his jammies and snuggling with Mom while she knits.

I always go with my dad when he votes. It used to make me feel grown up, walking into the big kids' school, holding Dad's hand. Now that I'm older, Dad takes me out for coffee after voting. Decaf mocha with whipped cream for me. Double espresso for him.

There's a knock on my bedroom door. "Ready, Els?" Dad asks.

"How's this for ready?" I'm wearing royal-blue leggings, a red shirt with a flag detail left over from the Fourth of July, and a white denim jacket.

"Your grandmother would roll over in her grave, Miss America," Dad says.

My smile crumples.

"Oh, no, Els. It was a joke." Dad puts an arm around me. "Your nan would have thought you look adorable."

"I miss her," I say. "We're not going to England for family Christmas, are we?"

Dad shakes his head. "Maybe next year. Aunt Louise doesn't have enough room for all five of us, and hotels are expensive."

I never thought it was strange that our Jewish family celebrated Christmas with Nan, Aunt Louise, and our English cousins. I love Christmas—the tree with its ornaments, visiting relatives with their houses decorated for the holiday, and carols on the radio, which Mom sings along to as long as Dad's not in the car. I never questioned it until everyone at Hebrew school started talking about bar and bat mitzvahs, which Mr. Yukht told us means "son or daughter of the commandments." Can I be a real daughter of the Hebrew commandments if I celebrate Christmas with my English family? I try not to think about it too much.

My birthday is in the summer, so my bat mitzvah is practically two years away. I'm sad that Nan won't be here for it. She made a special trip for David's ceremony. I took it for granted that she'd be at my bat mitzvah too.

There's always been a spot inside me where I keep Nan and England safe. It's more powerful than a memory because, until now, I've always known I'll go back. I'll see her again. We'll gather together for our traditional Christmas dinner of pheasant and Yorkshire pudding and sweet, creamy trifle.

I wonder if Mom feels the same way I do: if she thought she'd have another chance to share a cup of tea, shop for bargains at Marks and Spencer, or walk in Nan's garden. My whole life, I've known that sometime in the next year, I would get to help Nan pull warm eggs from the nests in the chicken coop and breathe in the lingering smell of coal in the air. Even though the village mine has been closed for decades, the scent is still there.

Now those memories are like a gray winter tree, sharp and bare.

"Let's head out before the lines get too long," Dad says.

I follow him to the car. "I was hoping Mom would get to vote today," I say as I buckle up.

"Hmm?" He's distracted, tuning to election news on the radio.

"She was supposed to get her citizenship, remember?"

Dad frowns at me in the rearview mirror. In his suit and slicked-back silver hair, he looks more like a school principal than my dad.

"It's been a rough year for your mother," he says. "We're lucky they let her postpone the test. She'll reschedule as soon as she's ready."

Not if she gets to London first, I think. What if she has so much fun with Aunt Louise that she never comes back?

"When will she be ready?" I ask.

How can I explain to Dad that when Mom lost Nan, she also lost a whole country, a huge part of herself? My dad grew up in three different states, all along the East Coast. He doesn't understand how Mom can miss a place almost as much as she misses a person.

But I get it. I feel England pulling at my heart, an echo calling to me like wind in a tree's branches, saying, *Come back, come back.*

"Let's help Mom get on track with small stuff first," Dad says. "You're doing a great job helping with the cooking, Els. That chicken you made this weekend was delicious."

"It was a curry. I learned it in cooking club." But I'm not ready to make polite conversation. "Dad, I wouldn't need to take over cooking if you were home more often," I say. "Mom's always worse when you're traveling. If you want her to get back on track so bad, do something."

Dad's hands grip the steering wheel. "It's not that easy, Elizabeth. We're five people living on one income."

And three children being raised by one parent, since you're never here, I don't say.

As we pull into the crowded school parking lot, I spot Maddy and her mom carrying signs. Mr. Montgomery is nearby, talking to voters.

Dad must notice my grim expression.

"Trouble between the Companions?" he asks. I have to give him credit for knowing what the people who travel with the Doctor are called.

"Dad, Maddy's not into *Doctor Who* anymore. She's into swimming. And *I'm* into *Salma Aunty's Desi Kitchen.*"

132

Before we can pass the sign that says NO ELECTIONEER-ING BEYOND THIS POINT, Maddy waves me over. Her mom nods. Over her nurse's scrubs, Mrs. Montgomery is wearing a sweatshirt with the incumbent county executive's name on it.

Dad takes my arm. "You can talk to Maddy after we vote. The last thing I need is a hard sell for their conservative candidate."

"What do you mean?" I ask as I wave back to Maddy.

Dad considers me for a moment before saying, "You're old enough to know. There've been some incidents of anti-Semitic and racist graffiti lately."

"Around here?"

He nods. "At the high schools. The county executive hasn't taken a strong enough stance against it, in my opinion. And my opinion counts. At least today."

"I wish Mom could help vote him out."

"Me too," Dad agrees as we line up to check in.

There's a tug on my elbow. For a second, I hope it's Maddy. But I turn to find Sara in line behind us. How does she keep showing up like that?

"Hi, Elizabeth! I love your outfit." She's standing next to a balding man with a goatee. His white jacket has his name stitched on the pocket, SAFDAR HAMEED. He's wearing khaki pants. And sandals, even though it's November. Mr. Hameed would get along great with Micah.

Before I know what's happening, our fathers are shaking hands and talking politics.

133

"What are you doing here?" I ask Sara. I lower my voice. "Aren't your parents from Pakistan?"

"My baba got his citizenship years ago." Sara's voice is loud. I bet everyone in line heard that. "He's like Mr. America. Every Election Day, I get a big lecture on what makes this country the best in the world."

A man in front of us smiles at her, and Sara grins back.

"Are you doing anything today?" I ask. "Maybe we can work on our recipe."

She shuffles her feet. "I have plans with a friend from my old school."

"Oh." I'm a little disappointed. I didn't know I was going to bump into Sara, but now that she's here, I wouldn't say no to an invitation to her house. I'd love to watch Mrs. Hameed cook in her own kitchen. "No probs."

Sara's father interrupts. "You're only going to the mall with Rabia. Elizabeth should come with you. I insist." He widens his eyes and tilts his head at her, which must be parent code for: *We talked about this. You need to make friends at your new school.*

"Great idea," my dad says, clapping me on the back. "You have a free afternoon and a mall filled with things you don't need."

"Are you sure it's okay?" I ask Sara.

She shrugs. "It's just shopping."

"I can't wait to meet your friend!" I link my arm through Sara's and jump up and down like a kangaroo, until she jumps

134

with me and we're both laughing. I'm glad Maddy and Stephanie aren't around to see us. They would not approve of our goofiness.

"We can research for our recipe at the food court. They have stands from all over the world. Mexican, sushi, Chinese, bubble tea." I count them off on my fingers.

"Fast food is not my idea of inspirational," Sara sniffs. "And what is bubble tea, exactly?"

"You've never tried bubble tea?"

Sara shakes her head.

"Trust me. You're going to love it." I wave goodbye as Dad gets his ballot. Hot chocolate with Dad and then bubble tea with Sara and her friend. This was going to be a great day.

As we're leaving, though, Maddy's father spots us. He leaves his place with the other electioneers and stops us before we get to the parking lot.

Mr. Montgomery isn't as tall as my dad, but he is big. Maddy told me his nickname is Mack, because he's built like a truck. The kind you wouldn't want to get flattened by.

He sticks out a hand for my dad to shake. "Voting red today, Josh?" he asks.

Dad is slow to take his hand. "You know the rules, Mack. No informal polling."

Maddy runs up. I'm glad to have someone to talk to so I don't have to listen to our fathers.

"Do you want to come over?" Maddy asks. She takes in my Election Day outfit, but if she has a comment about it,

135

she keeps it to herself. She's dressed in jeans, a gray hoodie, and Sperry's, the unofficial uniform of Poplar Springs Middle School students. The non-nerdy ones.

"I feel bad about ditching you on Halloween," Maddy is saying. "Stephanie really needed my help. She's raising money for this charity. They do special events for—"

I cut her off. "Sorry, I'm not free."

"Oh. Okay." She sounds so disappointed, I almost ask her to meet up with me, Sara, and Rabia. But Maddy doesn't have a great track record when it comes to getting along with Sara.

"Let's make plans over Thanksgiving break," she says. "Will your parents let you go to the mall? We can go shopping. I'll help you pick out some new clothes." She pauses and gives my red, white, and blue outfit a not-so-friendly once-over.

"I guess." I kick my TARDIS high-tops into the sidewalk. Dad puts a hand on my shoulder.

"Excuse us," he says to Mr. Montgomery. "I promised Elizabeth an Election Day treat."

I wave goodbye to Maddy.

We get in the car, but Dad doesn't start it. He sits, taking deep breaths in and out through his nose.

"Are you okay, Dad? Did you forget to charge the car?"

"It's not the car. It's that man!" He motions to the front of the school, where Mr. Montgomery is trying to convince voters to choose his candidate. "He's a—"

"A plonker," I fill in a non-swear word for Dad. "Mom would call him a plonker."

136

15

Sara

THE MALL IS CROWDED for a Tuesday afternoon. Mama settles down at a table in the food court with her cooking-club binder. "Stop fidgeting," she tells me as she looks over recipes. "Rabia will be here soon."

I see a girl in jeans and hijab waving madly at me. "There she is!"

Mama nods absentmindedly. "Remember, stay on this floor and don't leave the mall under any circumstance."

"What if there's a fire?" I ask, with only a little sarcasm.

Mama rolls her eyes. "Yes, Sara, you're allowed to leave the mall if there is a fire. Or another emergency."

Rabia reaches us and grins as if she hasn't seen us in forever.

Mama looks at her. "*Salaam alaikum,* Rabia. That hijab looks very pretty."

I turn to inspect Rabia's hijab. It's brown with bright yellow-and-green flowers like an overgrown garden. Yup, it's her usual style. She started wearing hijab last year, right after we came back from winter break. She told me she was going to do it, but it was still a shock to see her long hair covered for the first time. Her hijabs are always brightly colored, with flowers or geometrical designs.

Rabia's grin grows wider. "*Wa alaikum salaam,* Aunty, and thank you. Are you coming with us?"

"You're old enough to walk around by yourselves as long as you stick together," Mama replies. "Now, shoo! I have work to do."

We link arms and walk away. I breathe in and out like I'm winding down after a tough race. It's so nice to be with my old friend again. No stress, just being myself.

Rabia gives me a sideways glance. "Remember the time we made those stuffed bears at Build-A-Bear Workshop and strutted them around the mall, so proud of ourselves?"

I giggle a little. My bear was light blue with pink lips and a bow in her hair. I named her Bluey. She's still sitting on the top shelf of my closet with a few other precious memories. "Do you still have yours?" I ask. Her bear was a matching one with yellow fur.

"Nah," she answers, but we both know it's not true.

Thinking back, I figure it was Nasreen aunty and Mama who started this annual tradition. After shopping, they'd take us to the play area, eat ice cream, and chat. Then a few years ago, Nasreen aunty stopped coming because she got a job at Iqra Academy. I sort of threw a tantrum when I discovered our annual mall tradition was in jeopardy. Mama agreed to take us just to keep the peace. Last year she had the flu, so Baba trudged along, complaining the whole time.

I don't think we've missed a year since that first trip when we were little. I squeeze Rabia's arm, and she turns to me, eyebrows raised. "What?"

"Nothing. I'm just glad you're here."

"Stop being weird, Sara." She looks around. "So, where's this new friend of yours?"

Before I have a chance to reply, Elizabeth, still in her bright red, white, and blue outfit, walks up with an older boy who is a taller, skinnier version of her. He's all elbows and angles, even in his high school team jacket. She has an older brother?

A grin breaks out on her face. "I was looking for you guys everywhere!"

The boy says, "I'll be at Game Stop," and walks off. The back of his jacket, where it should have a football or basketball mascot, says GHS ROBOTICS.

Elizabeth says, "Let me guess. You're Rabia."

Rabia relaxes beside me. "I like this girl," she says, and we all laugh.

I jump in for introductions. "Rabia, this is Elizabeth, my friend from cooking club."

Rabia's already walking. "Come on, ladies. We have shopping to do!"

I follow, and Elizabeth falls in step next to me. On my left is Rabia, who represents the safe and comfortable life I've

139

known since I was born. She's not just my friend. Her family is friends with my family. On my right is Elizabeth, who is almost a head taller and twice as nerdy as either of us (in a good way, of course). She stands for everything new and interesting I've been experiencing recently. Middle school, cooking club, even the clashes with Maddy.

Our first stop is Claire's, where Rabia and I always get our fix of the latest bracelets and headbands. A big sign at the entrance announces FREE EAR PIERCING.

"Ooohhh!" I exclaim. "Rabia, how about it?"

Rabia scoffs. "You know we need an adult with us. Besides, I'm happy wearing one pair, thank you very much." She walks into the store and inspects a wall of long, dangly necklaces.

I can't take my eyes off the display of earrings, a different color for every month. "I could get a second one. My cousin Lailah in Pakistan has three piercings in each ear, and one in her nose." I turn to Elizabeth, wiggling my eyebrows. "How about it, Elizabeth? You with me?"

Elizabeth shakes her head. "I'm not allowed to get my ears pierced."

My smile vanishes. "Really? Not allowed? Why?"

She plays with the charms on her bracelets. "When you're Jewish, you're not supposed to harm your body. No piercings. No tattoos." She pauses to think. "There are some girls at my Hebrew school with pierced ears, so maybe it's only my family."

I have to smile at this. "I like that. Although . . . that means no ink when you're in college, young lady!"

She rolls her eyes at me. "I thought you wouldn't be allowed either. Getting your ears pierced is a lot more permanent than dressing up for Halloween."

I see her point. "It's a tradition for Pakistani girls to have their ears pierced when they're little. Rabia and I had ours done together, when we were babies. Noses come much later, usually when girls get married."

"Yeah, it's a cultural thing, not a religious thing," Rabia adds from the necklace wall. She turns, holding up a multi-colored necklace the size of a magazine page against her chest. "You likey?"

I drag her away because I know Nasreen aunty wouldn't approve. Next door to Claire's is a candle store, where Elizabeth gets a small candle marked "Tranquility" for her mom.

"That's it? You guys disappoint me!" Rabia teases, selecting a giant candle in strawberry cinnamon fragrance. "For our family bathroom." She laughs and walks up to the counter to pay. I know she gets a weekly allowance, unlike me. I also know she usually spends it all on gifts for other people.

I watch as Rabia and Elizabeth talk easily with each other. It's amazing how I'm the only one who gets tongue-tied at meeting others. Still, I'm happy that they're getting along. This is turning out to be an excellent day.

"I'm starving," Rabia announces. She leads us back to the food court, where workers are standing on ladders, putting up a gigantic Christmas tree.

"Already?" Elizabeth groans. "It's not even Thanksgiving

141

yet. Do they have to make it so over-the-top?" We pass more workers, hanging a sign that reads SANTA'S WORKSHOP. Elizabeth humphs. "No, I do not want some mall Santa asking me if I've been good this year. That's just creepy," she says.

I turn to her in surprise. "You don't celebrate Christmas?" Then I check myself. "Of course you don't. You're Jewish. Sorry."

Elizabeth shakes her head. "It's okay. We have Hanukkah at home, but we celebrate Christmas in England. Or, we did, before my nan died. She had a real tree and everything. On Christmas morning, there were pillowcases full of presents at the ends of our beds. That's an English tradition. It's way better than stockings by the fireplace. In England, no one talks about the fact that my family is Jewish. Or that my mom converted. It's like they're pretending it never happened."

I imagine her sitting in an old English house, sipping hot chocolate while snow falls outside, drawing a tiny menorah on a notepad, a Hanukkah celebration for her alone.

"I don't know what we're doing this year," she says.

I put out an arm to hug her sideways, and she hugs me back. Rabia gives me a glance but doesn't say anything. I wonder if she has anyone to hug sideways at Iqra now that I'm gone. I reach out with my other arm and hug her, too. The three of us giggle as we stumble, then straighten up again.

At the food court, we get slices of gooey cheese pizza and find a table not too far from where Mama's sitting, engrossed in her folders. "What's Aunty working on?" Rabia asks as she stashes her bags under the table and takes a long sip of Coke.

"Our school is having an international festival, and the cooking club is part of a showcase," I tell her.

"Have you decided what you're going to make?"

"Still working on it," I reply. "Something fusion, for sure."

Rabia points to our empty plates. "How about pizza? Like with chicken tikka or malai boti toppings."

"That's a great idea," Elizabeth says. "What's malai boti?"

I slap her arm lightly. "They're like kebabs, but the meat has a creamy texture. All the Pakistani joints sell them."

She opens her eyes wide. "Yum! Let's do that."

"It's too common. We need something unique." I have to grin at her expression. "Stop drooling, please!"

Rabia slurps the last of her Coke and stands up. "Okay, let's get back to shopping. I still have to buy a couple of tunics for school."

We head to Sasha's, a clothing store that Rabia and I discovered a couple of years ago, tucked into a corner of the mall. Rabia rushes to the clearance section at the back. I hang out in the front of the shop, checking out some new tops. There's one that's caught my eye: a brown-and-green-striped tunic with bell sleeves and a small collar at the neckline.

Elizabeth stays with me. "That would look great on you," she says.

"Maybe." I finger the rich fabric of the tunic. "I think I love everything in this store, actually."

"Why?"

"It's so hard to find what my mama calls modest clothes in the regular stores. You know, long enough to cover your butt, half sleeves or longer, not so tight you can't even breathe."

"I know what you mean." Elizabeth takes a tunic off the rack that says BOGO and holds it up. "Some of my *Doctor Who* tees are getting too small in certain areas. I don't like showing off all this." Elizabeth smirks, juts one hip out like a model, and waves a hand down the front of her chest.

I shake my head at her silliness. "It's a choice. Like Rabia wears hijab, but I don't."

"Did I hear my name?" Rabia pops out from behind the wall of clothes, holding a bunch of bags. I try not to think of Mama and her bills. It's not Rabia's fault her parents have good jobs.

Elizabeth turns to her. "Do you think I'd look good in this tunic?"

"Try it on!" she commands.

Before I know it, Elizabeth has pulled on the tunic over her T-shirt. She struts around the rack like a fashion model. I giggle. Rabia claps. If I had a cell phone, photos of this would be all over Instagram.

Before I can tell myself I'm being silly, I slide a matching tunic off the hanger and pull it over my clothes. Still giggling,

I join Elizabeth and we catwalk up and down the aisle between metal racks, almost knocking down a mannequin. Rabia's claps become louder.

When we pay, the cashier smiles at us in our identical tops. "You two look adorable," he gushes as he reaches to scan the tags on our sleeves.

We're still giggling and posing as we walk out of the store.

"Elizabeth!"

I stop cold. I'd recognize that voice anywhere. Maddy is standing in our path, gaping at us. I'm not sure why, until I look at Elizabeth and realize it must be the identical tunics. Suddenly I'm glad we're not on Instagram. Maddy's reaction tells me something is very wrong.

Elizabeth's smile disappears. "Oh, hey, Maddy. Hey, Stephanie."

I hadn't noticed Stephanie with Maddy. She's wearing jeans and a white top. The absence of her usual pink cupcake apron makes her almost unrecognizable, like an alligator outside of its swamp.

Maddy comes closer to Elizabeth. "You told me you weren't free."

"I'm not," Elizabeth says. "I had plans with Sara."

"You'd rather hang out with a bunch of Arabs than us?" Maddy hisses.

"Maddy!" Stephanie shrieks. "You can't say stuff like that."

Elizabeth frowns but doesn't respond.

145

My mouth is frozen so tightly shut, I can't even tell Maddy that not all Muslims are Arabs. Stephanie pulls her away, murmuring something under her breath. Maddy goes, but not without one last insult. She points at me as if I'm a criminal and she's a judge. "Go back to where you belong."

16

Elizabeth

I STAND FROZEN—half inside the store, half out. Before I can speak, Rabia rushes after those girls, shouting, "Go back to Abercrombie and Witch, where *you* belong!"

Stephanie drags Maddy away. I wish I could hear what she's saying. From her angry gestures, it looks like she's telling Maddy off. I hope so. I can't believe Maddy just said that to Sara. It was wrong. More than wrong. It was racist. Sara belongs here as much as anyone.

When I finally catch my breath, Sara is glaring at me. "You want to know why I'm so cautious with people, why I don't talk at school? It's because this is what happens." Her voice is shaky and quiet, as if it's taking all her effort not to scream. Her eyes are sizzling mad.

I step back into the store and pull off my new top. This shirt suddenly feels itchy, like Maddy's words are sticking to my skin.

Sara puts her hand on my arm. Her touch is gentle, but her voice is sharp. "Some of us look like this all the time." She holds up the bell sleeve of the tunic. "It's not a costume I get to take off when people are rude. Or racist."

Rabia comes into the store, tapping a foot at us. "Come on, you two. Forget them. We still have half the mall to check out."

Sara ignores her. "You didn't stand up for me, Elizabeth," she says, so loud that the cashier leaves his desk and moves in our direction. His smile is gone, probably because we're disturbing the peaceful environment of his store.

Rabia leans close to Sara. "Elizabeth's not used to hearing comments like that. Let's get froyo and forget it."

But Rabia is wrong. I have definitely heard comments. A memory washes over me—Maddy's sleepover birthday party in fourth grade, when her favorite younger cousin asked if I'm going to hell because I'm not Christian. I remember how quiet the room got, just for a second, long enough so I knew everyone heard her question. What if Maddy had stuck up for me in that moment and told her cousin off? I try to imagine it, but I'm not Doctor Who. I can't go back in time and change what's already happened.

As we walk through the mall, I focus on the sunshine pouring in through the skylights and try to think things through. I'm glad Stephanie yelled at Maddy. Has Maddy always been like this? Was I too little, or too clueless, to notice before now?

Sara walks beside me silently, her shoulders slumped. She's right. I should have stood up for her. "Are we friends or not, Elizabeth?" Sara finally asks.

My chest feels tight, like my ribs are a real cage, squishing my lungs and heart. We were having so much fun today, me, Sara, and Rabia. I haven't laughed like this with Maddy in a long time. Probably because being around Maddy doesn't feel good anymore.

"We're friends," I tell Sara firmly.

The sizzle in her eyes fades. Relieved, I pull some cash out of my pocket and wave it at both girls. "My dad gave me extra money so I could treat you to bubble tea."

Rabia says, "Oooh, fun!" She nudges Sara playfully, but Sara's face is still weighed down by a frown.

As the three of us walk back to the food court, Sara suddenly tells me, "If we're going to be real friends, not just cooking partners, that means we stick up for each other. If someone from school tells me to go back where I came from or asks if I live in a tent, you don't get to stand there with your mouth hanging open like an old goat. Tell them to shut up. And I'll do the same for you."

"I'm really sorry," I say. "I've never heard Maddy say anything like that before. Her dad, yes. Other people in her family. But never her." I'm doing my best, trying to find the right words. "You're right, I should have said something. I guess I was too shocked to speak."

"Okay . . ."

"I'll do better next time," I promise. And I mean it. "But if we're going to be real friends, not just cooking partners, I need something from you, too."

"What is it, then?" Sara prompts me.

149

Rabia looks from one of us to the other, as if she's watching an entertainingly tense moment in a TV soap opera. All she needs is some popcorn.

I say, "We're allowed to ask each other stuff. If I ask you why you can't trick-or-treat, you don't have to answer me, but please don't get mad that I asked. And you can ask me anything."

"Oooh, good one," Rabia says, clasping her hands together. "Can I have that one also?"

Sara pokes her arm. "I already tell you everything, Rabia." She turns to me. "Do I get to ask what's so great about this doctor show you're obsessed with?"

"It's going to take longer than one helping of bubble tea to explain the intricacies of the TARDIS," I say. "That's Doctor Who's time machine," I tell Rabia.

"I'm already confused," Sara jokes. That's a good sign.

I ask, "What if we get frustrated with each other? Like, really bad, almost-fighting kind of frustrated?" I can't believe Halloween was only a week ago.

Sara shrugs. "We say, 'I'm mad at you right now, but I'll get over it.'"

"I like that," Rabia says.

I wonder if being friends is going to be as hard for our moms as it is for us. Will they argue over dumb stuff, like whose house they're going to study at? Will someone give my mom grief when they see her hanging out with a lady in a

150

hijab? I suddenly wonder what Mrs. Montgomery would say if she saw my mom and Mrs. Hameed together.

I can't blame Mom for wanting to go back to England, where she blends in. Where no one notices her accent or who her friends are.

The bubble tea stand is humming with activity. I order my usual green milk tea with tapioca pearls. "Those are the bubbles," I explain. "You suck them up through this extra-wide straw."

Rabia and Sara both get mango milk tea with bubbles. "Desi people love mangoes," Rabia tells me with a wry grin.

We drink and talk about school. The differences between Poplar Middle and Iqra. The pains of being the kids of immigrants. "What do you think?" I ask, holding up my bubble tea. Rabia's cup is almost empty.

Sara studies the dark tapioca bubbles at the bottom of her cup suspiciously. "Tea isn't supposed to have chewy bits."

"I'll finish yours," Rabia says, happily taking Sara's half-finished drink.

As we throw our cups away, my brain starts worrying about what's going to happen at school tomorrow. Will Maddy repeat the awful things she said? I know Sara expects me to stand up for her, but what does that mean, exactly? Does she think I'm going to walk up to Maddy in the lunchroom and say, *Maddy Montgomery, you said something really hateful to my friend?*

For the rest of the week, I avoid Maddy as much as possible.

151

I am moving on. That's what Bubbe says when someone annoys her. "I've got no time for drama. Moving on!" But it's not easy. Maddy's locker is near mine. She's in my gym class. Until this year, we practically lived at each other's houses on the weekends. A few weeks ago, I didn't want to do anything unless she was doing it too. Now I'm not even sure I want to be her friend.

17

Sara

THAT FRIDAY, I meet Mama in the school parking lot as soon as the last bell rings. She makes me drag a twenty-pound bag of potatoes to cooking class. "Why can't everyone bring their own ingredients from home?" I complain. The bag is so heavy, my muscles strain the sleeves of my extra-long denim blouse.

"Choup!" Mama shushes me. "A little exercise isn't going to kill you, Sara."

"It might," I grumble.

"Hurry up — I want to get the potatoes boiling before class begins." She hands me a key chain with a faded yellow pineapple charm. "Mrs. Kluckowski won't be here today. She gave me an extra key for the FACS room. Go ahead and unlock the door. I have more groceries in the car."

It takes us two more trips to get everything unloaded. I make sure I complain the whole time. Mama doesn't ask for the pineapple key chain, so I slide it inside my backpack to give it to her later. We immerse the potatoes in pots of boiling water, then set out cilantro, green onions, and spices, plus yogurt and mint bunches for the chutney. By the time Elizabeth and the other kids get to class, the water is bubbling fiercely.

"Why didn't you wait for me after language arts?" Elizabeth complains.

I'm about to snap back that I was busy lugging a toddler-size bag of potatoes, but I don't. Elizabeth expected me to wait for her so we could walk to cooking class together. A few weeks ago, I didn't have one friend at this school. No one to talk to other than "Would you pass me that charcoal pencil?" in art class or "Are you done with the protractor?" in math. Now I have someone to look out for me, someone who worries when she sees me rushing off after class. It's weird, but also nice.

"Sorry. I had to help Mama with class prep today." I flex my biceps. "See how big my muscles are?"

She slides into the seat next to me. "Uh . . . wow?"

There's a slight noise from the doorway, or maybe I'm just on hyperalert. It's Maddy, a frowny look on her face, as if this is the last place she wants to be. I get it. It's the last place I want her in, but nothing about this afterschool club seems to be my choice.

Stephanie follows close behind Maddy, like a stern mother hen. "Remember what I told you," she whispers, loud enough for everyone to hear. "BEHAVE!"

The other girls look at the pair oddly, but I don't even try to hide my disgust.

"We have got to make a better showcase recipe than those two," Elizabeth whispers.

"You bet," I whisper back.

Mama calls us to attention with a little clap of her hands. "We're making aaloo tikkis today, class," she announces. "These are little potato cutlets, very easy to make. You can also call them aaloo kabab or potato kabab."

There's a murmuring in the room, like the buzz of excited bees before they embark on their morning mission to the garden, but it's quiet in Maddy and Stephanie's station.

While Mama tells the class the correct and incorrect ways of cooking vegetables—the microwave makes them soft but also wrinkles their skin—I zone out. This is child's play for me, and I have other things on my mind. I take out my sketchbook and make some last adjustments to my flyer. It's due Monday and I'm not sure about the colors yet.

Elizabeth jabs an elbow in my side. "That's awesome!" she whispers, nodding at my sketch.

I roll my eyes at her, but a warmth spreads in my chest at her words. "I can't decide between red or blue lettering," I whisper back.

She thinks. "Definitely red, but make it browner, like turmeric or cinnamon. The color red is supposed to make you hungry."

I didn't know that. I take out my maroon marker and color in the lettering of HAMEED'S KITCHEN. Elizabeth's right— the color is perfect.

155

While the potatoes boil, Mama shows the class how to make chutney. She throws mint leaves and a tiny bit of yogurt into the blender, adds lemon juice, and presses the button. Elizabeth is leaning forward, as if there's some sort of magic happening in the front of the FACS room.

I put away my sketchbook when Mama places the boiled potatoes on plates and passes them to everyone. "Be careful— don't burn your hands," she warns. "Let them cool by running water over them, then peel and mash them, please."

Before long, we've peeled and mashed, mixed in spices, and made the round tikkis. Mama shows everyone how to coat them with eggs and breadcrumbs, then fry them in a shallow pan with a little oil.

"I prefer to use chickpea flour instead of breadcrumbs," I tell Elizabeth.

Mama overhears, reminding me once again how sharp that woman's hearing is. "Sara is right. We can use many other things as substitutes," she says. "That reminds me: Mrs. Kluck-owski isn't here today, but she asked me to make an exciting announcement."

Mama goes back to the frying pan in the demonstration kitchen. The first batch of tikkis is browning nicely. "Sara, there's a paper on my desk. Why don't you read it out for every-one while I flip over these tikkis before they burn?"

I get the paper from her desk and stand in front of the class, feeling awkward. Maddy's looking down at her nails as if Mrs. Kluck's announcement is written on them, and I suddenly wonder if she's embarrassed to look at me after her outburst in the mall.

I clear my throat and read. " 'Poplar Springs Middle School is proud to welcome celebrity chef Alfonso Morgan as a special guest at this year's International Festival. Chef Morgan is the author of three acclaimed cookbooks and host of the local television show *Let's Get Cooking!* on WBAL. Chef Morgan will offer advice and encouragement to all students taking part in the International Festival recipe showcase. The creators of one recipe will be his guests on an upcoming episode of *Let's Get Cooking!*' "

Chatter breaks out in the class. Stephanie cheers and says something about raising awareness and peas — huh? — but Maddy looks sullen and grumpy. The other kids in our class are so loud, Mama shouts, "Time to eat!" twice before anyone listens.

Our potato tikkis have browned beautifully on both sides, sizzling with the aroma of cilantro and olive oil. Mama passes around dollops of mint chutney to put on top.

I turn to Elizabeth and clutch her arm. "If we win the competition, we'll be on TV!"

She gives me a blank stare. "That would be cool."

"Don't you get it? This would be perfect for my mama. If we win, we could get aprons like Stephanie's and advertise Mama's catering business to the entire city."

Elizabeth nods. "That would be awesome for your mom."

"We have to win this thing!"

She grins brightly. "Let's do it!"

The next day in art, Mrs. Newman collects our flyer sketches. "Very good, Sarah," she whispers as she picks up my sketch. "I like the border you've made."

"Thanks," I mutter. Everyone is peering at my flyer now. My face is getting hot.

Mrs. Newman stops me after class. "Sarah, I really liked what you did with the flyer." She waves her bangled arms to show her excitement.

An unexpected memory of Mama smiling politely at Mrs. Shainmark in Bean Heaven crosses my mind. "It's *Sa-ra,* not Sarah," I say before I lose my nerve.

"Pardon?"

I take a deep breath and try again. "My name is pronounced *Sa-ra,* not Sarah, the way you say it." Then I shrug. "It's no big deal, really."

She looks horrified. "Why didn't you tell me before? I'm so sorry."

"That's okay. It's a common mistake."

She leans forward and touches my shoulder. "Well, Sa-ra, as I was saying, I really like your flyer and I'd like to give you a special job."

I narrow my eyes. "What special job?"

"The International Festival needs a big sign for the entrance, and I think you're the perfect person for the task! You can use the henna patterns and the other cool ethnic designs you've

158

been adding to your drawings. Be creative—do whatever you like with it."

I don't particularly like her use of the word "ethnic," but I forgive her because I know she's trying her best. In any case, I can't believe what she's saying. My art is good enough to be showcased in front of the whole school? And a celebrity chef? "Are you sure?" I whisper.

"Of course I'm sure. Your flyer stood out from the class. And of all the portfolios I asked students to submit on the first day of class, yours was the most impressive!" She's grinning broadly, but I'm pretty sure she's dead serious. "I'll email you instructions for the sign by next week. And I'll give you all the art supplies you need. Come get them from me after school."

My mind is already speeding, thinking of designs and patterns and colors. The bell rings and I skip out, barely resisting the urge to give Mrs. Newman a hug. It's only when I'm sitting in Mama's car that afternoon, sketching out my ideas, that a horrible thought dawns on me: How will I make time for this project when Elizabeth and I have to plan our fusion recipe?

18

Elizabeth

Hᴇʙʀᴇᴡ sᴄʜᴏᴏʟ ᴀɴᴅ I have an awkward relationship. It's not quite an orange-juice-and-milk situation, but it's not a PB&J, besties-forever vibe either.

It's where I first met Micah, when we were both new to our synagogue's Sunday morning religious-ed program. On the first day, I was trying to spot kids I knew from Watersville Elementary. There was Lisa Greenbaum—in my grade, but not in my class—and Ari Marks, who played kickball every day at recess and was always in trouble for tracking mud inside. They waved at me, but there were no excited hugs, and neither one of them sat by me.

Mr. Yukht, our teacher, said we were the nicest group of kids he had ever met, even though he'd only known us for five minutes. But he meant it. Mr. Yukht has moved up with our class every year. He says he's sticking with us, so we all have to invite him to our bar and bat mitzvah parties. He's bald and wears khakis like a regular man teacher, but his red high-tops and suspenders make him super cool, at least to me and Micah.

There may be other kids like us at our Hebrew school, but Micah is the only one I'm comfortable talking about it with. He makes me feel like I'm not the only person in Mr. Yukht's class who gets mixed up when our class talks about Jewish holidays.

After Mr. Yukht wraps up the day's lesson, we stand in line, waiting to high-five him on our way out. Then Micah and I head to the synagogue's main entrance.

"Where's your dad taking us for lunch?" I ask Micah. "I vote IHOP."

Micah shudders so dramatically, his curls shake. "You call those pancakes? Have you been to the new crêpes shop on Main Street? *Those* are pancakes."

I'm about to argue when Mrs. Gruver steps out of her office and puts her long, skinny self between me and any chance of escape.

"May I speak with you, Elisheva?" she says, tipping her head down so she can stare at me disapprovingly over the tops of her glasses. I wonder if she knows her chin squishes into her neck when she does that.

I widen my eyes at Micah.

"I'll tell my dad you're with Mrs. Gruver," he says with a meaningful nod.

Mr. Perez is not a fan of our principal. "Hebrew school should be something you kids enjoy," he says. "She's too strict. Takes all the fun out of it."

Easy for him to say. He's never been to Hebrew school.

161

Micah's dad grew up Catholic. Unlike my mom, he never converted to Judaism. Micah's mom, Ms. Rosen, is the religious one at their house.

I follow Mrs. Gruver into her office. There's a giant picture over her clean white desk of her son, Noah, at his bar mitzvah. Mrs. Gruver and her husband stand behind Noah at the bimah. She's smiling and wearing a pretty floral dress. The way Mrs. Gruver is scowling at me right now, it's hard to believe she ever smiled in her life.

Mrs. Gruver sits down and interlaces her hands. Does she think that makes her look religious? More like a principal? I look up and realize that she's waiting for me to make eye contact.

"Sit, please."

I park it in the gray office chair across from her.

"Elisheva, where were you on Friday night?"

Friday night? She must be talking about services. My family only ever goes when Dad is home, which is not something I need to share with Mrs. Gruver.

I push the toe of one TARDIS high-top into the other until she speaks again.

"It was your family's turn for Oneg Shabbat. It may not seem like a 'big deal,' bringing fruit and cookies for Friday-night services, but it's important to our school, to our community."

That's what this is about. Hospitality.

Instantly, I think of Mr. Yukht. Back in September, he explained how our congregation supports the Hebrew school

162

and how we return the favor by bringing treats on Friday nights. I know I handed Mom the sign-up sheet. I remember her writing "Services: Cookies" on the family calendar in big letters.

Tears start to prickle in my eyes, but I will not cry in front of Mrs. Gruver. "We forgot," I say. "I'm sorry."

I pull my shoulders back and sit up straight, ready to hear my punishment. I feel better facing Mrs. Gruver with the good British posture Nan taught me. Sometimes when we were visiting England and Mom was out for a hen night with Aunt Louise, Nan would put on fifties music, get a stack of novels for each of us to put on top of our heads, and David, me, Justin, and Nan would dance around her parlor until the books dropped, or one of us laughed, or both. Usually both.

Mrs. Gruver shakes her head slowly, disappointed. I'm in big trouble. But then she mumbles, "Once a *shiksa*, always a *shiksa*," and I know it's not me Mrs. Gruver is disappointed in. It's my mom.

Mrs. Gruver writes something on a slip of paper, folds the note, and creases it with the back of her painted thumbnail, which creeps me out. Then she gives me that glare over the tops of her glasses, seals the paper in an envelope, and hands it to me. "Give this to your mother."

I know what *shiksa* means. A woman who's not Jewish. It's what Bubbe calls my mom. She thinks it's funny, what she calls a term of endearment. Whenever we invite Dad's cousins to Passover Seder at our house, Bubbe will get up from the table and say, "The *shiksa* needs my help in the kitchen." I know it hurts Mom's feelings. It makes her feel like she's never going to get the whole being-Jewish thing right. And getting chewed out by Mrs. Gruver for forgetting Oneg Shabbat isn't going to help. Besides, Hebrew-school assignments are my responsibility, not Mom's. If I'd paid attention to the family calendar, I would have remembered about the cookies. It's one more thing I'm supposed to do for myself, one more thing to prepare and remember and take care of.

A sob escapes my throat.

"What is it, Elisheva?" Mrs. Gruver is patting my hand.

I can barely get the words out. "My grandmother died this summer. She was my mom's mother, and that's how come we forgot. I know it's not an excuse."

Of all people to fall apart in front of, why did it have to be Mrs. Gruver?

She passes me a tissue, says something in Hebrew, then translates, "May God console you. I'm so sorry to hear this, Elisheva. I didn't know. Can I do anything for your family?"

I shake my head.

Gently, she slips the note out from under my hand. "How about I reach out to your mother? I'll call her. And we'll give you a new date for Oneg Shabbat. Maybe in the spring?"

"Can you send her an email instead?" I get it. Mrs. Gruver is trying to be nice. But I can't tell her that my mom hates talking on the phone unless you're Aunt Louise. And just like that, I've gone from crying to furious. Why can't I have normal

164

parents? A mom who remembers things like cookies for synagogue. A dad who's home and can remind her. I'm eleven. I have a hard enough time remembering to do all my homework.

In the car, I ask Mr. Perez to take me straight home.

"No pancakes?" Micah asks. "Not even crêpes?"

I shake my head miserably. Micah bumps my knee with the top of his hand.

After Mr. Perez drops me off, I stomp into the house. I'm yelling before I even close the front door behind me.

"Mom, we forgot to bring cookies to services! And now Mrs. Gruver is going to call you. MOM!"

All my shouting brings Robin Hood to the door, barking and bouncing, trying to get my attention.

Dad intercepts me. He's so tall, I can't get past him into the family room.

"Shhh. Robin, sit," Dad says. "Mom is studying, Elizabeth." He tilts his body so I can peer down the hallway.

Mom is sitting at the table with a cup of tea in one hand and her citizenship book in the other. David's across from her, taking a screwdriver to the guts of what might be our old toaster.

"Justin's at Taemin's house," Dad says.

I should be glad Mom's studying. I should be thankful that Mrs. Gruver is going to give us a new cookie date. But I'm not. I'm so angry, my voice shakes when I say, "I hate it when people treat Mom like she's not really Jewish."

"People?" Dad asks, tilting his head.

"Mrs. Gruver. Bubbe!"

165

He puts an arm around my shoulders, walks me to the stairs, and sits on a carpeted step. There's barely enough room for me to squeeze in next to him. Robin heads back to the kitchen, convinced he's done a great job keeping the humans in line.

"Take a deep breath and tell me what happened," Dad says.

"Mom doesn't like it when Bubbe calls her *shiksa*. Why do you let her? Why don't you stand up for Mom?"

Dad pulls at his T-shirt collar, the same way Justin does when he's anxious. "Bubbe's teasing, Els. And I thought we were talking about Mrs. Gruver."

"You should tell Bubbe it's mean. It makes Mom feel left out."

"Fair enough. For the record, I'd rather stand up to Mrs. Gruver than your bubbe." He winks at me.

"Dad! It's not funny. We forgot Oneg Shabbat at synagogue. I know it's my responsibility, but Mrs. Gruver acted like it's Mom's fault."

Dad nods thoughtfully.

"None of this would have happened if you weren't traveling all the time." I say it right to his face.

He sighs. "Not this again. Elizabeth, until your mom's ready to go back to work—"

"Money's tight. I know." I'd give up bubble tea and half-price tunics and seven of my eight Hanukkah gifts if it meant Dad didn't travel so much.

"We're all making sacrifices right now," Dad says, standing

166

up. "I'll talk to Bubbe about the *shiksa* business, okay?" He pats me on the head, like that's supposed to make me feel better.

That week, Sara and I work on recipe ideas during lunch. Ever since Sara moved to our table, Maddy has been sitting with Stephanie. At first, she stopped by sometimes to talk to me and Micah. Now she stays away. Micah thinks the two of us had a fight.

"Worse than that," I tell him.

"Details?" he asks.

"Not worth repeating."

Sara brings out a special notebook dedicated to our project. On the cover, in glittery purple calligraphy, she's written "OSAWR."

"It stands for Operation Secret Award-Winning Recipe. I don't want the whole school to know what we're doing." She tilts her chin in Micah's direction. "The less the competition knows, the better."

"My taste buds are neutral territory, I swear." Micah puts a hand over his heart.

I wonder if he'd feel differently if I told him what happened at the mall. Micah's abuela, Cookie, is his favorite person in the world. He hates when people talk down to her because—as Micah says—she's small, brown, and Latina. But I don't say anything. Sara would hate it if Micah, or anyone else, felt sorry for her.

As Micah eats his lunch, Sara and I create a work schedule

and dream up recipes. I've watched every *Salma Aunty* episode. The ones where she makes golden, fluffy parathas are my favorite. My heart is set on making them.

"I eat parathas every day," Sara says. "They're not special enough to win."

"They will be if the filling is something no one expects." Soon, we have three pages of ideas for how to stuff parathas. We've already eliminated peanut butter and jelly (boring), apple pie filling (slimy), and meat (overdone, according to Sara).

This is harder than I expected.

"We're out of ideas," I complain to Micah. "What's your favorite food in the whole world?"

"S'mores," he says. "My family's having a backyard bonfire this weekend. Cookie's secret ingredient is homemade marshmallows."

I grab his arm. "You can *make* marshmallows? From scratch?"

"Forget it," Sara says. "We are not making marshmallow parathas."

"No," I say. "But we are making s'mores parathas."

Sara shakes her head like she's some sort of cooking expert. Which she is not. "Parathas are made on a hot griddle," she says. "Not the best place for chocolate."

I cross my arms on my chest. "We won't know if it works until we try it—unless you have a better idea."

"Okay, fine!" she groans.

168

"I'll trade you Cookie's homemade marshmallow recipe for a taste of the finished product," Micah offers with a sly smile.

Sara says, "Don't make this even more complicated."

We make a shopping list: flour, eggs, ghee, marshmallows, chocolate chips, crushed graham crackers. That takes up a whole page in our notebook because Sara insists on making little drawings of each ingredient.

I don't mind in the least.

As Thanksgiving nears, the cooking competition is all I want to talk about. And I'm not the only one.

Stephanie and Maddy are always in the sixth-grade hallway, asking their friends to taste their latest baking experiment. More than once, I've heard Maddy telling kids how much Steph wants to win the TV spot so she can promote some care-package thing she's into. Probably a new part of her baking business. Because baking cupcakes and being on swim team is not enough for Sweet Stephanie.

Maddy and I don't even look at each other anymore. She's been my friend for so long, it feels wrong passing by her and pretending we don't know each other. But every time I see Maddy, the words she said to Sara whirl in my mind as if they've been thrown into a blender and whipped into a sloppy mess.

Enough thinking. We should be *doing*. I want to be in the kitchen so Sara and I can show Maddy that Pakistani parathas and American s'mores belong together. "When do we start cooking?" I ask Sara on Friday as we make a mixture of ground meat and spices for today's project. "If all we do is make lists, we'll never have a recipe ready in time."

Thanksgiving break is next week. Two half-days followed by Wednesday through Sunday off school. I'm dreading being stuck at home, where Mom's sadness hangs over everything like the smell of burnt toast. She knits, talks on the phone with Aunt Louise about their London trip—which they're still secretly planning—and reads her citizenship booklet. I keep hoping she'll invite Mrs. Hameed over for coffee, or to get their nails done while they discuss the three branches of government. But maybe she's not as ready to make a new friend as I was.

Sara crosses her arms at me. "I like my lists. They're organized."

"I know. And we need them. If you set me loose in the kitchen without a plan, I'd end up with some weird, barf-inducing concoction."

Sara tilts her head toward Mrs. Kluck, who's bustling around the display kitchen with a measuring tape, totally getting in Mrs. Hameed's way.

"I'd like to give Mrs. Kluck a barf-inducing concoction," Sara says under her breath.

I stifle a laugh and say a silent prayer that our recipe doesn't taste like Mom's Pepto-Bismol sardine sauce. "You're a planner. I'm a doer. That's why we are the perfect team. How about coming to my house next week so we can practice parathas?" I ask her. "We've got mad culinary skills, if these kiftas are any

170

evidence." I pat my mouth with a napkin, like a polite British lady.

Sara laughs at me. "*Kofta,* not kifta, silly. It's Urdu for 'meatballs.'"

"They're a million times better than any meatball I ever had." I take another bite. "We're ready. Next week, when we have time off, we are getting together to cook."

19

Sara

ON THE SATURDAY before Thanksgiving, Rabia sends me a Google Hangouts invite for another *America's Got Talent* watching. It's a video we've watched three times already. A seventy-year-old lady does gymnastics as if she's fifteen, then a man sings a rap song while dancing like a robot. After ten minutes, Rabia says, "Forget this, Sara! I already know this entire episode by heart."

I'd been looking forward to the magician later in this episode, but I say, "Yeah, I know," and mute the video.

"I can't believe we still watch this stupid show," she continues, making a face.

I shrug. "I don't know. I like it. We've been watching it together since we were little."

"Yeah, but why?" she persists, chewing on her juice straw. "There are so many other things to watch. Cat videos, baking shows . . ."

I shrug again. "I like the way it equalizes everyone, you

know? Most competitions are only for one thing, but in *America's Got Talent,* you can do anything. Be anything."

She grins, but I know she secretly agrees with me. "Like the American dream."

"Exactly! We're all different here, you know. But we're all American!"

"Spoken like a true daughter of Pakistani immigrants!" She laughs, then takes a final sip of her mango juice. "Okay, you've convinced me. We can keep it."

I nod, satisfied. Some schoolchildren are singing a song from *My Fair Lady,* and my hand itches to turn up the volume.

"Oh, cute, those kids look just like your brothers." Rabia points. She's watching the show on mute just like I am. "How are they, anyway?"

"The same. Brats."

"Oh, come on, they are adorable." Rabia's an only child, so she thinks siblings are the best thing that could ever happen to anyone. "Remember the time they came into your room while we were studying and spilled your paints on the floor?"

I shudder. "How could you ever find that adorable?"

"They made such cute 'sorry' faces." She laughs. "Plus, they did clean up, like, immediately."

"Of course they did. Mama would have been furious if she'd found my bedroom floor covered in paint." I try to imagine Mama's reaction and have to close my lips over a little giggle.

Rabia giggles too, just a bit. Then her face changes, and she whispers, "I miss studying together."

I pause to peer into the screen. "What do you mean? I bet you've made lots of new friends since I left." I try to tease her, but the words come out uncertain.

She shrugs sadly. "Not really. Everyone's already got friends."

My heart is thumping. I've been feeling so bad for myself lately, I never even realized how my leaving Iqra has affected Rabia. "At least we'll be together for Thanksgiving," I remind her.

She blinks rapidly. "Actually, we're spending Thanksgiving break in Boston, with my grandparents."

"Oh, that's cool." I feel nauseous. Sharing Thanksgiving with Rabia's family is our long-standing American tradition. If Rabia's family doesn't visit like always, everything is going to change. I just know it. Mama and Baba will probably not even bother to celebrate the holiday because it's not something they did "back home."

The magician is stepping onto the stage, bowing deeply. I reach over to close the video. "Listen, Mama's calling me from the kitchen. Gotta go. Bye!"

I disconnect Hangouts without waiting for Rabia to reply. My heart is thumping at my lie, and I tell it to stop being a baby and quiet down.

Monday is a half-day because of parent-teacher conferences. Elizabeth and I have made plans to work on our Secret Award-Winning Recipe at her house. Now that the prize is a television show appearance, we need to up our game.

"Are you excited about Thanksgiving?" Elizabeth asks as we walk to her house after school.

Rabia's quietly dropped bombshell the day before has sucked out all the usual happiness of my favorite holiday, but I focus on the delicate embroidery at the edge of my tunic sleeve and reply, "Sure, are you?"

Elizabeth nods hesitantly. "With my mom the way she is lately, I'm worried Thanksgiving's going to stink. My grandmother usually cooks for us. I dream all year about her apple cake."

"I thought your grandmother died."

"That's the English one. This one lives in New York. Somehow I got two grandmothers who are amazing cooks and a mom who thinks Thanksgiving stuffing should come from a box. That's why I'm so glad we're working together on this contest, Sara. It'll keep my mind off having to eat instant mashed potatoes."

I pull my arm loose. "Okay, let's not get mushy here," I caution. "I'd rather be anywhere than at home, putting curry in plastic boxes for customers. Mama is cooking up a literal storm this week, much of it Thanksgiving-related."

"Mmmm, I love Turkey Day."

175

I shake my head. "We're not big turkey fans in my house. Mama and Baba haven't developed a taste for it. They don't have turkeys in Pakistan."

"So what do you usually eat on Thanksgiving?"

"Pakistani food, like the recipes we cook in club."

"Sounds like heaven," she says. I roll my eyes, but I don't disagree.

Elizabeth stops in front of a brick townhouse. The street is a cul-de-sac with lots of trees and almost identical groups of five townhouses on each side. Elizabeth's is the only roof covered with solar panels. I smile. Her house is as nerdy as she is.

"This is it," she says grimly, reaching for the door. She seems nervous.

I notice a small brass cylinder on the frame of her doorway. "What's that?" I point, trying to distract her.

"It's a mezuzah. Jewish people put them on their doorways."

"What for?" I don't want to seem nosy, but the curving design on the front of the mezuzah is fascinating. It reminds me of the Arabic verse from the Quran on top of our front door.

"There's a rolled-up prayer inside. My parents aren't very observant, but having a mezuzah on your front door is like level-one Judaism."

I like this little piece of evidence that Elizabeth and I are somehow similar. We enter the hallway to the sound of high barking, although there are no dogs in sight.

"That's Robin Hood, our schnauzer," she explains. "He must be in the basement."

I follow Elizabeth down a hallway, past a kitchen strewn with used mugs. Nearby is a wooden table piled with small machine parts.

"David's trying to fix our toaster. So far it's a disaster," she explains, which raises more questions in my mind until I remember her brother is into robotics.

There's a faint scent of lavender in the house. Elizabeth sniffs, then seems to relax. "I think someone cleaned today," she whispers, almost to herself. "Mom! Sara is here!" she calls into the family room, but I don't spot Mrs. Shainmark and she doesn't say hello. Elizabeth grabs a laptop off the table and leads me upstairs.

"At least you don't have the smell of spices attacking you as soon as you enter," I joke, trying to put her at ease. This is a different Elizabeth, less confident, more like . . . me? I recall all the things she's told me about her mom, and I want to pull her into a hug.

Upstairs, Elizabeth opens the door to her bedroom. "Quick, before my brother lets Robin Hood out," she says. I stumble inside.

Elizabeth's room, unlike the rest of her house, is very tidy, with hardly any clutter on the floor or her desk. The walls are painted a calming peach, or at least I think it's peach—it's hard to tell what's wall and what's not because they're almost completely covered in *Doctor Who* and Harry Potter posters and postcards from cities all over the United States. Two bookcases, double-stacked with novels, frame the window. On one side of her neatly made bed is a bureau with *Doctor Who* figurines, and on the other a chair filled with stuffed animals.

"Wow, I like your postcards," I say, not at all teasing.

"My dad sends them when he's away. I'm up to fifty different cities."

This is the true Elizabeth, in all her nerdy glory. I realize we all hide some parts of ourselves, crowding them into our bedrooms, where only our best friends can see. I peer at her books. "Wow! I love your graphic novel collection. Can I borrow a few?"

"Consider my bookshelf your personal library," she says, bowing as if I'm a British royal.

I move on to the dressing table, which has lots of framed pictures. I lean in to get a better look. Among family photos is one of Elizabeth and Maddy wearing costumes. "Where was this?" I ask, trying to keep my voice neutral.

She doesn't look at me when she says, "A science-fiction convention in Baltimore."

The memory of Maddy's words at the mall is still a fresh ache in my stomach. "She . . . are you guys still friends?" I finally ask.

She shakes her head once, a small, painful movement. "We're definitely not speaking."

I smooth the embroidery on my sleeve again, feeling its cool pattern against my fingertips. "Really?"

Elizabeth continues quickly. "I never thought of Maddy as a bad person. She's loud and says exactly what's on her mind. But that was what made her fun. Until now."

"Now that you know she's racist," I mutter, turning away from the photograph.

"Her parents are super conservative. My dad says they're scared about the way society is changing. Maddy is with them all the time. She doesn't know any better."

I know exactly what Elizabeth's dad was telling her. Changing times equals more people like me coming to stay in white neighborhoods, standing in line at the carnival, wanting to see the doctor. Changing times means an America that's different from a hundred years ago. Nobody likes change, not even my parents, with their treasured memory of how things were done in the villages of Pakistan long ago.

I say, "How will she know any better if no one tells her? She should hear it from a friend. From you."

"That sounds easier than it's actually going to be," she replies.

We are quiet for a moment, both lost in our thoughts. Elizabeth sighs and opens up the laptop. "Let's not be sad. YouTube time, right?"

She presses a few keys. A video of a woman in orange hijab with plump hennaed hands and lots of jewelry fills the screen. She's making a beef dish, stirring the pot while talking nonstop in a friendly Pakistani accent. "Today we will teach you meat cooked in a special pot called a karhai."

179

"Introducing *Salma Aunty's Desi Kitchen*!" Elizabeth announces excitedly.

"She reminds me of Mrs. Newman, with all those bangles," I murmur.

Elizabeth doesn't respond. Her eyes follow every move of Salma aunty's hands with their pumpkin-orange nails. I settle down next to Elizabeth on her bed. Salma aunty makes Pakistani food sound like the most deliciously irresistible cuisine on earth. Despite myself, I'm grinning from ear to ear.

The door opens with a whoosh. A boy with curly hair and freckles rushes in like a messy whirlwind. "I'm bored, Els. Watcha doing?" He flops his sweaty body down on the bed with a grunt.

"Ew! Justin!" Elizabeth shrieks, shutting the laptop. She jumps up and points to the door. "Go take a shower! You stink."

Justin rolls back and forth. "Mom said I don't have to," he sing-songs.

"You're making my sheets wet with your disgusting sweat."

His smile disappears. "I'm hungry, but there's nothing good in the house. Even the pretzel jar is empty. Mom has her headphones on and she said not to bother her unless I'm bleeding."

"Not really," Elizabeth is quick to explain to me. "She's exaggerating. It's a joke."

I stand up. "I can whip up something for you really quick," I offer to Justin. "I do it for my brothers all the time."

He jumps up with a bound and pulls me to the hall. A little black dog with the funniest gray beard and eyebrows rushes at my knees, barking and bouncing. I squeal a bit. Elizabeth shouts at Robin Hood to quiet down.

We make a little parade, Justin in his bright green soccer uniform and knee socks, the barking black dog, me, and Elizabeth calling, "You don't have to . . . the kitchen is a mess." She trails behind us like she's been called to the principal's office. We pass the living room, and I catch a glimpse of Mrs. Shainmark lying on the couch. Then we're at the kitchen.

Baba says truth is stranger than fiction. I have an image of a kitchen full of food scraps and broken dishes, like the A-Team after one of their bar fights. Thankfully, it's nothing like that. It's a small kitchen close to the front door, with a huge window that makes it bright and cheerful. I smile at the glass jar with yellow and blue wildflowers sitting on the windowsill. The kitchen is a little shabby, with old-fashioned white cabinets full of handprints, unwashed mugs on the counter, and a sink full of dishes. Nothing a good cleaning can't fix.

Elizabeth tosses Robin a dog biscuit. He munches happily, then settles down to watch us, hoping for more treats. "I'll wash the dishes before we cook," she mumbles.

"You should see my kitchen," I tell her. "There's a ton of dirty pots and pans at all hours of the day."

She relaxes. I ask Justin to find some potatoes, tomatoes, half an onion, and three eggs. I cover the potatoes with plastic wrap and heat them in the microwave. "My mama would be so mad if she saw me using this shortcut," I say. "But boiling potatoes takes forever."

"You can always use potato flakes. There's a big box in the pantry," Elizabeth jokes.

While the potatoes are cooking, I mix eggs, tomatoes, a little onion, a sprinkle of salt, and black pepper.

"You're not gonna put stinky cheese in those eggs, are you?" Justin asks with a smirk.

Elizabeth shoves him in the arm. "Hey! That was one time."

He grins at me. "I almost barfed."

"No cheese. I promise," I assure him.

The microwave beeps. "As soon as they cool down, peel the potatoes like this, Justin." I demonstrate, feeling just like Mama in front of her cooking club.

He hurries to comply. I wish Rafey and Tariq were so obedient.

I scramble everything together in a pan, letting it bubble. "If you had cilantro and cumin, you could make this even yummier," I say, scraping the scrambled potato-egg mixture onto a plate and handing it to Justin with a flourish.

He sits at the kitchen table, pushing aside the pulled-apart toaster, and wolfs the eggs down. "This is delish," he says with his mouth full. "What's it called?"

I hesitate, then tell him. "Khagina. Scrambled eggs, South Asian–style."

"Kha-gee-na," he repeats, stumbling a little on the *Kh* but getting it mostly right. I'm so pleased, I give him a little pat on the back.

When Justin and the dog are gone, I teach Elizabeth how to make a simple paratha. We knead the dough, then divide it into little balls. Elizabeth is literally hanging on my arm, eyes wide. She's a great student, listening carefully as I show her what to do. I motion for her to take over. "Now roll each ball out until it's in a flat circle."

Elizabeth doesn't have a proper skillet, so we make do with a shallow pan. She surprises me with a jar of ghee. "I was so excited when I saw this at the grocery store," she confides. "I used it for cooking French toast. It was scrumptious!"

The paratha is beginning to burn. It comes out stiff and elongated, nothing like Mama's fluffy creations, but we gobble it up anyway. "We need to do this about a hundred more times, until we get the hang of it," Elizabeth announces.

"Don't tell my mama what a bad cook I am, and you have a deal."

Elizabeth opens a cabinet and takes out a packet of puffy marshmallows. "Want to make our Secret Award-Winning Recipe?"

Paratha s'mores turn out to be a terrible idea. The gooey marshmallow sticks to the pan, our hands, even our teeth. Both of us get chocolate on our clothes. But we're laughing so hard, neither of us cares that we'll have to come up with a new idea for the competition.

The bell rings. "Sara's mom is here!" Mrs. Shainmark calls.

By the time we enter the living room twenty minutes later, Mama and Mrs. Shainmark are sitting on a beige corduroy couch. Mama's eyes are so creased with laughter that I can barely see them. "Best show on earth! I can't believe the actors didn't crack up."

"And the one with Chandler's mom. That's hilarious!" Mrs. Shainmark gasps.

"I can't believe your mom likes *Friends.* My mom watches reruns all the time," Elizabeth whispers.

I rub my hands with glee. "Operation Citizenship seems to be a success."

Mama turns to us. "Hello, girls. Guess what! I invited Elizabeth to come spend some time with us on Thanksgiving Day, since Nasreen's family will be out of town."

Elizabeth shrieks so loud, I jump. "That's fabulous! Can I, Mom?"

Mrs. Shainmark is smiling. "Of course. You can take Justin with you, and I can spend the afternoon studying."

"Perfect," we both whisper together.

20

Elizabeth

"THANKSGIVING! TODAY'S THANKSGIVING!" I pull the turkey tea cozy off the giant jug of pretzels where it usually sits, stick it on my head like a hat, and dance around the kitchen.

Mom is curled up in her usual spot, still in her dressing gown. She laughs at me, so I put on a show, making bird wings with my arms as I sing, "Turkey day is here, sitting on your rear, eating all the treats of fall, my favorite time of year."

Then Mom comes into the kitchen and starts dancing with me. She snatches the tea cozy and puts it on her own head.

I am still disappointed that we aren't seeing Bubbe today. Bubbe usually takes over our kitchen and cooks turkey, chestnut stuffing, mashed potatoes, two types of pie, and Jewish apple cake. Food is the one area where my grandmother likes being traditional. But every few years, Bubbe goes to the West Coast for Thanksgiving. Dad only has one sibling (lucky). His name is Uncle Ted and he's a doctor in Oregon. It's his turn to have Bubbe, so there will be no delicious apple cake today, because my mom can't bake and Bubbe still hasn't taught me the recipe. She says she can't write it down.

"You have to know it up here," she always says, tapping her head. "And you have to know it in here," she adds, dramatically putting a hand over her heart.

That's when Mom rolls her eyes.

Enough thinking about Bubbe. I will miss her apple cake, but I'm happy that I get to spend time at Sara's house. Mrs. Hameed said I could come over to cook as long as Justin comes too. He's going to play with the twins, to keep them occupied while Mrs. Hameed finishes packing her Thanksgiving catering orders and Sara and I come up with a new recipe.

I plan to eat as many Pakistani Thanksgiving treats as possible, because we are not having a home-cooked holiday at my house.

Mom wanted to go to a restaurant, but Dad found out it was cheaper to order a precooked turkey, gravy, stuffing, and sides from the grocery store. "Plus, we'll have leftovers," he said last weekend as he finished grilling hamburgers for our dinner. We also had sweet potato fries—frozen, but deliciously salty-sweet—and a salad kit. Not bad for my parents. I like it when they work side by side in the kitchen. They bump into each other on purpose and pretend to argue about whose fault it is.

"I'm going to Sara's today, remember?" I remind Mom more than once.

Mom twirls me around and pulls me into a hug. "Sara's mom and I have a surprise for you," she says.

186

But before I can beg her to spill the beans, Justin rushes into the kitchen and pulls the turkey tea cozy off Mom's head. She chases my brother down the hallway, shouting, "Come back with that turkey, you turkey!"

I love when Mom acts like a big kid. Even when things were normal, when Nan was alive and my mom was only depressed some of the time instead of all of the time, moments like this were rare. Mom hasn't made me laugh so hard since that time she took a balled-up sock out of a laundry basket and threw it at Dad's butt. Next thing I knew, the five of us were having an all-out sock war. David even found a pair of Mom's tights and made a slingshot. Socks flew across the upstairs hallway like giant cushy snowballs. Robin was barking, of course. He hates to feel left out.

At ten o'clock, I walk and Justin rides his bike to Sara's house. It's a few streets away from our townhouse, in the Old Oaks neighborhood. While the two of us are gone, Mom will go pick up our holiday dinner. Dad and David are busy changing the oil in Mom's car.

Justin rides ahead of me, zipping along the sidewalk. I yell at him to stay in my sight. I should have guessed that he knows the Hameed twins from school. When we find Sara's address, I realize I remember this place from Halloween because it looked so dark and spooky. It's kind of a tragedy that the Hameeds don't celebrate Halloween. Their house has a rambling front porch that would be awesome decked out in spiderwebs and bedsheet ghosts. Before I can ring the bell, Sara throws open

187

the door. Two small boys with dark hair come flying out. They scream, jump off the top step, and land on the path, right in front of Justin.

I haven't even said hello to Sara, and these three are already playing tackle tag in the front yard.

Sara and I look at each other. "Brothers," we say at the same time.

I enter a small hall lit with a couple of warm lamps on a table. Sara motions for me to put my shoes on a rack in the corner. I'm glad I'm wearing socks.

There's a giant painting in Arabic script across from the doorway. Its bright colors remind me of the Ketubah hanging in my parents' bedroom. Uncle Ted's husband, Rory, is a graphic artist, and he wrote out my parents' Jewish marriage contract in calligraphy, decorated with colorful flowers, vines, and stars. When I was little, I loved to trace the vines with my finger. I like the way they wind around the Hebrew letters.

I follow Sara to the living room, where Mr. Hameed is sitting on a brown leather couch. His feet are propped up on a small ottoman and there's a teacup sitting on his belly. I peek at the TV.

"You like cricket?" I blurt out before I even say hello. Sara raises her eyebrows at me, so I backtrack. "I mean: Hello, Mr. Hameed. Thank you for having us over."

"Nice to see you, Elizabeth," he says. "You enjoy cricket?"

"Not me. When my cousins visit from England, they always complain that there's no cricket on American TV."

"Hello, Elizabeth." Mrs. Hameed walks in from the kitchen, smiling. It's strange to see her without her hijab. Her long black hair is shiny and smooth. I can't stop looking at it. "Would you girls gather some tindas from the porch, please?"

Sara begs, "Mama, please. We talked about this! Can't we have normal American sides? Stuffing. Cranberry sauce."

Mrs. Hameed flourishes the wooden spoon she's holding, as if she's the new Doctor Who and the spoon is her sonic screwdriver. "We can have those things and some traditional Pakistani food as well. Now, go." She points toward the back door.

Sara leads me out to a small sunroom, where there are planters lined up along the glass walls. In each container, herbs I recognize from class are growing next to vegetables I've never seen before.

Sara shows me the cutest little baby green pumpkins growing on a prickly vine. "Let's get this over with." She snaps a tinda off the vine and puts it in my hand. It's about the size of a small green apple but hardly weighs a thing. Sara pulls more fruit off the plant, making a little basket with the bottom of her tunic to hold them.

"They are adorable," I declare as I pick a few more tindas. "I want to take a Sharpie and draw little faces on them."

"You wouldn't think they were adorable if you actually had

189

to eat them," Sara says. "They are as sour and disgusting as Maddy Montgomery's heart."

I stop for a second and take a deep breath. I've tried to imagine pulling Maddy aside in the lunchroom or the PE locker room for a conversation. But what would I say to her? *Hey, former bestie. The racism thing? I know you can do better. Okay, Mads? Good talk.* I know I'm not ready. Will I ever be?

I ask Sara, "Can we not talk about Maddy today?"

"Sure. Let's just cook and have fun."

I can't help it—even with two tindas in each of my hands, I wrap Sara in a hug. She's so surprised that she drops the edge of her tunic. Little green gourds spill out.

"Escaping tindas!" Sara shouts. "Look out, they're making a run for it!" Then we're both laughing and picking up gourds, making sure none of them have cracked.

At dinner tonight, when my family shares what we're each thankful for, I'm going to say, "I'm thankful for my new friend." And for my mother's new friend too.

21

Sara

ELIZABETH AND I deposit the tindas on the kitchen counter. She stands in the middle of the kitchen, closes her eyes, and smiles, as if she's asleep and having a wonderful dream. When her eyes open, she sighs and says, "Everything smells so good, Mrs. Hameed. It's like chicken and mashed potatoes decided to dance a ballet with your spice cabinet. What are you making?"

I drag her away. "No time for that! I want to show you my room."

Mama is fiddling with the oven. "I'm baking zeera cookies —come back soon."

In my room, though, I pause, suddenly shy. I wish I'd cleaned up a little more. Elizabeth looks around. What is she thinking? Thankfully, my bed is made. My stuffed animals are in a tidy row on the top shelf above my desk like welcoming hosts. The desk itself is messy, but it's a contained mess. Paints, markers, and piles of sketchbooks. On the wall, a few pencil sketches are pinned to the corkboard. "I like it!" Elizabeth announces. She notices the poster spread out on my desk. "What is this? It's so good!"

I touch the lacy sleeves of my tunic. "You think so? Mrs. Newman asked me to make a sign for the International Festival. These are preliminary designs."

"Whoa. She asked you instead of an eighth-grader? The whole school is coming to the festival." Elizabeth puts up her hand for a high-five.

I give her a weak slap. "I'm not used to people looking at my art."

"Well, get used to it. You're going to be famous!"

I feel an excitement inside me. *Famous.* A few months ago, the thought of the entire school looking at my art would've made me hide under the bedcovers. Not anymore. I'm done being invisible. "Any ideas for the white spaces?" I ask Elizabeth. I've painted the border with flags of different countries and the middle with smiling faces. The rest is empty.

"A cupcake emoji would look great here."

When I glare at her, she laughs. "Kidding! Your artwork is amazing. Why are you even in cooking club? You should be in art club. You should be *president* of the art club."

I flop down on my bed. "My parents don't think art is a viable career option."

She frowns at me like a stern teacher. "We're kids. It's too soon to think about careers. Our brains haven't even developed yet." Elizabeth taps the side of her head. "Our gray matter is still, like, ten percent mashed potatoes."

"Please. My brain is perfectly well developed, especially the creative side." I pat my head. "But my parents want me to be good at math and science, not art."

"Have you actually talked to them about this? Have they ever said, *Art is beneath you, Sara?*" She says the words in a fake adult voice.

I think about that. There have been no actual conversations about my art. Baba always tells me how good I am, but since sixth grade started, Mama hasn't even looked at my drawings. She's always running around juggling ten jobs at once. I sometimes wonder if she sees me at all. "They always say immigrants should go into scientific fields, like medicine or computers," I finally reply. It's what I've heard from every South Asian parent or teacher my entire life.

Elizabeth puts her hands on her hips. "But your parents are nice."

"You've met my dad, what—twice?" I protest, throwing a pillow in her direction. "And you see my mom once a week for an hour."

"What can I say? I'm an excellent judge of character!" She throws the pillow back, and I catch it with both hands. She plops down on the bed next to me. "Seriously, Sara. You need to stop worrying about what people will say and be yourself."

"Oh, yeah, Miss Philosopher?"

"Yeah. Just look at Maddy. She's turned into a carbon copy of Sweet Stephanie, and it's enough to make me puke. She's a carbon cupcake."

"Maddy's not sweet enough to be a cupcake," I mumble.

Even though we agreed not to talk about Maddy today, Elizabeth's right. In every interaction with kids at school, I always worry about saying the right thing, being the right way. I always obsess on what others think of me, even stupid mean girls like Maddy and Stephanie. It's just how I am.

Elizabeth softens. "I am simply pointing out that you've got to be more chill. Try being less intense."

"Intense?" I want to be mad at her, but she's right.

"Yes! Intense." She pushes her glasses up and brushes her bangs out of her face. "Which is good when you're drawing, not so much if you're trying to make friends in middle school."

"Enough lectures." I pull my laptop toward me. "Since we've decided not to make paratha s'mores for the competition, we're starting from scratch."

"That means more cooking videos!" Elizabeth is so excited, she bounces up and down on my bed. "Salma aunty dropped a new video about appetizers yesterday. I haven't watched it yet."

"Less intense, please!" I mock.

She throws a pillow at me.

All the cooking videos make us hungry, while giving us zero recipe ideas for the International Festival. We peek into the dining room, where Mama is putting the finishing touches on a pile of catering orders.

"I'm sorry—I forgot I'd promised to help you!" I groan. Now she's going to look all tired out, and it will be my fault.

She hardly looks up. "Don't worry. Your father helped me this morning while you were snoring away. I'm almost done."

Elizabeth comes closer. "Can I help you with anything, Mrs. Hameed?" I can tell she's trying to read the labels on the boxes and figure out what's inside.

Mama waves to the box of labels on the table. "I need these fixed on the smallest boxes, then the words 'Chicken Tikka' written on them."

Elizabeth gives me a knowing look. "Wouldn't it be nice if you had an actual label with a logo for your business?"

Mama looks up, startled. "What?"

I step on Elizabeth's foot to shut her up. "Nothing," I say loudly. Nervously. I'm not ready yet to reveal my business ideas to my family. I don't know if I ever will be.

Elizabeth shakes her head at me and picks up a plain white sticker. "Yeah, nothing," she repeats.

I relax. That was a close call.

Mama goes back to her labeling. "What were you girls doing upstairs for so long?"

Elizabeth sniffs at the box she's holding in her hand. "Watching videos."

"To get inspiration for our Secret Award-Winning Recipe," I add. "We still can't think of what to cook."

Mama looks up in surprise. "You'd better hurry up and decide. You don't have much time left."

Elizabeth dazzles Mama with a smile. "Can't you give us some ideas, please, Mrs. Hameed? You're the expert, after all."

Mama shakes her head. "Sorry. That would be cheating. I can't help any of my students, because I'm the event organizer." She picks up an armful of plastic boxes and a blue hijab from the back of a chair. "I'm off to deliver these orders. You two are on your own."

Elizabeth and I sit at the kitchen table after she's gone, munching freshly baked zeera cookies. Baba's cricket match is still going, but he's sleeping on the couch with his cup of chai still balanced on his stomach. I bring my recipe notebook with the glittery purple lettering on the cover, and we go over our notes again. And again. I can't believe how many ideas we've discarded. Parathas. Sandwiches. Samosas. Even a strawberry lassi mixture that I'm secretly dying to make.

"Too bad Mama won't help us," I complain. "What's the point of having a cook for a mother if we can't use her expertise?"

"We could do something Jewish, like matzo balls," Elizabeth suggests, rubbing her eyes under her glasses. "My bubbe would help us."

"What's she like?" I imagine an old white lady with gray hair and old-fashioned glasses hanging from her neck.

"She's the best! She wears bright colors and funky jewelry and her hair is all spiky. Mom says I get my sense of style from

196

her." Elizabeth grins and shows off her very colorful autumn-leaves leggings. "She's coming to visit for Hanukkah. I hope you get to meet her." She pauses. "What about you? You never told me about your grandparents."

"They live in Pakistan. I don't see them very often," I say slowly, trying to conjure them in my mind. Nana and Nani, who are Mama's parents. Dada and Dadi, who are Baba's parents. Or in the case of Dada, that grainy, serious picture of him.

Elizabeth looks at me with big eyes. "That's so sad. When was the last time you saw them?"

I tell her about our summer vacation in Pakistan three years ago. My first international air travel. The heat of the season. The crowd of cousins, aunts, and uncles. The food. The fragrances. The noise. We flew first to Karachi, where Mama's parents live, in a poor but bustling city. Then we traveled by train to Lahore, where my dadi lived on a sprawling village farm outside the city, complete with chickens, cows, and fields of turnip greens.

It's kind of cool, though. My parents were a city girl and a village boy, but they still found each other thousands of miles away in America.

Elizabeth closes the recipe notebook and listens to everything I'm saying as if it's the most interesting thing she's ever heard. I get a happy feeling inside, like I'm made of bubbles.

But I know bubbles don't last forever. There's another part of me, my brain, perhaps, that's telling me this is too good to be true. Elizabeth's real friends are Maddy and Micah and the other kids she's grown up with. Sure, we have some similarities. We both go to religious Sunday school. We both have at least one parent who comes from another country. But exchanging secrets and being there for each other is still easier with Rabia.

Yeah, but we're getting better at it, my heart reminds me.

22

Elizabeth

MOM ARRIVES AT the same time as Mrs. Hameed. The cricket match on TV is ending. Mr. Hameed is clapping for the home team. He gives Sara's brothers high-fives and fist bumps.

Mrs. Hameed pulls off her hijab and brings out some fresh tea and fruit. "Sara, boys, everyone! Come into the family room, please. We have something to tell you." It's obvious that tea—chai—is a big thing in the Hameed household.

My mom's bright pink cheeks tell me it's surprise time. Justin, Tariq, and Rafey tumble onto the couch. They're adorable, but sweaty and fidgety, so I take a spot as far away from them as possible. Sara sits on her father's ottoman, and he pats her shoulder. He's grinning. He must be in on the secret.

Our mothers stand, facing us all. My mom is tall and regal. She's wearing a navy blue dress. An actual dress! Next to Mom, Mrs. Hameed is petite, but her lifted chin as she motions to my mother means she's the one in charge.

"Nicole and I have something to tell you."

"You won the lottery?" Mr. Hameed jokes. Okay, maybe he's just as clueless as the rest of us.

She gives him her teacherly *Settle down, now* face, but she's holding back a smile. "No. We both received our interview dates for citizenship."

My mother's smile rises like a sweet golden cake. "We got the same date! And if we pass, we'll be at the same ceremony."

Sara and I exchange glances. I can't believe it. It's happening. Even if Mom goes through with her plans to visit London, she's going to go as an American. This is huge.

"I won't feel as anxious, knowing Hina is with me the whole time," Mom says.

Justin rushes over to give her a hug. "I'm proud of you, Mom!"

Mr. Hameed clears his throat. "Congratulations, ladies. Now, let's talk about dinner. Nicole, are you sure you won't join us?"

I want to jump up and say, *Thanks, Hameeds! Of course we will join you for dinner. Don't know why we didn't think of it earlier.*

But Mom is making excuses. "You have enough to do, Hina. And we wanted a quiet holiday this year." The three boys have tumbled off the couch and are wrestling on the floor.

Now that the couch is open, Sara slides next to me. "I guess we've got another event to plan, after the festival."

It takes me a second to catch on. "A citizenship party. Yes! I'm in."

"We'll need flags," Sara says. "I may need another notebook. Operation Citizenship Party."

"I'll bake cookies. With striped icing and star sprinkles."

Sara lifts one dark eyebrow. "Should we hire Stephanie to bake cupcakes for the occasion? She *is* the cupcake queen."

"If she does say so herself," I add.

Mr. Hameed says, "Flags, cookies, cupcakes. This sounds like a big celebration."

"I hope it's after the festival," Sara whispers to me. "We need to focus. We only have a month left to get our recipe ready." She crosses her fingers and turns to her mother. "Mama, you haven't told us the date yet."

Mrs. Hameed checks the calendar on her phone. "Wednesday, January ninth," she tells us.

My chest tightens. "It's on a Wednesday?" I ask my mom. I touch the charms on my bracelets—Star of David first, then flag, teacup, TARDIS. "What if Dad's traveling?"

"Let's talk about that later. At home," Mom says. She reaches for her cup of tea and focuses on Mrs. Hameed. Away from me.

I cross my arms at her, even though she won't meet my eyes. *Let's talk about that later* means bad news. It means Dad won't be there for Mom's citizenship ceremony.

Mom drives me and Justin home, but I refuse to go into the house. I am boycotting this family. They can eat their

201

grocery-store Thanksgiving dinner while I sit out here on the cold front steps.

Mom pushes Justin inside and hesitates in the doorway. "Elizabeth, stop being so dramatic. I don't need Dad at the swearing-in. I'll have you and your brothers."

"It's not right," I insist. "I am protesting. I'm doing a sit-in."

"Looks more like a sit-out," David says as he pokes his head out the door.

"Mind your own business," I tell him.

He pulls Mom inside. There's some emergency with the meat-thermometer app that David insisted on using for the turkey. They leave me out here to shiver and fume.

When the door opens a few minutes later, I'm surprised that it's Dad. He likes to joke that he's in charge of car repair, compost, and recycling. He leaves friend trouble and "minor emotional sprains" to Mom.

Dad sits, long legs stretched out in front of him, and wraps an arm around me. "I hear you're staging a sit-out," he teases.

"Humph. Sit-in."

"Want to tell me what happened?"

Usually when I'm sad, Dad's deep voice resonates in my chest, soothing my hurt feelings. But not this time. When my parents sent me away this summer, I shut down all my sadness about Nan being sick, about missing home and Justin. I couldn't show those feelings to the girls in my cabin. They would have started singing *"The sun will come out tomorrow"* at

202

me. But today, all the sadness I've been holding inside wants to burst out of me.

"Dad, you can't skip Mom's citizenship ceremony," I say. "We're supposed to go together, as a family."

Dad shakes his head. "It's not that easy, Elizabeth. I have to work."

"Take a day off."

"You don't understand."

"*You* don't understand. If you don't come, it's like you don't care. I thought you wanted Mom to be an American, so she can vote, and go through Customs with us at the airport, and stay here forever."

"Of course I want those things. The ceremony isn't that big of a deal."

"Did Mom say that?" I ask. "Because if she did, she was lying to make you feel better about not being there."

Dad pulls his knees awkwardly into his chest. "We'll give Mom a party on a weekend, when it's convenient."

I face my father and tap his chest with two fingers, the way Bubbe does when she argues with him. "You'd better be at that ceremony. I need to know that I have at least one parent who's not going anywhere."

Dad gapes at me. I glare right back.

"What does that mean?" he asks.

I shift on the cold concrete step. "Mom's been talking to Aunt Louise about going back to England. She's always checking airfare sales and making packing lists. If she goes, how do we know she's coming back?" Tears start to flow down my cheeks. I bat them away with my knuckles.

Dad's forehead furrows. "Any chance you overheard something your mother said and blew it out of proportion?"

I make a sound in my throat. "Why does everyone in this family think I'm some kind of drama queen?" I complain.

Dad doesn't answer that question. He asks, "And where do you think I'm running off to? Tahiti?" The way Dad's lips are smirking makes me want to storm into the house, but I'm determined to do this sit-in. Sit-out. Whatever.

"It's not funny, Dad. You're never home. Never. Mom has been so sad, and sometimes she doesn't do basic stuff like laundry or cooking or leaving the house. It feels like our family is buried under a blob of gray, lumpy gravy. When you're home, she tries to act like everything's fine, but it's not. That's just for show."

Dad takes a deep breath too. His exhale makes a cloud of steam.

The door opens before he can speak. It's Mom. "Dinner's on the table," she says.

"No more moping on the steps." Dad pulls me up by the arm. I guess my protest is over. "We'll talk more later," he says.

Dad is home for all five days of our holiday break. He gets up early, pours boiling water into a proper teapot, and puts the tea cozy over it to keep it warm. I add a dainty flowered teacup and

204

some English digestive biscuits to the breakfast tray so Mom can have tea in bed. She loves this tradition. It was something her father used to do for Nan before he passed away. I was little when Granddad died, but I used to love crawling into bed with Nan for morning tea.

The sadness falls off my mother a little bit each day, like peeling the ugly brown fuzz off a kiwi fruit and finding the sweet green goodness inside. I can't tell if it's because of Dad being home, or because the citizenship test is finally happening.

Dad spends Saturday in the garage with David and Justin, trying—finally—to put the toaster back together, so Mom invites Mrs. Hameed over for a study session.

Before Sara's mom arrives, Mom calls me to the table and hands me a steaming cup of milky tea.

"I hear you think I'm a flight risk," Mom says.

"Huh?"

"Just because I want to visit Aunt Louise in London, it doesn't mean I want to leave you, Elizabeth. I love England. I miss the countryside, and fruit pastilles, and lighting the Christmas pudding on fire, but there are other traditions we can do here."

"Don't tell me Dad's going to be okay with a Christmas tree. And angel ornaments."

She laughs. "Maybe not, but I think we can talk him into Christmas pudding. The point is, I love you, and Dad, and your brothers more than all of those things put together."

I blow on my tea to help it cool. "What about Aunt Louise?"

"She has her own family to take care of, and she has her hands full selling Nan's house. She doesn't need to solve my problems. And she will—try to solve my problems. She is my big sister, after all."

"David doesn't try to solve my problems," I grump.

"Count yourself lucky," Mom says. "He can't even fix the toaster."

I sip my tea. "What about Dad? You're happier when he's home. And that makes the whole house feel better."

"He's working on it, Elizabeth. I promise," Mom says.

"Working on what? Coming to your swearing-in?"

"We'll see. You need to trust us. There are some things you're too young to worry about. Let the parents handle it."

Before Mom and I can finish talking, Mrs. Hameed arrives and the two of them get busy studying. I hear their happy chatter as they quiz each other on historical facts and dates.

It's fine for Mom to say *Let the parents handle it* when Dad is home. As soon as he's gone again, Mom's mood will crash and David, me, and Justin will be handling everything she can't.

On Sunday afternoon, my whole family gathers at the table for tea, Jaffa cakes that my mom found at the supermarket, and a game of dominoes. We all laugh when she tells a story about the time Nan's chickens escaped their coop. There were eggs hidden everywhere. In the hedges, in the flower beds, and one in the dry birdbath. Mom pats her eyes with a tissue, and for a second, I can't tell if she's laughing or crying. Maybe both.

After dinner, all of us crowd onto the couch to watch Mom's favorite episode of *Doctor Who*—the one where the hero of Nottingham, Robin Hood, is a real historical person. It's the Sheriff of Nottingham's knights who turn out to be evil robots.

"Your nan could never understand why Louise and I loved this show." Mom sighs. "She thought it was scary, no matter how fake the special effects were."

It's been such a great few days with Dad home. Now that I know Mom isn't going anywhere, it's time to convince my father that we need him here, and not only on the weekends.

23

Sara

MY HEAD IS ACHING. I had a nightmare just before dawn and wasn't able to get back to sleep. On the Monday after Thanksgiving break, school feels too bright, too loud, too . . . everything. I wish I could crawl back into my room and pull the covers over my head. Instead, I'm in Ms. Saintima's language arts class, trying to focus.

The weekend was brutal. Baba worked late and Mama had a ton of catering orders. My job was to keep the twins entertained. I took them cycling in the neighborhood, wrapped in our jackets and scarves. I watched superhero videos with them on my laptop in my room, closing the door so that Mama and Baba weren't disturbed by their laughter. I even taught them how to bake brownies on Sunday, and I didn't get a bit mad when Tariq spilled batter all over the counter.

Okay, I got a little mad. But he gave me a lopsided grin and cleaned up like an angel, so I rolled my eyes and said, "Good job."

"Antonio said there's a new ice cream shop across the highway that sells the most amazing brownie sundaes," Rafey told us. "Can't we have those instead of these homemade brownies?"

I smiled even bigger and replied, "Nobody makes brownies like me." I didn't let on that I'd seen the menu of that new shop and the sundaes cost almost ten dollars. Dollars we can't waste on dessert.

As Ms. Saintima settles our class down, I keep thinking of the dream from the night before. Mama and Baba were fighting loudly. Rafey and Tariq were running around the house, their faces twisted like monsters. And the walls of our living room were plastered with white papers. I took a closer look at the papers, scrunching up my eyes to read the tiny red words. LOAN PAST DUE. LOAN PAST DUE.

Ms. Saintima's voice pulls me out of my thoughts. "Poetry today," she announces. The room bursts into a mixture of cheers and groans. "Food poems," she clarifies, raising a hand to stop the chatter.

I wipe a hand over my eyes, wishing I'd asked Mama for some Tylenol at breakfast. Elizabeth is turned in her seat, wiggling her eyebrows at me. "Food poems!" she whispers.

I don't see why this is a big deal. Who even writes poems about food, anyway? But Elizabeth's not alone in her excitement. Micah grins at me, rubbing his hand over his stomach in a totally exaggerated way. Across the room, I notice Stephanie sitting up straighter, ready to write an advertisement about her latest cupcake flavor, I'm sure. I have to smile. All this because of Mama and her afterschool club. Well, mostly.

I'm surprised to realize that I don't hate cooking as much as I used to, at least when I'm in the kitchen with a friend. I sit up and get ready to take notes. Ms. Saintima's activities are always interesting.

"Who loves hot dogs?" she asks. A number of hands go up, but not mine.

"Hot dogs are gross," Stephanie calls out. I agree, but I'm not going to say so.

"Well, we're reading about them, not eating them." Ms. Saintima switches on the smartboard, and a poem pops up. "Good Hotdogs," by Sandra Cisneros. Our teacher perches on the edge of her desk in her bright batik pants, careful not to upset the stack of fantasy novels on the corner. We all settle down to listen. Ms. Saintima's accent, with its hint of something special from when she grew up in Haiti, adds music to the poem. The rhythmic words take ahold of me, like Selena Gomez's latest single, luring me to the table.

My headache grows lighter, and my eyelids get heavy. To stop myself from dozing, I focus on the poem. It's about a girl and her older sister who get to leave school and go to the hotdog store for lunch. We figure out it happened a long time ago, because it costs the girl fifty cents for a hot dog, fries, and a soda. Every one of my senses is tingling as Ms. Saintima asks us to imagine pulling the door of the store open and breathing in the steamy, meat-scented air. She has us close our eyes while she rereads the description of the hot dog slathered in toppings and wrapped up with crunchy french fries. I'm ashamed to realize that my mouth is watering.

"Why do you think the poet is telling us about a hot dog she ate when she was a kid?" Ms. Saintima asks.

Micah raises his hand. "It was a really, really good hot dog. It's right in the title."

Our teacher chuckles. "Fair enough, but what made it stick in her mind?"

I take a deep breath and raise my hand. "At the end it says, 'We'd eat, you humming and me swinging my legs.' It's a happy memory of being with her sister."

Elizabeth turns again to look at me, her face slightly shocked. I don't think I've ever said anything much in class before. She gives me a thumbs-up. Raising my hand in class, making friends with Elizabeth and Micah; I'm very different from the girl I was at the start of sixth grade.

"Good eye, Sara. Everyone, that's your assignment for today," Ms. Saintima says. "A food memory. Yes, your goal is to use all five senses to describe your food, but also think about who you're sharing the food with, and how you feel in that moment. If your family has a special food tradition, that would be a great topic to write about."

Immediately, my headache comes back. It's not that I can't write poetry. At Iqra, we started doing simple poems in fourth grade. Ms. Saintima would never call on me to read my poem aloud unless I wanted to. Which I wouldn't. But my mind isn't

211

on food at the moment. Mama's bills scurry through my mind like noisy, demanding children. LOAN PAST DUE.

I pick up my pencil and doodle. What's my best food memory? Everything I remember about food is associated with hard work. I remember Ms. Saintima telling us many weeks ago that writing poetry could begin with something as simple as coming up with some words to describe your feelings. Almost like brainstorming, but in rhythm. I try.

Fragile rice cooked with spices.
Chicken adorned with garlic and ginger.
Frowns and pursed lips.
A sweaty hijab.
Money.

"Ugh, this is terrible!" I whisper to myself, throwing my pencil down on the desk. A few kids look up and stare at me. I scowl at them, and they look away. *That's more like the old Sara,* I can almost see them thinking. I go back to my notebook, determined to try again. For several minutes, the only sound in the classroom is pencils scratching against paper, and the ticking of the clock on the wall.

Soon, Ms. Saintima looks around the room. "Who'd like to read their draft out loud?" she says in an encouraging tone.

I swallow and look away. Elizabeth raises her arm straight into the air. Ms. Saintima nods in her direction to give permission.

"Ahem," Elizabeth begins. "'Mushy Peas.'"

Micah makes a sound in his throat. "Mushy peas? That sounds disgusting."

Elizabeth frowns at him and continues.

"One pound fifty pence
for mushy peas.
Our shopping done,
we climb
a flight of stairs
to the fish market,
then the stall
that smells of vinegar.
Two orders of mushy peas
slathered in tangy mint sauce,
bright green heaven
in Styrofoam cups.
We walk
through the old market square,
Nan and me
window shopping.
We eat, never thinking
this is the last time."

When Elizabeth finishes, everyone claps loudly, including me. She smiles, but her eyes are a little sad. I know she's remembering her grandmother.

"Okay," Micah admits. "Mushy peas don't sound too bad, but I still wouldn't eat them."

Ms. Saintima is about to say something, but the bell rings. "Work on your poems tonight, please. I'll collect them tomorrow."

In the hallway, Elizabeth asks to see my poem. "I know you were writing something. Show me!"

I clutch my notebook as if she'll grab it from me. "It's really bad. And very short."

"I don't care," she insists. "I read everyone the poem about my grandmother. I'm dying to see what your favorite food is."

"It's not a food I've ever had. More like my dream of the perfect pizza." Slowly, I open my notebook and show her my poem. It's not a poem yet, just the start of one. She reads it soundlessly.

> Pizza with bihari beef
> trapped in gooey cheese
> telling me I'm the queen
> of the food court,
> my best friend's laughter
> the only topping
> I could ever need.

Her face is comical. "Pizza? I was sure you'd write a poem about samosas or curry. Even tindas."

"Pizza's my favorite—what can I say?"

214

"But why?"

I struggle to explain. "Pizza is . . . delicious."

Micah comes up behind us. "You know it!" He puts up his hand for a high-five, but we both roll our eyes at him.

I keep talking, my voice becoming louder. "I don't always have to eat immigrant dishes, do I? I can enjoy American foods once in a while."

"Pizza *is* immigrant food," Micah reminds us. "Italian, remember? Except for Chicago-style deep dish. That's one hundred percent American."

I nod vigorously. "Exactly. Pizza changes to suit the culture of the people eating it. It's basically like America itself. We all come from different places, and then we settle here and try to be American, but still retain our distinct flavors."

I'm proud of my analogy, but Elizabeth and Micah look puzzled. "What are you talking about?" Micah asks. "Pizza is like America, even though it's Italian?"

"Exactly. It's Italian but it's also American. Like my family is Pakistani but also American."

Elizabeth smiles. "And I'm British on one half, and American on the other!"

Micah raises his hand. "Make my pizza half Jewish and half Puerto Rican."

I tell him, "My favorite afterschool snack for my brothers is shredded cheese and red pepper flakes on packaged naan from the grocery store. I heat them in the toaster oven and voilà —naan pizza!"

Micah is hanging on my words like a hungry man visualizing a banquet. "I wish today was pizza day," he says, licking his lips. "Hey, where can we get that packaged naan? Your pizza idea is genius. My mom's working when I get home from school. I can never find anything good to snack on."

"You can always eat mushy peas," I tease.

He groans. "Okay, don't tell me. I will ask Google. She's my friend."

Near the water fountains, a bunch of boys are gathered together, laughing. I see Ahsan Kapadia in the crowd. He gives me a little half nod, half smile. Almost as if he's saying, *Look at us, away from Iqra Academy and already making new friends.*

I nod back. Then my smile freezes, because just behind him, Maddy Montgomery is giving us the blackest scowl I ever saw. "What's up with all the Arabs at this school?" she practically screeches. "It's like Saudi Middle over here."

I'm not sure who she's talking to. Micah and Elizabeth look shocked. Ahsan's smile disappears. His shoulders slump. He turns from the other boys and walks away.

"Ignore her," I manage to utter, even though my eyes are smarting.

Elizabeth's mouth is set in a thin, straight line. "No. I can't ignore her anymore."

216

24

Elizabeth

"You should come to cooking club today," I tell Micah as we walk to the cafeteria. "Sara won't give me details, but we're making dessert."

"Chocolate lava cake?" Micah asks.

"I doubt it. I don't think there's much chocolate in Pakistani cooking."

"Pass," Micah says as we walk through the double doors into the lunchroom. "Unless it's ice cream. If it's ice cream, text me."

"You're going to be waiting a long time for that text. No phone until I turn thirteen, remember?"

"I pity you," he says. "My phone is where I keep all my favorite drum solos. Stewart Copeland is my dude." Micah drums his fingertips on his lunch bag.

I lead him through the noisy cafeteria, avoiding Stephanie and Maddy's table.

"This is dumb," he says. "Can't you just tell her to stop acting like a jerk, have a fight, and go back to being friends?

That's what my brothers and I do. I have the scars to prove it." Micah stops and makes me look at a small gray dot on his knee. "Nathan stabbed me with a pencil when I was seven," he says.

I shake my head. "It's not that simple."

But it used to be. Until last year, my friendship with Maddy was perfect. We were the Companions. She was loud and loved being silly and having dance-offs in the basement. Plus, Maddy was the only person at school who would gush about *Doctor Who* with me. Who I could be myself with. Not like at home, where Mom was always asking me to calm down, keep quiet, or act my age.

Micah sniffs the air. "Ribique today. God bless Cookie for packing my lunch." He lifts his brown bag to his face and kisses it.

My mind is not on lunch—it's on Maddy. When she made another dig at Muslims yesterday, I thought back to fifth grade. This popular kid, Troy Jansen, sat behind Maddy. He started complaining that her hair was so short that he had to stare at her neck freckles all day. He started calling Maddy "Neckles." It was mean, but all the boys still wanted to play touch football with Troy at recess. All the girls still laughed at his jokes. Except Maddy. And me.

That's when Maddy started growing her hair long and wearing the same thing as everyone else. Maybe it's also when Maddy decided that popular equals mean.

As Micah and I take our seats, I feel a tap on my shoulder. Stephanie.

"Hi, Steph." Micah grins hungrily. "Giving out samples?"

Stephanie shakes her head. Her high blond ponytail flips back and forth. "Not today."

She's traded her usual pink-and-white Sweet Stephanie's shirt for a cartoon of three adorable green peas, still in their pod.

"Can I talk to you, Elizabeth?" Steph asks. "I need to ask you a favor."

"Sure, I guess. Unless you want me and Sara to back out of the recipe contest, because that is not happening." I raise my eyebrows mischievously.

"Would you do that for me?" she jokes right back. "You two are our biggest competition. But seriously . . ." Stephanie lowers her voice. "I need to talk to you about Maddy."

I let Stephanie pull me to a half-empty table. We sit side by side on the bench and turn to face each other.

"It's about what happened at the mall," Steph begins. "I've been trying to tell Maddy to apologize. I can't believe what she said to Sara. Will you talk to her?"

My jaw wants to clench, to keep the words in, but I say, "You're her new best friend. Anyway, why do you care? You never even talk to Sara."

Steph looks at her hands. "I'm not a bad person, Elizabeth. And I actually like Mrs. Hameed. A lot. She's the best cooking teacher I ever had. The point is, Maddy shouldn't talk to anyone that way."

I can't believe we're agreeing on something. "So, what are you going to do?"

"The thing is, she won't listen to me. She says I should stick to my charity work." Stephanie motions to the logo on her shirt. Underneath the cartoon, it says PROJECT SWEET PEAS. "If you don't talk to her, it's going to get worse."

I wonder if Steph heard about Maddy's outburst yesterday.

I get it now. This is exactly what Sara's been saying. If I don't talk to Maddy, get her to understand why she has to apologize, nothing is going to change. Maybe some other kid, someone like Troy Jansen, will tell Sara to go back where she came from. And then they'll say it to Micah, or Ms. Saintima.

"I'll try," I tell Stephanie.

She doesn't clap her hands or bounce up and down with her usual glee. She says, "I knew I could count on you." Steph isn't my favorite person, but it makes me feel good when she says that.

When I get to our table, Sara is pulling at the edge of her sleeve. "What was that all about?" she asks.

I don't want her to know I'm talking to Maddy until after I do it. "Steph's charity work," I fib.

That afternoon, Mrs. Kluck lets us into the FACS room and rushes away, mumbling something about the janitor. Sara and

I settle into our cooking station. Class is always more relaxed when Mrs. Kluck's not here. Stephanie keeps glancing my way.

I'm too distracted to cook. The things Maddy said at the mall, the things she shouted in the hallway the other day, take up all the space in my brain. *Go back to where you belong. Nobody wants you here. What's up with all the Arabs at this school?* How many times have I felt like nobody wanted me around? It's the story of my whole summer at sleepaway camp.

"What's this dish called again?" I ask Sara.

"I told you three times. Doodh ka halwa." She pronounces each syllable carefully, then points to the milk on our counter. "It's milk curd."

"Like lemon curd?"

Sara crosses her arms. "It's not at all like lemon curd. I tried to talk Mama out of doing this recipe. It's made from curdled milk." She throws up her hands, so I know her mother didn't listen to Sara's advice. "Everyone is going to be so grossed out."

"What about Mrs. Kluck?" I ask. "She has a huge sweet tooth. I know your mom's been buttering her up — bringing her Pakistani candy, making her sweet chai tea."

Sara gives me a not-so-patient blink. "*Chai* literally means 'tea,'" she corrects.

I wince. "Sorry. Still learning."

Normally, I'd be smiling and laughing as Sara and I cook together, but I keep glancing at Maddy's station, wondering

221

when I'm going to find time to talk to her, and what I'm going to say.

"I think Mama's plan to sweeten Mrs. Kluck up is working," Sara says. "Did I tell you she gave Mama an extra key to the FACS room? That means she's starting to trust Mama."

I'm surprised. I didn't think Mrs. Kluck trusted anyone. "She did?"

Sara nods proudly. "Yup. It's on a silly little pineapple charm, something you'd buy at a tourist shop."

Mrs. Hameed claps her hands for attention. I try to focus on her smiling face. We boil milk, sugar, and spices, as if we're making vanilla pudding. Then Sara squeezes fresh lemon juice and water into the mixture and, as promised, it curdles.

I don't say anything to Sara, but the mixture we just made looks vile, like pale gravy full of lumpy flour. It's supposed to cool and set for several hours before the so-called treat gets decorated with pistachios and coconut, then cut into something like bar cookies.

We're each going to take home the batch we're cooking so it can cool. Sara says her mother made a panful in advance so we can all taste it now. Hooray?

"If this milk was in my fridge, I'd vomit," I hear Maddy say. "Indian food is disgusting."

Sara grits her teeth. By now, Maddy knows the Hameeds are from Pakistan. "Keep stirring," Sara tells me, calling my attention back to the pot. "If it burns, we have to start over."

Before I can answer, Mrs. Kluck bursts into the room.

222

Behind her is our janitor, Mr. Brody, who is usually all smiles, but not today. Today, he is huffing and puffing as he pushes a gigantic wooden box.

Mr. Brody works as a birthday clown on weekends, so lots of kids have known him since they were toddlers. He's the closest thing our school has to a celebrity.

Mrs. Kluck throws out her arms. "Gather around, everyone. The ice cream machine is here." Finally she's the center of attention in her own classroom.

"Children, children," Mrs. Hameed calls over the commotion. "Do not leave your stoves. Your halwa will burn."

When no one listens, Sara rushes off to help her mother. They go from station to station, removing pots from stoves and turning off the heat.

This is my chance. "Maddy," I say, as she walks over to join the group.

She stops. Her dark hair pulled back into its too-tight ponytail makes her expression look hard. She's wearing lip gloss and mascara. When did she start wearing makeup?

"What's up, Els?" she says. She takes in my outfit, which is pretty tame for me: navy sweater, stone-gray jeans, and my TARDIS kicks. "Still got your *Who* gear."

"*Allons-y,*" I say, quoting the Tenth Doctor's catchphrase. "I have to talk to you. About what happened at the mall."

Maddy is focused on Mr. Brody, who is opening the mysterious box. "That was weeks ago. Can't you just forget it?"

"No," I say. "Sara is my friend. You shouldn't have

223

spoken to her like that. And I heard what you said to Ahsan yesterday."

She takes a few steps back from me. "Thanks to Sara, Stephanie's been on my case. I don't see why it's such a big deal. We're in middle school. People say mean things all the time."

I narrow my eyes. "There's a difference between being mean and being racist, Mads."

I follow her gaze back to the demonstration kitchen. A shiny silver contraption emerges from the box. I know what that is. An ice cream maker, the rapid-freeze kind they use on television cooking shows.

"Is that all?" Maddy asks. "'Cause I kind of want to see that thing."

"You need to apologize," I insist.

She shrugs. "Sara shouldn't take things so seriously. And neither should you." She walks away. Stephanie gives me a thumbs-up from across the room. I shake my head at her. That did not go well.

Everyone but Sara and Mrs. Hameed fusses over the ice cream machine, which gleams on the counter. Micah's words pop into my head: *If it's ice cream, text me.* Because who can say no to ice cream?

That's it! Ice cream is the secret element we need for our festival recipe.

I rush back to our station and stick a teaspoon in the pot. The flavor reminds me of Dad's favorite cake, German chocolate. Not the cake itself. The halwa tastes like caramel and coconut icing. The texture is weird, though—chewy and . . . curdy.

When Sara comes back, I announce: "This doodh stuff would taste great mixed with ice cream. Like our own version of cookies and cream."

She groans. "Don't tell me you've got ice cream fever too. Mrs. Kluck's machine is ruining Mama's class."

I'm relieved that in all the confusion, Sara didn't notice me talking to Maddy. I stir the pot and tell her, "Sara, I have the answer to our recipe prayers."

25

Sara

THE HOUSE IS QUIET on Saturday morning. I lie in bed, staring out my window. My room seems different since Elizabeth was here. Lighter. Airier. I wonder if she feels the same way, if we leave a tiny bit of ourselves behind when we leave a space.

Someone is coming up the stairs. Baba was supposed to take the twins to a movie, so that must be Mama. She knocks on my door and enters without waiting for an answer. I grit my teeth. Typical Mama.

"*Salaam alaikum,* sleepyhead," she says, and starts picking up my clothes from the floor. "I need to do laundry, so . . ." She gives me a disapproving look.

"Sorry," I say sheepishly. I watch as she tidies my room, picks up clothes, straightens the things on my desk. I should help her, but it feels nice to see her doing these little chores for me. Her entire attention is focused on my room, my stuff, me. I can't remember the last time that happened.

When I was little, Mama and I used to do everything together. This was before the twins were born, before Mama started her catering business. Before I somehow changed from being the daughter to being the helper. The responsible one. One time we went to a carnival, just Mama and me together. We sat in a bumper car, laughing every time another car banged into us. We ate popcorn, throwing pieces to the pigeons that hopped toward us with eager beaks. Mama used to laugh a lot then. And hug me all the time.

"Yeh kya?" She's looking through my sketchbook.

I scramble out of bed and take it from her. "It's nothing," I stammer. "Just my . . . art." I'm suddenly thinking of what Elizabeth said at Thanksgiving. *Be less intense.* Do I even know how? My shoulders sag, and I offer the sketchbook to her hesitantly. "Want to see?" It comes out as a whisper. Maybe she won't hear.

Mama's got a full laundry basket tucked under one arm, but she reaches out with her free hand. Just then, the cell phone in her back pocket chimes. "Hello?" She gives me an apologetic look, then turns and walks away.

When I go downstairs for breakfast, she's loading the washing machine. "What are your plans for today?" she calls out to me.

I shrug, even though she can't see me. "I don't know. I need to work on some projects for school. But I've got some free time. Do you need help with orders?"

She emerges from the laundry room with a smile. *"Nahi.* I have zero orders today!"

"Wow," I say. "I mean, that sucks, but still!"

227

"Don't say 'sucks'—it's not nice," she tells me. "You want to go to the grocery store with me?"

I slurp some cereal. "Can we go to Burger Palace for lunch?"

She rolls her eyes. "If you insist on eating bland, unhealthy food instead of home-cooked yummy meals, then sure."

I swallow quickly and grin at her before she changes her mind. "I do insist."

By the time we finish grocery shopping and get to Burger Palace, it's almost two in the afternoon. I order a double cheeseburger with fries and a chocolate milkshake. Mama gives me an *Are you sure you can eat all that?* look and orders a salad for herself.

"It's called Burger Palace, Mama. It should be against the law to order a salad here."

She gives me a little grin. I smile back. I like this version of Mama. Having a day off without a sky-high pile of catering orders or a couple of hyperactive boys leaping around is good for her.

"So, about my sketchbook," I prompt when we're digging in to our food. Or at least, I'm digging in. Mama's nibbling on lettuce leaves.

"I'm sorry. I forgot to take a look like I promised," she replies. "I'll do that when we get back."

"It's okay." I chew on some fries for courage, and whisper, "I've got some great ideas for your business. You might like them."

228

She gives me a confused look. "My business? What's that got to do with your art?"

I gulp down some milkshake. This is going to be hard. "You'll understand when you see. I'm just trying to help you with your bills."

Mama pushes away her half-eaten salad. "Sara, jaanoo, worrying about my business is not your job. Your job is to study hard, get good grades, and one day get a good job that will make me proud. None of this cooking business for my daughter, okay? Be a doctor, or a teacher, or a journalist maybe. Your baba and I are working so much because we want you to have more opportunities than us. That's the reason why we came to this country."

My head is aching, and my cheeks feel hot. I've heard this lecture about sixty thousand times. *Study hard. Get good grades. Be a doctor or something. You owe it to us because we left our homes and came to America. For you.*

"Nobody told you to come to the U.S.," I mutter. "It's not fair. I just want to help you."

"Sara!" When Mama is angry, she doesn't yell. Instead her voice becomes hard like glass. Right now, I feel encased in a glass box of her fury.

I don't care. I'm angry too. I go back to my burger as if it's the most interesting thing in my life, even though I can't swallow another bite. I should apologize for being disrespectful, but I don't.

On Friday, Elizabeth is waiting for me impatiently outside the FACS room. We're the first ones to arrive, as usual. Mama is busy setting up the classroom. The music room next door is open, and a few students are practicing drums. I catch a glimpse of Micah, eyes closed, head bopping to the beat.

"Come in and close the door, girls!" Mrs. Kluckowski shouts over the noise.

I grit my teeth but do what she says. The room quiets down a bit. Elizabeth says, "So have you thought about my brilliant idea?"

I rack my brain. I've spent the entire week being mad at Mama for not taking me and my ideas seriously, so I'm not sure what Elizabeth's talking about. "Which one?"

"Our winning recipe—what else?" She does a little dance. She's that excited. "Ice cream with chunks of doodh ka halwa."

"What flavor ice cream?" I ask. "We have to make sure it goes well with the halwa."

She nods as if I've answered a difficult trivia question correctly. "Exactly. It has to be the perfect flavor combo. Something slightly floral." She pauses to take a breath. "Like Earl Grey."

"Tea?" She knows I'm not a fan of chai.

She waves her hand in the face of my doubt. "Not plain old tea. Earl Grey. It's British. It was my grandmother's favorite. I thought, 'What if we make Earl Grey–flavored ice cream and put the halwa in it?' Like a British-Pakistani version of cookie

230

dough ice cream. Nobody will think of that, not in a million years!"

My mouth is already curving upward. I have to admit, it's pretty genius. "Yes! That's perfect."

Elizabeth pushes her glasses back up her nose and says, "Only problem is, they don't sell Earl Grey ice cream in any store I've seen. We need to make it ourselves."

"How?"

She's staring at something in the far corner of the FACS room. Something big and metallic and gleaming. Mrs. Kluck's ice cream machine.

"No!" I whisper in horrified fascination. Mrs. Kluck has specifically told us about a million times that no one is allowed to touch the new machine. I'm surprised she hasn't got it locked up in padlocks and barbed wire.

Elizabeth gives me the side-eye. "I've watched a hundred videos about making ice cream. I can do it in my sleep. Trust me."

I clutch the trim on my tunic so hard, it gives a little protest rip. Trust her? How can I? She's not the one with everything to lose. Mama will be in so much trouble if anything goes wrong. Mama and Baba have enough to worry about without me acting like a disobedient daughter.

Elizabeth gives me a little nudge with her leg. "Sara, you want to win that competition and get your mom on TV, right? This is our big chance to tell people about her business. And don't you want your parents to take you seriously?"

231

"More than anything," I whisper over the frantic beating of my heart.

"I want to win too. I want us to beat Maddy and show her that immigrant food is awesome, because immigrants are awesome. I want my mom to be proud of me. That ice cream machine is the ticket to our dreams." She unzips her backpack and points inside.

I see a box of Earl Grey tea stuffed between her notebooks and binders, plus a plastic Tupperware box. "What's that?"

"My own doodh ka halwa," she replies proudly, and I blink. She's recreated the dish Mama taught us in cooking club. She actually likes my culture, my food. How can I refuse her? I squeeze her hand tightly in a *yes*. Yes, let's make British-Pakistani flavored ice cream with halwa chunks and show the world what fusion food means.

I have a feeling it's not that different from fusion friendship.

The other girls start arriving, including Maddy and Stephanie, but I hardly notice. The ice cream machine is taking up one hundred percent of my vision. I swear it's staring back at me in glee.

Mama puts away groceries with quick, economical movements. Everything else we need for the ice cream is in the FACS room already: sugar, milk, cardamom.

I have no idea what we cook in class. Something with ground chicken, something steaming hot that splashes on my fingers and makes me yelp. Elizabeth and I alternate between whispering, making notes in our OSAWR book, and nodding

232

at Mama. It helps that the drumming from next door is getting louder, covering up our plotting.

The class ends and the other students leave. The music room is booming now, as loud as a thunderstorm. Finally, Mama stands before us with her hands on her hips. "Sara! Elizabeth! We're all done. Let's go." She's supposed to drive us both home today.

Elizabeth and I exchange a glance. "Er, can we stay behind and listen to Micah's percussion group?" I stammer. "We can all walk home together."

Elizabeth gives Mama a thousand-watt smile. Not suspicious at all. "Please, Mrs. H.?" she begs. "Micah's been asking us forever."

I gulp. I can't believe we're lying so easily. I can't believe I've changed from Good, Obedient Daughter to Scheming, Dishonest Daughter. The noise from the music room hammers around us in emphasis, copying the beating of my heart. *Boom-ba-boom-boom!* Mrs. Kluck is pushing all three of us out, looking at her watch. She locks the door and leaves without saying goodbye. "Not more than one hour, okay?" Mama says, turning to leave.

I freeze. "She locked it. How are we supposed to . . . ?"

Elizabeth waits until Mama's gone, then gives me a huge grin. "Do you still have that pineapple-charm key chain?" I rummage through my backpack until I find it in the bottom, under all my books. Elizabeth unlocks the FACS door and rushes inside like a secret spy. "Let's get to work."

233

Making ice cream isn't as easy as it sounds, even with a sleek, metallic machine like the Breville 3000 Ice Cream Maker. Elizabeth fiddles with the buttons and dials on the top as I chew my nails. "Wish I had a phone so we could look up the instructions," I mutter.

"We've got this. It's not rocket science."

I want to tell her that cooking is basically chemistry, which is a kind of science. But she waves me toward the cupboards, so I ignore the bubbles in my stomach and gather ingredients for making ice cream. My heart is still thumping in time with the percussion group, making my hands tremble, but I steel myself. This is me taking charge. This is me forcing my parents to take me seriously. This is me creating a prize-winning recipe. Me and Elizabeth.

I use the frozen custard recipe she's brought with her to make a thick, creamy mixture. We add a dash of steeped tea and pour chunks of the halwa mixture into the machine's churning bowl. I'm muttering all sorts of Arabic prayers under my breath as we push the START button and watch the bowl spin.

Elizabeth hugs me, grinning broadly, and I try to grin back. How comes she doesn't seem even a little bit nervous?

Oh, right—her mom isn't responsible for this ice cream machine, this FACS room, and everything inside it. She probably thinks we're having some secret adventure straight out of

234

a *Doctor Who* episode. In the meantime, I'm planning to beg forgiveness on my prayer mat for the next year.

The bell dings. The first batch of ice cream is so bland, it tastes like paper. We take two more tries to get the ratio of sugar, Earl Grey, and halwa right, but finally it's ready. The mixture is a little soft, but as Elizabeth pours the ice cream into ziplock bags, she assures me that a few hours in the freezer at home will make the texture perfect. There's silence as we sigh in relief, then gobble some of our creation down like starving puppies. The halwa pieces are the perfect addition of chewy crunch. "This is nothing like chai," I announce gratefully.

Elizabeth claps her hands. "International Festival, and Alfonso Morgan, here we come!"

26

Elizabeth

ON SATURDAY MORNING, Robin Hood waits for me at the bottom of the stairs. He tilts his head, hairy gray eyebrows raised in that adorable schnauzer way. "Robin, Bubbe's coming today," I say. I'm so glad that Bubbe is going to be here. Dad may not listen to me about coming to Mom's ceremony, but he'll listen to Bubbe.

Mom is the only one awake. She's working on a red blanket. I was hoping when she finished the last one, she'd take a break.

I pick up a ball of red yarn and brush it against my cheek. It's like sticking my face in a bowl full of marshmallows. "This color makes me happy. And it's so soft."

Mom smiles. "You have Bubbe's sense of style. The brighter, the better."

Robin lies down and rests his bearded chin on Mom's toes. Mom hides a yawn behind her hand and holds out her mug. "Put the kettle on and pour me another cuppa, sweetheart?"

My feet jiggle. I can't wait for Sara to meet Bubbe. I can't wait for her to taste my favorite Hanukkah treat, sufganiyot—Bubbe makes the jelly-filled donuts from scratch. And I can't wait for Bubbe to see the wreath Mom put on our door. It's electric blue with little silver dreidels. Wreaths aren't exactly a Hanukkah tradition, but at least Mom is trying.

Most of all, though, I can't wait for Bubbe to talk to Dad.

An hour later, my brothers are eating massive bowls of cereal and—miracle of miracles—Mom is dressed. But I feel itchy. There are dishes in the sink and papers strewn over the coffee table, and the toaster is in bits. My bed still needs to be changed for Bubbe to sleep in. I'll have an air mattress on the floor. Bubbe hates it when she visits and the house is a mess. I touch the charms on my bracelets, one by one.

"Mom?" I'm about to suggest that we spend the morning doing a massive cleanup, but Mom is putting on her coat. "Where are you going?

"To the grocery store."

Justin follows her to the door, chewing on the collar of his pajama top. Robin's tags jangle nervously. "Can I go too?" Justin asks.

"Not today." She leans down to kiss his forehead. "Help your brother and sister tidy up. There's a good boy."

"Wait. What?" I ask. "You want us to get the house ready without you?"

Mom sighs. "I have a long list for the latkes and donuts. We'll be cooking all afternoon. David, you're in charge." And then she's gone.

237

David smirks at me. He loves being in charge. "Justin, get dressed," he orders. Justin salutes and heads upstairs with Robin Hood. David leans his long, spindly body against the kitchen counter and pokes at toaster parts, like he's got nothing better to do.

"Why does Mom do that?" I ask him.

"Do what?"

"Disappear. She does it whenever things are hard," I say.

"Els," David says in his *I'm in high school, so I know everything* voice, "that is our whole family's MO."

"Huh?"

"Modus operandi. That's how we operate. Mom tunes out with her knitting and podcasts. And food shopping, apparently. Dad travels all the time, so he doesn't have to see how depressed Mom is."

"Aunt Louise says Mom is practicing self-care. Like, 'Keep calm and carry on,'" I argue. But then I stop and think about what David is saying. "If Mom is depressed, shouldn't we help her?"

"What does it look like I'm doing?" David says.

"Fiddling with the toaster."

"Very funny, little sister."

"Is that why you're always at school for clubs?" I ask. "Are you checking out too?"

David's face is serious. "Sometimes being at school is easier than dealing with home."

I lean an elbow on the counter and put my chin in my hand. "If Mom was a kid at our school, I think she'd have to go see the guidance counselor," I say. "Or the school psychologist."

David nods. "You're pretty smart, you know that, Elizabeth-Like-the-Queen?"

I push him away, because otherwise I'd have to hug him. When I was little and people asked what my name was, I always said, "Elizabeth, like the Queen."

"But convincing Mom she needs professional help? That's above my pay grade," he says.

"Huh? Above your what?" I'm convinced my brother uses terms I don't know on purpose, to confuse me.

He rolls his eyes and opens the family laptop. "Let the so-called grownups figure it out."

"But—" I protest. David waves me off.

"I figure we have three hours, max, before Bubbe gets here." David types furiously, filling out a spreadsheet. In moments, my brother has created a plan for cleaning the house, broken down by task, time allotted, and which kid is doing what.

I can't help it. I hug David around his bony ribs.

"Hey," he says, awkwardly patting my arm. "We've got this."

Two hours later, the bathrooms are wiped down, my bedroom is visitor-ready with clean sheets, the family room is vacuumed, and the old magazines are in the recycling bin. Mom returns with bags full of potatoes and onions, applesauce and sour cream, flour and jam. Nobody asks her why groceries took more than two hours. We just smile and show her how hard we've worked.

By the time we put the groceries away, Bubbe is here. She pinches all our cheeks in turn, then wraps Mom in a big hug. Bubbe is wearing chic dark jeans, yellow flats, and a long black sweater. There's a plastic spiky yellow thing hanging from her neck.

"What is that?" Justin asks, pointing.

"Wearable art," Bubbe says. She leans down so Justin can touch the spiky yellow fingers, which bend and bounce back.

"You're wearing rubber french fries," he says.

"French fries are delicious, just like you," Bubbe retorts. She gives Justin a ton of kisses on his cheeks, making him laugh until he pushes her away.

"And how is my favorite granddaughter?" Bubbe asks, her royal-blue glasses focused on me.

"Your only granddaughter," I correct, earning me an extra cheek pinch. "I can't wait for you to meet my friend."

That afternoon, Dad video-chats with each of us, including Bubbe, who holds Robin on her lap. After we say goodbye, Mom and Bubbe argue over latkes. Mom pulls a bag of something called "potato shreds" out of the freezer.

"I can taste the freezer on those," Bubbe complains. She insists that her potato pancakes can only be made from freshly grated potatoes. It's scary how Bubbe is reminding me of Mrs. Kluck right now.

Mom puts up two hands. "I give in," she says, taking the grater from Bubbe, "but only on one condition."

Bubbe narrows an eye at Mom. "Well, what is it?"

I hold my breath. Is Mom going to stand up to Bubbe? Is Bubbe going to call her *shiksa* and brush her off?

Mom says, "You give me cooking lessons. Jewish apple cake, charoset for Passover, challah — the recipe and the prayers. I want to learn. Will you teach me, Nadya?"

"It would be my pleasure," Bubbe says, pulling Mom in for a hug.

Hanukkah really is a season of miracles.

The next morning, I wake up on a partly deflated air mattress, too excited to go back to sleep. Dad is coming home! Sara is coming over! And we're making sufganiyot.

The kitchen still reeks of onions from last night's latke extravaganza, but I'm too happy to care. Everything is finally going right. Was it only two days ago that Sara and I made the ice cream? The ziplock bags are hiding in the bottom of our freezer. *Freeze well, my frosty delights,* I think. *You're our ticket to fame and fortune.* The floral Earl Grey flavor goes perfectly with sweet chunks of doodh ka halwa. It's the winning combination we've been searching for.

Dad gets home right after breakfast.

"You eat, Dad," I say. "Bubbe can drive me to Hebrew school."

Bubbe is practically elbow-deep in the dough she's

241

kneading. "I can?" she asks. I give her a meaningful nod. Luckily, she takes the hint. "Of course I can. I'm happy to drive my best granddaughter wherever she needs to go."

"Thanks, Bubbe." I get another pinch on the cheek, but I don't complain.

We leave the donut dough to rise as Dad eats his favorite Hanukkah dish, fried eggs and leftover latkes.

"So what's this all about?" Bubbe asks when we're alone in the car. She pushes her glasses up her nose and starts the engine. Bubbe has the biggest, weirdest rings. Today it's a giant green butterfly on one hand and a spiral fossil on the other. Her fingers must be freezing without gloves on. I am wearing the *Doctor Who* mittens that Aunt Louise sent me as an early Christmas/on-time Hanukkah present. The whole holiday-gift thing is a little confusing in our family. But that's not what's on my mind.

"Bubbe, I think Mom needs someone to help her talk about her feelings."

Bubbe slows down at a stoplight and looks at me in the rearview mirror. "Tell me more, Elizabeth."

I try to get the words out before the light changes. "Aunt Louise says she's doing 'Keep Calm' but I think she's not so good at the 'Carry On' part. That's why she forgets to do laundry and gets upset if we ask her for stuff while she's knitting."

Bubbe nods as if to say, *I'm listening.*

"I think Dad needs a person like that too. Someone to tell him that being away all the time makes life better for him,

242

because he doesn't have to see Mom being sad, but it makes things worse for us."

"Bubbeleh, have you been worrying about all of that?" Bubbe asks.

"Yes." I nod. "For a long time. For months."

"What's going on with your mother?"

But I'm tired of talking about problems all the time. I'm eleven. I want to eat donuts, hang out with Sara, and win the recipe contest. I lean forward in my seat. "Can't you talk to her? Please?"

Bubbe pulls into the synagogue's drop-off lane. Outside, Micah is waving to me. I'm bundled up in a parka, hat, and mittens. He's in his usual hoodie and cargo shorts.

"I'll do my best," Bubbe says. "Pinch Micah's cheek for me."

"No way, Bubbe." I smile. "That's grandma stuff."

I follow Micah inside. It's ridiculous to hope that something will be different when I get home, that I'll walk through the door and an alternate version of my family will be there: Happy Mom, Stay-Home Dad, Cool Older Brother. Justin can stay exactly the way he is.

But hours of watching *Doctor Who* has prepared me for the possibility of other dimensions. As long as we're still making donuts in the alternate universe, I can deal.

That afternoon, Sara and her mother arrive wearing identical outfits—jeans with floral tunics, plus Mrs. Hameed's bright pink hijab. I introduce them both to Bubbe, then point to the family room. "Mom's in there, Mrs. H."

She holds up her tote bag. "I made lots of notes," she says, hurrying away.

"It took them long enough to get serious about that test," Sara says. She's carrying a grocery bag with coconut flakes and pistachios to garnish our ice cream.

"Interesting ingredients," Bubbe says as she sips her coffee. "I can't wait to watch you two in action."

While we roll out and cut the donuts, Sara calls Rabia for a video chat. "Hellooo!" Rabia's smiling face fills the screen. She insists on staying online while we cook. "Someone has to make sure you guys don't burn the house down," she says.

"Don't worry. My grandma is in charge of the fryer," I tell her. After we say goodbye to Rabia, it's time for Bubbe to help us fry donuts.

Soon everyone is packed into our small kitchen: me, Sara, Bubbe. Dad comes in, asking, "How are the study buddies?"

"Are you talking about us or the moms?" I ask. Sara giggles.

Then Justin appears. "Hi, Sara! Are you making kha-gee-na? Bubbe gave me astronaut Legos for Hanukkah. Want to see?"

"Not right now, Justin," I say. "Let's teach Sara how to play dreidel while Bubbe cooks."

I wish I could freeze this afternoon in my memory—the sound of the dreidel spinning on the table, the way Mrs.

244

Hameed's and my mom's laughter carries from the other room, even the longing glances Robin Hood gives Bubbe, hoping she's saved a bit of Hanukkah donut for him.

Last year, my family spent the holidays in Nottingham. We all stayed in Nan's rambling old house, where David, Justin, and I each had our own room. Nan bought us new pajamas and laid them out on our beds for when we arrived, tired from the long flight and the drive up from London.

If I'd known it was my last-ever visit to Nan's house, I would have paid more attention to everything: the carpets with their busy floral designs, the giant soaking tub in the bathroom, Nan's gentle hugs and lavender perfume.

"Your bubbe should sell her recipe to my mom," Sara says as she fills a just-fried donut with jam. "Yum! What do you call these again?"

"If I can learn to say doodh ka halwa, you can learn sufganiyot. Repeat after me: soof-gah-nee-yoht."

David shoves a whole donut in his mouth and says, "Shoofgan-ee-yummm." I punch his arm.

Bubbe pats her belly. "Every culture has fried dough," she says, "because it's delicious."

Even though we're celebrating Hanukkah, I can't stop thinking about Nan. If she were with us today, she'd be sitting in Mom's corner, knitting, talking quietly with David. She didn't always do so great with people she didn't know. When Nan visited for David's bar mitzvah, I introduced her

245

to Maddy. I wanted Maddy to love Nan as much as I did, but they never exchanged more than a hello.

I'm lucky that I had two different grandmas. One who was as soft as bird feathers and loved sharing quiet cups of tea in the morning. And one who is loud, and pinches our cheeks, and makes great Hanukkah donuts.

The Hameeds are leaving before sundown, when we light the Hanukkah candles. It's starting to get dark, so I pull Sara aside.

"Are you ready?"

I take our ice cream out of the freezer. Sara scoops big dollops into glass bowls.

"Let's make it look pretty, at least," she says. Typical Sara. She's always thinking about design. She sprinkles a few extra flakes of coconut on each serving. "Ready."

We're about to go into the family room and offer tastes to everyone, when I notice a ziplock bag of ice cream melting on the counter.

"Go ahead," I say, picking up a damp sponge. "I'd better clean this up before . . . Oh, no."

Sara stops cold. "Oh, no, what? Did we forget the cardamom?"

My stomach drops. I wish I hadn't eaten so many donuts. "Sara, we forgot to clean the ice cream machine."

27

Sara

I ALMOST DROP THE TRAY of glass bowls. My hands are suddenly numb. "We did."

My mind runs frantically over the events of last Friday. We'd scrambled to use the machine before anyone caught us. We'd giggled and eaten way too much ice cream in the name of flavor testing. We'd even divided the cleanup duties as we waited for the machine to ding. I'd wiped down the counters and mopped the floor, and Elizabeth washed the pans. Then the thunderous drumming from the music room went silent and we'd rushed out before anyone walked past the FACS room and saw us.

We'd been so proud of our division of labor, we forgot the most important cleanup task of all: Mrs. Kluck's brand-new ice cream machine.

I lean against the wall for support. *"Ya Allah,"* I whisper.

"We would make terrib—" Elizabeth hiccups, then swallows. "Really terrible criminals."

Her joke falls flat.

I set the plate carefully on the counter and turn to face her. My heart is thumping so loudly, it drowns out the sounds of laughter in the other room. "This is serious, Elizabeth. We weren't supposed to touch that machine."

"Maybe we can go to school early tomorrow and fix it before anyone notices."

"What if Mrs. Kluck finds out? Who knows what she'll do?" Elizabeth bites her thumbnail. I've never seen her do that before. "What if she tells Mama and they figure out that we made the mess?"

Elizabeth picks up the tray I just put down. "We didn't leave any clues," she tells me. Her voice trembles a little. "It's not like they'll dust the place for fingerprints. Your mom probably doesn't even remember that you have the extra key."

Elizabeth walks out of the kitchen, her posture rigid. I follow her with lead feet into the family room, where everyone is gathered to taste our recipe before Mama and I head home.

Elizabeth passes around bowls and spoons. "Earl Grey ice cream with halwa chunks," she tells everyone, but her voice is flat. Nothing like the excited way we planned. I am supposed to say *Ta-da!*, but my mouth won't open.

"What is halwa?" her grandmother asks, passing bowls around.

I don't say anything. My throat is closed tight. Mama gives me a puzzled look, then explains. "It's a milk-based custard I taught the girls to make in my cooking club."

"This is delicious, Elizabeth," Mrs. Shainmark says in a surprised voice.

"Huh?" Elizabeth pushes her glasses up her nose and gives her mom a blank expression.

Mrs. Shainmark pauses and puts a hand on Elizabeth's forehead. "Are you coming down with something? You look flushed."

Elizabeth shakes her head.

"AAAH!" Justin clutches his throat and pretends to choke. "I've been poisoned!"

For a split second, I think he's telling the truth, that our recipe is so bad, it could kill someone. My breath stops.

But everyone is laughing.

Elizabeth's dad says to Justin, "Too much sugar for you, kiddo. I'll have to eat your share." He picks up Justin's bowl and takes a spoonful. "It really is delicious."

I let my breath out with a whoosh. A silver lining in the very cloudy sky that is my life right now.

"You invented this recipe?" Mama asks me quietly.

I can't even look at her. All my anger at her over the last week evaporates in a haze of worry about the ice cream machine. I nod way too fast. "It's no big deal."

Mama frowns. "Take it as a compliment, Sara. From one chef to another!"

"What's it called?" Justin asks.

"You need a snazzy name for the contest," Elizabeth's grandmother says.

Everyone looks at me. I can't stand it. How am I supposed to think of a name for something I wish I'd never created?

"How about Halwa Cuppa Tea?" Mrs. Shainmark exclaims. Mama nods. "Perfect!"

"Can we go home, please?" I beg Mama. My head is starting to pound. We put on our coats and say goodbye. Outside, everything seems strange and downcast, as if a storm is coming.

Elizabeth's grandmother gives me a warm hug, her necklace digging into my neck. "I'm so glad you're Elizabeth's friend," she tells me, the corners of her eyes crinkling in exactly the same way my own nani's used to. I don't have the heart to tell her that right now we're having a bit of a crisis.

Can you be friends with someone when you're so mad at them you want to scream until your breath is gone?

"Kya hua?" Mama asks in the car.

"I'm tired." It's true. I am so exhausted from feeling stressed-out and worried—even angry—all the time.

At home, I ignore the half-done poster on my desk and crawl into bed without even changing. I'm sure I won't sleep a wink, but I'm wrong. I fall asleep, only to be chased in my nightmares by a screaming Mrs. Kluck riding her ice cream machine like a horse.

On Monday morning, I rush to the FACS room before first bell, but Mrs. Kluck is already there, setting up for a class. A few kids are waiting outside. I see one of the Muslim girls from the mosque, so I know it's an eighth-grade group. She smiles at me, but I can't smile back.

250

Throughout the day, Elizabeth and I keep running into each other in the hallways. She waves at me each time, but I can't wave back because I'm sick to my stomach. What's going to happen when Mrs. Kluck sees the ice cream machine? I wish I'd never joined the cooking club or become Elizabeth's partner.

"What's up with you two?" Micah jokes at lunchtime. "You look like someone just ate the last jelly donut on earth."

Elizabeth shrugs. "Everything's fine. Right, Sara?"

"No, it's not."

Elizabeth touches the charms on her bracelets. The motion is so familiar now. She's as anxious as I am, no matter what she says. "Why do you always expect everything to go wrong?" she asks.

Micah drums on the table with his fork and spoon. "Els, don't be so harsh."

"I'm being realistic," I say to Elizabeth. "You're pretending everything is fine when it's not. Even if the sky fell on your head, you'd tell everyone, 'No big deal. Ignore the massive head wound. I'm great.'" My voice rises more than I mean it to.

Elizabeth crosses her arms. "It's better than acting like everything is a red-alert disaster."

I stand up so quickly, my milk spills all over the table. I quench my instinct to clean it up. "Sometimes. It's important. To make a big deal," I hiss. "Especially when our actions affect other people, like our families."

251

"What do you know about my family?" Elizabeth says, but her voice is thin and tearful.

"C'mon, you two." Micah stops drumming the table and gives us a stern face.

I bite my lip. I shouldn't have mentioned her family. I've seen how she worries about her mom, how she wishes her dad was around more. She's always trying to help make things right at home.

The laughing kids and the bland smells of the cafeteria press at me like a fog. I stand up and leave before I puke.

In last period, Mrs. Newman gets a call on her wall phone. She motions me over with a wave of her bangled arm and whispers, "You're wanted in the principal's office."

My knees shake. "Why?" I squeak, but I already know. My nightmare is about to come true.

There's a crowd of cooking-club girls inside the principal's office by the time I get there. Elizabeth stands in the corner, elbows pressed to her sides, looking as aghast as I feel and paler than usual.

Mama and Mrs. Kluck are almost toe to toe, arms akimbo. Mrs. Kluck looks like a ferocious tiger. Mama's in an old shalwar kameez and the threadbare pink leopard hijab that she keeps in her purse for emergencies—the one she wears when she needs to run out for an errand without warning.

She's been called to the school without warning.

Principal Harrison is the only calm presence in the room. He holds up his hands and calls for quiet.

"Mrs. Kluckowski reports that someone used the new ice cream machine without permission." Mrs. Kluck's nostrils flare and her eyes bug out, prompting Principal Harrison to add, "This is a serious matter. At Poplar Springs Middle, we treat our equipment with respect."

Elizabeth hangs her head so her brown hair shields her face. I grip my tunic sleeves tightly and pray under my breath.

Mrs. Kluck can't hold it in anymore. She interrupts loudly. "Someone vandalized my machine!"

I bite my lip to stop myself from protesting. We definitely didn't vandalize anything.

Principal Harrison puts up a weary hand. "There was no mechanical damage, Mrs. Hameed. The machine just needs cleaning."

Mrs. Kluck's face is bright red. "Just needs cleaning? That is a delicate piece of equipment. I can't spray it with Fantastik and call it clean. It has to be professionally sanitized."

"Better call the ice cream police," someone whispers loudly from the crowd. A few of the kids giggle. Was that Maddy?

To be honest, I can almost understand what Mrs. Kluck is talking about. Cleaning kitchen equipment is a big deal in my house too. Mama spends almost the same amount of time washing her pots and cleaning her blender as she does actually cooking. *Cleanup is a critical part of cooking,* she always tells me.

253

Mrs. Kluck puts her hands back on her hips. "Rancid milk is stinking up the insides. That's what happens when milk and sugar are left to pool for three days. My own classes haven't even had a chance to use it."

Mama takes deep breaths. Her jaw is tight. "I was there on Friday. Nobody used the machine during my class. The room was clean when we left, and I'm sure I locked the door."

Mr. Harrison rubs his forehead and gives Mama an apologetic look. "Still, Mrs. Hameed. The classroom was your responsibility. I trust that you make sure students don't touch anything that they don't have prior approval to use."

Elizabeth sniffles next to me as Mama says, "I know that. I trust all my kids. They wouldn't do anything like this."

Mrs. Kluck scoffs and wags a finger at Mama. "I've seen what happens in that cooking club," she says, practically spitting. "I'm surprised no one's lit the classroom on fire. They're barely supervised."

"That's not true," someone shouts. It's Stephanie, glaring at Mrs. Kluck with her arms crossed defiantly over her chest.

"Yeah," Maddy adds. "Mrs. Hameed is a great teacher."

I throw a shocked glance at her.

"Mrs. Kluckowski, let's not say anything we'll regret," warns the principal. He faces us. "Girls, this is a very serious matter," he says again. "Does anyone know who used the ice cream machine?"

Elizabeth stares at her ridiculous time-machine shoes. I

254

catch a glimpse of the dark circles under her eyes. She shuffles one foot forward. Is she going to tell? Should I?

No one else moves. The entire class is as still as a mass of mannequins after the mall closes. Elizabeth's breath rattles unevenly beside me. I want to move, but my feet are stuck to the ground.

I keep hoping Elizabeth will be brave and stand up for Mama. But I remind myself to get real. Elizabeth didn't stand up for me at the mall. When Maddy said, "Go back to where you belong," she did nothing. Mrs. Kluck might as well be saying *Go back to where you belong* to Mama right now. She is like Maddy's parents, like our old neighbor who complained that our house smelled, like every person who makes my family feel like outsiders. That's been Mrs. Kluck's problem since Mama took over the club. She never used the term "PLU" like Maddy, but I bet she feels it in her bones.

Mama adjusts the edges of her hijab. "I don't know who did it, but if it's one of my students, I'll make sure there are consequences." I can't bear the firmness of her voice. She will be the one who suffers the biggest consequence.

Mrs. Kluck isn't satisfied. "Your cooking club should be banned," she threatens. "That's the consequence I'm recommending to the school board."

The girls all start shouting. The dismissal bell rings. Mr. Harrison holds a palm up and closes his eyes. "We'll discuss this later."

255

Mrs. Kluck gives Mama one last glare and storms off, leaving us all looking dazedly at each other.

Maddy looks shattered. She actually makes eye contact with me, dips her head, and mouths, *Sorry*. Sweet Stephanie has lost almost all her annoyingly upbeat attitude. Mr. Harrison checks his watch. "I'll call you this evening, Mrs. Hameed," he calls out as he leaves. "I'm sure Mrs. Kluckowski will listen to reason once she calms down."

Mama looks like she's about to cry, but she straightens up, squares her shoulders, and addresses the class.

"Settle down, children," she says so quietly, I strain to catch her words. "I will email your parents tonight with an update."

"What about the International Festival?" Maddy asks. "What about the recipe contest?"

"And the TV spot?" Steph adds, her voice trembling. "I was hoping . . ."

Mama shakes her head slowly. "I'm sorry. I don't know."

The enormity of what's happened is hitting me in waves. Big red words—LOAN PAST DUE—flash in my mind. Mama taught this club in order to make some much-needed extra money, to pay her bills. No wonder she looks as if she's been flattened by a Mack truck.

"I hate whoever messed with that stupid ice cream machine," someone to my left grumbles.

Elizabeth looks at me. She takes a step toward Mama.

"I . . . We . . ." she stammers, then stops.

There's a huge bubble in my stomach, but this time it's

256

anger. Not only at Elizabeth, but at myself, too. Angry that my dumb mistakes could cost my mama her job. How could I have been so stupid, so reckless? I feel the anger growing inside me, filling up my eyes and mouth and nose. I can't take it anymore. I stumble away from her and out into the hallway with the other girls.

"Sara, wait!" Mama calls. Does she see the tears that are almost blinding me? Does she know what I did? How badly I let her down?

I can't face her. I just can't.

28

Elizabeth

BEFORE MRS. HAMEED can follow Sara out, I touch her sleeve. "Wait."

"What is it, Elizabeth?" Mrs. Hameed's eyes are glassy and tired, reminding me of my mom.

I take a deep breath and let it out. "I used the ice cream machine on Friday after class. I'm really sorry."

Mrs. Hameed touches the spot on her throat where her pink leopard headscarf is gathered. "You did what?"

Now that I've confessed, the words tumble out. "It was me. Sara had your FACS room key, and we went back inside after you left on Friday because we needed to test our recipe."

"So that's where the key went. I thought I'd lost it," she murmurs.

"It's not Sara's fault," I explain. "The whole thing was my idea. Sara kept telling me no, but I didn't listen."

Mrs. Hameed's entire body sags like a soufflé that's lost its air. "Thank you for telling me, Elizabeth. I wish you and Sara had spoken up straightaway."

I wish I had too. And I wish I'd never talked Sara into using the machine. Once I decided ice cream was the winning ingredient for the contest, I blocked out every other thought. I didn't consider how angry Mrs. Kluck would be that we used her brand-new machine. I didn't consider that Mrs. Hameed might get blamed. And I didn't consider Sara.

Mrs. Hameed puts a hand on my shoulder. "We will figure this out. Sara's father always says his favorite type of problem is a fixable one."

"What if they shut down the club?" I ask.

"Let me worry about that. Right now, we must find Mrs. Kluckowski so you girls can apologize. I'll let your mother know you'll be home late."

As I follow Mrs. Hameed out of the office, dread hangs over me, as heavy as the smell of burned popcorn.

Sara is sitting on the floor in the hallway, hunched over her sketchbook. Her face is blotchy. She's been crying. "Come, Sara," Mrs. Hameed commands, handing her a tissue. "You had a part in this too."

Talking to Mrs. Kluck isn't the doom-filled explosion of fury I'm expecting. She sits at her desk as I make my confession. Next to me, Sara is silent, eyes glued to the wall behind Mrs. Kluck.

"I am disappointed in you girls," Mrs. Kluck says, her words all scratchy. She must have hurt her voice when she screamed at us in the principal's office. "You took advantage of your club

259

teacher, Elizabeth, and your mother, Sara. That is unacceptable. But I also made some . . . unfair assumptions."

I shoot Sara a surprised glance, but she ignores me.

Mrs. Kluck clears her throat, and I almost offer her a cough drop. "The previous leader of the cooking club was 'borrowing.'" Mrs. Kluck makes air quotes with her fingers. "She used school equipment for her catering business, without permission. When she was let go, it was my opinion that the cooking club should be disbanded."

Mrs. Hameed listens calmly to Mrs. Kluck admit that Chef Elaine was fired for stealing. No wonder Mrs. Kluck flipped out when she saw someone had used the ice cream machine. No wonder she always watched Sara's mom so carefully.

"I understand, Mrs. Kluckowski," Mrs. Hameed says. "Girls, I'd like to speak with your teacher." When we don't move, she adds, "Privately," and shoos us out of the room.

I stand in the hallway, leaning so my backpack is pressed against the wall. Sara stands across from me. Some band kids pass between us, staring. Haven't they ever seen a kid cry at school before?

"We survived the plaid tyrant," I say, trying to get Sara talking. Her face stays frozen, expressionless.

She doesn't even twitch an eyebrow.

When the band kids are out of sight, Sara lets me have it. "All I wanted was to be quiet, do my work, and not get in trouble at this school. I was invisible, and I was *fine* with that until you came along."

260

"I said I was sorry." I kick my TARDIS high-tops at the floor. "But it's not like I was the only one there. You were with me."

Sara crosses the hallway, coming closer. "Why didn't you say something in Mr. Harrison's office? You let Mrs. Kluck talk to my mother like that, in front of everyone."

"I was scared," I admit.

I think about all I've learned over the last few weeks. What if it had been my mom in the principal's office instead of Mrs. Hameed? Would Mrs. Kluck have let her anger boil over if our club leader was someone like my mom, who speaks perfect English? Who is white? Sara's always talking about respecting her parents. It must have hurt her heart to see a teacher yell at her mom, especially in front of a bunch of kids.

"I told your mom that the whole thing is my fault. You're off the hook."

"I don't care about myself," Sara cries. "My mama needed this club. She needed the money."

"Money?"

"Yeah, remember that stuff? People use it to pay for groceries, clothes. It takes money to run a business, Elizabeth. My mother can't afford to lose this teaching job."

The door opens, interrupting us. Mrs. Hameed comes out. We follow her through the building in silence.

I'm surprised to see Mrs. Hameed put an arm around Sara's shoulders. When my mom is angry with me, she shuts off like a broken oven light. I try to see what's going on, how Mom is feeling inside, but it's too dark in there. I can't tell her what happened. There's no way she'll understand. Tomorrow, when I walk into school, everyone will know Sara and I went into the FACS room without permission and used the new ice cream machine. For most kids, it will be a day's worth of gossip. But when the cooking club finds out I stood there and let Mrs. Kluck blame everyone, they're going to hate me.

Outside, Mrs. Hameed says, "Elizabeth, your mother is waiting." She points to the carpool lane.

In the car, I pull the hood of my sweatshirt over my head. I yank the strings and pull the fabric closed over my face. Mom asks what's wrong, what she can do to help, even what I'd like for dinner. But there's nothing—there's no one who can comfort me. I go to my room and pull down the shades.

Justin opens my bedroom door an hour later. "Aren't you coming down?" he asks. "Bubbe says we have to do candles at sundown."

"No."

Robin noses his way into the room and jumps onto my bed.

"But it's the last night of Hanukkah," Justin whines. "Mom has a surprise for us. And Dad's leaving in the morning."

If Bubbe talked to Dad like she said she would, it didn't make a bit of difference. Dad's taking off for another business trip. Who knows how long he'll be gone?

Justin pulls my arm. "Come *on*." He drags me off the bed, which makes Robin bark. The only way to stop the noise is to get up.

Everyone is sitting around the table. Dad came home early from work, since he's leaving tomorrow before breakfast. He helps himself to a piece of gelt from the candy bowl, peels the gold foil, and pops the chocolate coin into his mouth before reciting the prayers in Hebrew. Then we all say them together in English. My favorite part is when we thank God for working "miracles for our fathers, in days of old." I wish there were a prayer to ask for another small miracle, a small light to revive the friendship Sara felt for me. As long as I'm asking, a prayer for Maddy, too, so she'll see that there are no "people like us." Only people.

And there is a kind of miracle that happens. As we watch the candles burn and play our last game of dreidel, Mom goes into the family room. Instead of sitting down to knit, she pulls three silver-wrapped packages from behind her chair. Mom hands one package to David, one to Justin, and the last to me. Justin rips open his wrapping paper. David holds his present on his palms, weighing and poking it. "Squishy," he says, raising a curious eyebrow.

I don't feel like I deserve a gift. Not today. I lift the tape halfheartedly.

"Oh," says Justin at the same moment I peek inside my package. Bright red.

263

Justin unfolds his gift. It's a navy-blue blanket. Not big enough to cover a bed, but the right size for snuggling up on the couch. David has a matching gray one.

"They're lap blankets," Mom says. Her cheeks glow in the candlelight. "For when you're reading or watching TV."

I hold my blanket to my face and breathe in the lavender smell of my grandmother.

"I wanted you each to have something of Nan's," Mom says. "But all I had was her unused yarn—unless you want the Queen's Jubilee plates."

David laughs. "No, thanks. What's the point if you can't put a Hot Pocket on it?"

Mom shoves his arm playfully. "Louise will send other things, once the house sells. But I wanted you each to have something now."

"They're beautiful, Nicole," Bubbe says.

Dad puts an arm around Mom. She tilts her head to his shoulder.

All this time I've been complaining about Mom and her endless knitting. I wish I'd known she was making something to keep us connected to Nan, to wrap us in her smell and the good memories of our times together in England. It doesn't fix everything, but it helps.

Sometime before sunrise, Dad comes into my room, kisses my forehead, and says goodbye.

I reach my arms around his neck for a hug.

264

"Didn't mean to wake you, kiddo," he says.

"Don't go, Dad. I need you here. I kind of got in trouble at school."

He nods. "Mrs. Hameed called."

"You knew?" I sit up. "Why didn't you and Mom say something? Or punish me?" I almost wish they had. Then I'd know they were paying attention.

Dad sits on my bed and strokes my hair. "Your mother and I know how hard you are on yourself. There's no punishment that's going to make you feel more miserable than you are right now."

"I wouldn't be so miserable if you stayed home. Can't you leave tomorrow? You're good at fixing things. I need to fix things with Sara."

"I wish I could. But this isn't a problem I can solve with solar cells and computer systems, Elizabeth. Your mother's best at dealing with friend stuff."

"That's not fair, Dad. You're my parent too."

"You sound like Bubbe," Dad says. "Is this some kind of conspiracy?" He cocks his head so I know he's joking, but it's not funny.

"Bubbe's leaving too," I point out. She flies back to New York today. By the time I get home from school, my family will shrink down to Mom and us three kids. We'll probably be eating tuna, peas, and mayo for dinner.

Dad kisses my forehead again. "You'll be fine," he says, and before I can argue, he's gone.

265

I should get up. I should finish the homework I was too upset to do last night. I should get dressed, go to school, and face Sara.

Instead, I close my eyes.

When Mom tries to wake me, I say, "I'm sick," and pull the covers to my nose.

"No fever," she says. It's her favorite test of whether or not David, me, or Justin should go to school. She heads downstairs.

Bubbe shuffles into my room in her ridiculous fish-shaped slippers. I peep at her with one eye. My bed dips as she sits. "No school today, bubbeleh?"

I shake my head.

"I hear you've contracted a serious case of the friendship flu." Dad must have told her the details. Bubbe sighs and rubs my back.

"Don't leave, Bubbe," I say. "Mom needs help."

"I know she does, Elizabeth. We're working on it. Before I leave this afternoon, we're going to get her an appointment with the doctor."

"You are?"

"Promise," she says. Bubbe convinces Mom that I need a day off from school, but I wouldn't need one if Bubbe stayed.

The next day is Wednesday. Mom drives David to school so he can hand in some giant science project on a trifold display. "Get yourself to the bus stop, Elizabeth," she orders. But I don't go. I reorganize my books into categories—Obsessed,

Beloved, Can't Part With. When I hear her car pulling into the driveway, I rush back to bed and pretend I'm still sick.

Mom sends Justin in to talk to me.

"Elizabeth, you're late for school. You love school!" he says. Justin pats my covers to make Robin jump onto my bed. Robin snuffles my morning breath, but I don't budge.

"Tomorrow," I mumble.

I picture myself sitting in class, all the kids from cooking club glaring knives at me. I can't handle that. So instead, I shut off. I reread my Doctor Who comics and try not to think about Sara.

Sara was counting on me. If our recipe won that TV spot, it would have meant tons of orders for her mom's catering business. Not only from Pakistani and other South Asian families, but from all kinds of people who love delicious food. Now that's never going to happen.

I wish ice cream had never been invented.

29

Sara

THE ANGRY BUBBLES have taken up permanent residence inside my stomach. Tuesday is a painful, dizzy blur. I keep remembering Mrs. Kluck's ferocious frown when she yelled at Mama in front of everybody. School takes on a nightmarish quality, like a house full of ghosts that won't quit bothering me. There's the memory of the water fountain, where Elizabeth and I had our first real conversation, and of the FACS room, where our friendship was cemented.

Elizabeth is not in school today. It's as if she existed only in my dreams. I should pick up the phone and call her, but my angry bubbles get in the way. I want to stay home too, pretend none of the last few months ever happened. But that's never an option for the Hameeds. *Perfect attendance is the first step to greatness* is one of Baba's favorite cheesy lines.

I guess he didn't get the memo that his daughter is far from perfect.

I keep my head down, the way I used to before Mama's

cooking club started. Back to square one, back to being invisible and unnoticed. The only problem is, it's difficult to be a nobody when everyone in school knows you and your mother, when your artwork is going to be on the entrance of the building.

It's lunchtime, and I'm hiding away in the farthest corner of the cafeteria, gobbling up my food quickly so I can leave.

"Hey, Sara, want a sample? I'm trying out a new flavor."

I look up. It's Stephanie, holding out a red velvet mini-cupcake and wearing none of her usual snark.

"Uh, sure," I mumble. She's never offered me a sample before.

She smiles, a mix between a concerned pout and a grin, which makes her face look lopsided. She tilts her head and her blond ponytail swings to the side. "Are you doing okay?"

I've seen this smile before. People offer it when someone is really sick or your pet dies. OMG. Sweet Stephanie is feeling sorry for me. This is worse than being invisible, honestly.

I get up from my chair so suddenly, she startles. "I gotta go," I say. I gather up the remains of my lunch and hurry away.

"Don't be sad—we'll think of something!" she calls.

The hallway is quiet after the laughter and chatter of the cafeteria. I bite my lip, wondering where to hide before I'm accosted by any more kids feeling sorry for me. The art room door is open. Maybe it'll be empty and I can sit there for a few minutes in peace, surrounded by the comforting smell of oil paints.

Inside, I find Mrs. Newman eating at her desk. "Oh, Sara, come in." She says my name the right way, the way I'd told her.

"Are you sure? I just came in to be alone for a while."

She nods. "Yes, I can imagine. Mrs. Kluckowski was talking about the cooking club in the teachers' lounge."

I wait for more, but she goes back to her food. It's some sort of salad, with a cluster of dark leaves like kale mixed in with carrots. After a few seconds, I walk to my regular seat and sit down. It feels odd to be here without other students. I stare at the wooden whorls on my desk, the nick that's been there from the first day of class, and also the blue paint I smashed in the corner in my first week and never bothered to clean. *How we leave our marks in tiny ways, wherever we go,* I think.

"You could work on your poster," Mrs. Newman calls softly. "During lunch periods, I mean."

I look up, startled. "I can do that?" My rough draft is done. I emailed it to her last week. Her reply had been a dozen smiley faces, which I'd taken to mean she approved. Now I have to do the real thing, in time for the International Festival, ten days away.

Mrs. Newman nods again, her mouth full of kale leaves. "Uh-huh," she replies. "I'll tell the front office you're going to work in here during your lunch period. Does that sound good?"

There's a rush in my body as some of the angry bubbles

in my stomach evaporate, and my shoulders relax. "Yes, thank you!" I say, my eyes smarting. "That would be perfect."

She smiles and goes back to her food. I wonder if she's going to ask me questions, or smile that awful smile Stephanie sent my way earlier. Nope. She's engrossed in her salad.

I go to the supply shelves at the back of the room and select some paints. The big sheets of poster paper are rolled up on the top shelf. I reach up and pull out the longest one. Six feet should do it. I'd been fearing the International Festival since Monday's drama, cursing the day I'd heard about it. But preparing to make the poster is calming. As if I can gather all my pain and anger and pour it into the poster, into my art.

Baba also says another thing often: *Work is the best healer.* I guess it's time to get to work. Show the bubbles who's boss.

Mama is deathly quiet that night at dinner. It's been a whole day since Mrs. Kluck yelled at her, but her eyes are still red, and she and Baba exchange tense little glances. I'm feeling sick, but I force down some food for the sake of the twins. "I don't want to eat vegetables!" Rafey shouts, pushing his plate away. He's always been that way, refusing to eat anything the least bit healthy.

"Yuck," agrees Tariq. He's eaten his tandoori roast chicken, but the curried peas and potatoes are piled in a lumpy hill on the side of his plate.

Baba frowns and opens his mouth to say something, but I

271

beat him to it. "Come on, we'll race!" I tell the twins. "First one who finishes their food gets a scoop of ice cream!" Inside, I'm shuddering. Ice cream again. I can't get away from that stuff.

They cheer and start gobbling. I'm deliberately slow, my stomach heavy with a sick feeling every time I peer sideways at Mama. She knows what I'm doing, trying to lighten her load, help her with little things, but she doesn't seem to care.

"I win!" Tariq pushes his empty plate away and shouts. "I ate all the vegetables."

"Me too! I come second!" yells Rafey. "Can I have ice cream too?"

I abandon my uneaten food to get their treat. Mama leaves the kitchen and heads toward the formal dining room, where her catering orders are waiting to be packed and labeled. I watch her go, ice cream scoop in my hand.

Upstairs in my room after dinner, I lie on my bed, staring out my window. Baba usually reminds me to pray the *isha* prayer, but he's too busy putting the twins to bed. I finally take out my prayer mat and pray, my tears seeping into the lush fabric.

Baba knocks on the door quite late. "You asleep?" he whispers. I shake my head. I'm lying down on the prayer mat, my hair spread out like a fan under me.

He comes in and sits cross-legged on the mat with me, breath huffing with the effort of lowering himself to the floor. "How's school?" he asks in that tone he uses when he's not really interested in getting a response.

272

I shrug. "I'm working on a poster."

I don't really expect an answer. Mama never did ask to look at my sketchbook again. I don't expect Baba to show any interest either. He surprises me. "Can you show me?"

I stare at him for a moment, then get up and bring the practice poster to him. "This isn't the real thing," I say. "The real thing will be six feet long. I'm still working on it."

"*Shabash!* This is really good, jaanoo." He's looking at me as if I've burst into song in front of him.

I shrug, but a smile is pulling at the corners of my mouth. "Thanks. The real poster will hang at the entrance of the school."

His goatee quivers. "Wow. The daughter of a lowly farmboy immigrant representing the entire school. Impressive."

I don't think he's lowly, but I say, "I know, right?" The honor of having my painting front and center is deliciously heavy on my shoulders. Even with all the stuff going on at cooking club, this little part is all my own, giving me some comfort. How far I've come from being that invisible girl with zero friends.

Of course, these days I wish I was back to being invisible. Anything would be better than the pitying glances of the entire school.

Baba must have read my mind. He puts down the poster and sighs deeply. "Sara, your mama told me what happened at school. We all make mistakes. We aren't mad at you."

"Mama is definitely mad."

"*Nahin.* She's just worried."

I fling myself back down on the prayer mat. "That's the problem. I know she's worried about money and stuff. I know her business could be doing better. I wish she'd let me help her. I have such good ideas, but nobody's interested in hearing them!"

He gives a reassuring thump on my back. "We want you to focus on your studies, that's all. Leave the worrying to me and your mother."

I sit up. "Baba. That's not going to work. If your dad had a problem, would you sit back and let him take care of it? Or would you want to help?"

He's quiet, his head bowed so I can't see his expression. I wonder if he misses his father, then tell myself I'm being stupid. Of course he misses his father.

"Yes, I'd want to help," Baba admits softly. "I used to help on the farm, you know, during summer vacation. But he'd always tell me he had plenty of workers in the fields. He wanted me to study hard so I could leave the village and live in the city."

I'm a little shocked, because he hardly ever talks about Dada. "You did that, though, didn't you? Not only leave the village, but you came to the U.S. and made something of yourself. I bet he was proud."

Baba frowns and clears his throat as if he's not sure. Maybe his father never told him that. "Well, your mama and I are equally proud of you."

I don't believe it, but I nod.

274

He stands up with a grunt. "There's an episode of *The A-Team* on tonight. Want to watch it with me?"

I sniffle. "No, thanks."

"Pity the fool," he says, and ruffles my hair on his way out. I stare at the wall for a long time after he's gone.

30

Elizabeth

MOM DOESN'T BOTHER to wake me up on Thursday. Good. I win. I never have to go to school again. But at nine o'clock, when Mom and Robin return from walking Justin to the bus stop, I hear her climbing the stairs.

Mom sits on my bed and pushes my bangs back from my eyes. "Are you ready to talk about it?"

I want to sleep, not discuss my feelings. I shake my head. "If you get to stay home and knit all day, why can't I stay home and read?"

Mom says, "I see. You're angry with me."

I prop up on my elbows. My hair's gotten greasy in the last few days. Gross. "Mom, no. Why would you think that?"

Mom notices the postcards filling my wall. Each one represents a time when Dad has been away. For the first time, I wonder if they make her sad.

"I'm not like you," she says. "It's hard for me to make friends. Sometimes it's hard to leave the house." Her eyes go soft, and I think she might cry. "You love being around people, Elizabeth.

People give you energy. They make you happy. One bad decision doesn't mean you have to hide away from everyone."

"I'm not hiding," I say. "I'm staging another sit-in. A sleep-in."

"No, you're not. You're avoiding Sara. If you want to stay friends with her, you need to put effort into it. That means going back to school and talking to her. Staying in bed seems easier, but it's not. Believe me."

It's weird to see Mom's hands motionless in her lap. I almost miss the knitting needles.

"That's not fair, Mom. You've been so sad since Nan died. Everything in our family shut down."

She closes her eyes and lies down next to me. "When your mother dies, even though you're a grownup, it feels like the person who's supposed to protect and love you most in the whole world is gone. And you're very alone."

I roll over to face her. "But I still need you, Mom. I need a parent who knows when I'm upset, or happy, or having problems with friends. Dad's away all the time, so that person is you."

Mom breathes in and out so slowly, for a second I think she might fall asleep, right here on my bed. "Your father and Bubbe and I talked this weekend," she says. "He's going to apply for a new position, one with less travel. And your grandmother's going to visit more often."

"Really?"

"Really." Mom sits up.

277

"And you're going to the doctor?"

"I am." She runs her fingers through her cropped hair. "Next week."

There's one more thing bothering me. I sit up and ask, "You're not going to go visit Aunt Louise and decide to never come back, right? You really are going to get your citizenship?" I'll feel better if I hear my mom say she belongs here, with us.

"You've been carrying around worries like a heavy rucksack, haven't you?" Mom asks as she stands up.

"I guess."

"Of course I'm not leaving you, darling. This is my home, with you and Dad and your brothers." She ruffles my yucky hair. "School tomorrow, Elizabeth. Every day you don't go, it will get harder."

I know what she means. Every day that Mom didn't leave the house, every day she spent knitting on the couch, pulled her deeper into sadness.

Mom takes my chin and tilts my head up. "I don't want you to be like me. Not in that way. In England they say, 'Stiff upper lip.'"

"What does that even mean, Mom?"

"It means act as if everything is fine, even when it's not."

"Do I have to?"

"No," she says. "And neither do I."

I take a shower, then make tomato soup from scratch for lunch. As I puree tomatoes in a blender, Mom leans on the kitchen counter, sipping her tea.

"You know that comes ready-made in a tin," she points out.

"Canned soup isn't made with love," I say.

"Love is messy." She points to the tomato-splashed spoons, pots, and measuring cups piled in the sink.

"Worth it," I reply.

It's three o'clock by the time the dishes are clean and we're ready to eat. We sit at the table together, but before I can take a taste, the doorbell rings, sending Robin into a barking frenzy. Mom gets up to answer.

"Maddy!" I hear her say in her brightest voice. "I'm so glad you're here. Elizabeth could use a friend."

Maddy comes in and stands next to the table, waiting for me to look up from my soup. A few months ago, she would have plopped down next to me as if she lived here.

"Hi" is all I say. I pull a chair out for her without getting up from my seat.

"I'll get you some soup," Mom offers. "Elizabeth made it."

Maddy lowers her voice. "Everyone at school is saying you kissed Micah and got mono."

"Gross. Micah's like my honorary brother." I shudder. "Wait. Is Micah sick?"

Maddy shakes her head. The ponytail is gone. Her hair hangs loose and dark around her shoulders, longer than she used to wear it, but she looks more like the old Maddy. "No. It's the usual stupid rumor. He left Tuesday to go to Puerto Rico for winter break." She sits across from me. "And also, I know you're not sick."

I sip my soup. I don't owe her an explanation.

She says, "Remember in fourth grade when you said you put your math assignment in the homework basket, and Mr. Hartack said you didn't, and he tipped your desk out and dumped everything on the floor?"

I was so embarrassed. And Mr. Hartack was so mean.

"You didn't come to school for two days," Maddy says.

"I told my mom I wasn't going back until they let me switch math teachers."

Mom brings out an extra soup bowl and a box of saltines. Maddy takes a sip from her spoon. "This is delicious, Els. Really. Steph always says you and Sara are the ones to watch out for in the recipe contest."

"Can we not talk about that?" I was enjoying this moment of no drama with my former best friend.

Maddy puts both hands flat on the table. "I need to talk about it. I've been thinking about what you said. I'm so sorry for what happened at the mall." Maddy's face squishes into a grimace. "Stephanie told me I shouldn't have said those things, but I didn't get it. I thought, *This is middle school. People are mean all the time.*"

"But not you, Mads. You're not mean. You weren't before." I can't believe Maddy is finally apologizing.

"I really wanted us to stay friends. I wanted it to be the three of us, you, me, and Steph. It hurt my feelings that you wanted to spend time with Sara and not me. I kind of snapped."

Tell me about it.

280

Maddy leans down to pat Robin's head. She slips him a cracker. "Can I tell you something? Ever since we moved up from elementary school, my parents have been nagging me to make new friends. They say Steph is more like us."

There it is again. People like us. "Not Muslim, like Sara," I say.

Maddy's chin drops to her chest. She nods slowly.

"And not Jewish, like me."

"I guess. I never thought about it before. You're normal. I mean, aside from the *Doctor Who* obsession."

I don't smile. "Maddy, I don't want to be your kind of normal. Not if it means making fun of kids because they have brown skin, or dress a certain way, or their parents are immigrants. Don't you get it? That's racist." I force myself to say the word.

"That's what Steph said too." Maddy closes her eyes for a second. "You're my two best friends. Maybe you're right. You've known me forever, and Steph is a really good person. Did I tell you she doesn't keep any of the cupcake money? It all goes to the NICU charity. Steph told me she was a preemie, and they weren't sure she'd survive. That's why she bakes. To raise money for families with preemies."

"That explains a lot," I admit. I try to picture Stephanie Tolleson as a tiny baby, small enough to rest in my palm. Once the image is in my mind, all my mad feelings about Steph dissolve. I realize I never looked past her blond ponytail and perfect smile. "I guess I didn't bother getting to know her."

281

"She called a cooking-club meeting at lunch today. Everyone was there, except we couldn't find Sara." Before I have time to wonder where Sara ate lunch, Maddy rushes on. "All of us are mad at Mrs. Kluck for being so gross to Mrs. Hameed. So I came up with a great idea." She pauses to make sure I'm paying attention and crinkles up her freckled nose. "Trust me. You're going to love it. What if we have the last class before winter break at Sara's house and cook for Mrs. Hameed? We can bring all the ingredients and show off what we've learned. Steph found a biryani recipe and assigned everyone something to bring."

Wait. Maddy likes South Asian food now? When did that happen? I think back over the last couple of classes and realize Maddy's been complaining a lot less.

I'm starting to grin. "I love this idea," I say. "As long as we clean everything up. And I mean everything." I look right at Maddy. "But you still need to apologize to Sara. It's not enough to say you're sorry to me."

"Can I help with this plan?" Mom says, coming in from the kitchen. "Sorry for eavesdropping, but the Hameeds are my friends too. Let me call Hina and let her know what you're planning."

We talk over details with my mom. My mood is as light and sunny as a lemon meringue pie. I think this is going to work. I can't wait to go back to school and plan our cooking-club party.

31

Sara

THAT ENTIRE WEEK, I go to Mrs. Newman's art room instead of the cafeteria and paint away my misery. The bubbles in my stomach scatter and settle down when I'm working. The poster fills my mind, leaving no room for anything else. The bold flags in the border, the faces of the kids in the middle, give me strange comfort. Mrs. Newman sometimes checks my progress but mostly leaves me alone. The art consumes me in a deeper way than it has before, the colors on the poster more real, throbbing with all the emotions in my heart. Once, I coat my brush with red and think of Elizabeth's advice about using a warm color for Mama's business flyer. Another time, I mix my palette with peachy tones and I'm reminded of the color in her room. No matter how hard I try to avoid thinking about Elizabeth, her friendship warms me like a mug of hot chocolate.

Painting isn't my only therapy. That week, I spend hours talking with Rabia on Google Hangouts. We don't discuss Iqra or Poplar Springs Middle. We talk about other things, like the first-grade field trip we made to the Smithsonian Museum, when I got so scared of the life-size dinosaurs that I cried in the bathroom. We talk about how Rabia's neighbors all have Christmas lights strung on their houses in the most intense competition she's ever seen. We complain about our parents insisting we speak Urdu even though we butcher it completely. We even go over the Arabic alphabet again like we're little kids, singing "Alef Ba Ta" over and over. And of course there are at least a dozen *America's Got Talent* episodes, the ones where Simon is the meanest.

"I wish you'd come back to Iqra." Rabia sighs more than once.

I realize I haven't told her the real reason why my parents moved me to Poplar Springs. Money isn't something Rabia's family worries about. I finally open up and share all the details. The bills. Mama and Baba's arguments. The ice cream machine fiasco. At one point she even brings her Cheetos to eat as I pour my heart out. I should be offended, but it feels okay, like we're still telling each other stories.

Talking about everything with Rabia makes it seem less heavy.

The bubbles in my stomach have completely disappeared by Friday afternoon. When I get home from school, I find Mama in the kitchen, her citizenship study guide open on the counter as she stirs a curry on the stove. She's dressed in black trousers and a long, colorful kameez. Her hijab hangs on the back of a chair.

"*Salaam,*" I say, glad to see she's doing okay after this rough week. "Are you going somewhere?"

She gives me a mysterious smile. "*Nahin.*"

"You're wearing lipstick," I point out.

She picks up the booklet and sticks her nose into it. "Just studying," she replies, which makes no sense at all.

I forgive her because I'm starving. I grab some zeera cookies from a plate on the counter and take the booklet from her. "What territory did the United States buy from France in 1803?"

Another smile. "Louisiana," she replies confidently. "You know how I remember that? Your father and I visited the French Quarter in New Orleans when you were a baby."

"Really?" I crinkle my eyebrows. "I didn't know we ever went on vacation."

She sighs and goes back to the pot on the stove, which is giving off a sweet, milky fragrance. I see the rice bin on the counter and guess that she's making kheer.

"Money has been tight recently. You know that."

I nod fast. Are we really going to have a conversation about money? Finally? I can hardly breathe as I wait for her next words.

RRRING! The doorbell breaks the spell. I go to open the door, and my mouth drops in shock. A group of girls stands on our front porch, with Mrs. Shainmark behind them. Elizabeth, Maddy, Stephanie, and all the others from our cooking club. Plus Rabia.

285

"Surprise!" they yell. Their faces are happy, even Maddy's.

"What's going on?" I whisper.

Mama comes up behind me, draping her hijab quickly around her head. "Welcome to our house," she gushes, and now I know why she's wearing lipstick. This is not a surprise for her, apparently.

Mrs. Shainmark takes pity on me. "The girls asked to have the last class at your house, since the FACS room isn't full of great memories."

"It's our final class before the festival, and we want to celebrate everything we've accomplished," Stephanie adds, beaming at me.

Maddy is standing right beside her, and I look away quickly. I take in the scene in my tiny foyer. The girls from our cooking club all talk excitedly. Rabia stands a little bit to the side, looking skeptical but also highly amused. Elizabeth has her arm around Mama, but she's looking at me, as if sending a silent signal to my brain.

I want to break into tears, but Mama beats me to it. Her eyes are already wet. "Girls, you are awesome!" she whispers.

"Let's make some biryani!" somebody shouts from the back. I think it's Maddy. I want to tell her not to enter my house, want to stand in the doorway with my arms held out to block her, but Mama would faint at such a lack of hospitality and respect.

The girls move inside like a wave in the ocean, taking Rabia with them. A few of them are holding grocery bags. Stephanie has a bag of Zebra basmati rice in her arms. Did they actually go to a Pakistani store for Mama? For me?

Elizabeth and I let the other girls pass, and in a minute we're alone in the foyer. I reach out to hug her. It's awkward and quick, but it feels right. She hugs me back and says, "You can't get rid of me that easily."

"I'm still upset with you," I tell her severely.

"I know. But it wasn't a hundred percent my fault." She has a pleading look on her face.

I sigh. "'It takes two hands to clap,' as Baba always says. I was right there with you. I had the key. You didn't force me to do anything."

She relaxes. "Thank you for saying that. I don't want to fight. We've got to stay friends. We complement each other."

Rabia walks back from the kitchen. "Good, you've made up. Let's cook some food!"

I look from Rabia to Elizabeth and back again. My two friends, so different from each other, stuck with weird old me in the middle. I hold out my hand to Rabia. "Thanks for being here."

She wrinkles her nose. "I wasn't expecting a bunch of Poplar Springs girls to be so nice, but I'm happy to be proven wrong."

"Even Maddy?" Elizabeth says hopefully.

Rabia is quiet for a minute, staring at the palms of her hands. She does this when she's thinking deeply and isn't sure how to frame her words. The sound of giggling girls floats to us from the kitchen. "What Maddy said to Sara in the mall was . . . terrible. But my mama always taught me—all her students—that in the same way we seek forgiveness from God, we should also forgive others." She finally looks up. "Has Maddy apologized?"

Elizabeth nods, and whispers, "To me. But not to Sara. She knows what she said was wrong. Maybe she's waiting until she can talk to you alone."

I smell chicken cooking on the stove. Biryani spices hang in the air around me. I hold out my hands, one to Elizabeth on my right, and the other to Rabia on my left. They reach out too, and we stand in a little circle of linked hands. I say, "We have a competition to win."

32

Elizabeth

As we clean up the Hameeds' kitchen, everyone gets a chance to describe their recipes to the whole group. We give each other feedback and ideas for different spices to try. It feels less like a competition and more like the way a class should be, all of us working together.

As the other girls start to leave, Maddy and I stand on the Hameeds' front steps. Steam rises from the containers of chicken biryani we're both holding. I shiver in the cold. Mom is still inside, chatting with Mrs. Hameed. I could have stayed inside too, but I wanted to talk to Maddy alone. I don't know if we'll be friends again, not the way we were before, but I'm relieved that we're speaking to each other.

"This was a great idea, bringing everyone to Sara's house," I tell her. "Sixth grade has been rough for her. She used to go to a religious school. Less than a hundred kids in all the grades."

Maddy's mouth opens in surprise. Her breath makes a cloud of steam when she says, "No wonder she hardly ever talked."

"Right? From a hundred kids to nearly a thousand just like

that." I snap my fingers, but it's so cold that they don't make a sound. Maddy laughs. Her cheeks are pink from the chill. It makes her freckles stand out.

"Remember when I tried to teach you how to snap?" she asks.

Fourth grade.

I say, "Remember when I tried to teach you how to blow a bubble?" Fifth grade.

"We both ended up with gum in our hair."

"Peanut butter shampoo!" we say at the same time.

"You busy this weekend?" she asks.

"Yeah. Sara and I have to figure out how to make ice cream without an ice cream maker."

"Steph and I are still tweaking our recipe too."

I motion to the Hameeds' house. "How did you talk your parents into letting you come here?"

Maddy tucks her chin into the collar of her pale-blue parka. It's North Face brand. Popular-kid approved. "I didn't tell them," Maddy says. "Stephanie's mom drove me."

I wonder if Maddy's parents are even coming to the International Festival. If they do, I hope they are polite, for Maddy's sake.

Steph bounces out of the house, cell phone in hand, as a big SUV pulls up to the curb. She gives me a quick hug. "Bye, Elizabeth."

Maddy waves before she gets in the car. "Good luck," she calls. "I mean it."

290

The next morning, Sara comes over with her mom so we can give our ice cream a final run-through.

"So can we make the name official?" I ask Sara. "Halwa Cuppa Tea?"

"Can't think of anything better," she says, and writes the name down in her notebook with plenty of swirls.

I know she's stalling. We still don't know how we're going to make a big batch of ice cream without Mrs. Kluck's machine. We sit together at the kitchen table, leafing through Sara's recipe notebook.

David pops a Hot Pocket in the microwave, which makes us both stick out our tongues in disgust. "You don't know what you're missing," David says.

I love looking at Sara's notebook, remembering all the changes our recipe has gone through. We admire Sara's doodles of each dessert we tried, and laugh at the exploding s'mores parathas. She shows me sketches for the International Festival poster and for her mom's business logo.

"Did you show it to her yet?" I ask in a low voice. In the family room, a few feet away, Mrs. Hameed is quizzing my mom on the citizenship booklet. I hear laughing, so I'm not sure how much work they're getting done.

"Not yet," Sara says. "Let's focus on the ice cream problem. Can't we just pour the mixture into plastic bags and stick it in the freezer?"

"Then it won't be creamy," I argue. "You're supposed to

291

churn it. Otherwise it gets gritty and crunchy." I shudder. "If we want to win, we have to do it right."

"For once, I agree with my sister," David says as he sits at the table. He chomps on his sad excuse for a pastry. "Mmm. Pepperoni pizza."

Robin Hood looks up at David, a mixture of hope and longing in his eyes. David breaks off an edge of crust and tosses it to the dog. "As I was saying," he continues, "you're correct. Ice cream has to be churned or it forms ice crystals. And crunchy ice cream is gross."

"Says the guy who eats microwave pastry," I say.

David puts on his *I'm smarter than you* face. "It's basic chemistry. I wouldn't expect sixth-graders to understand."

"See why I always say younger brothers are better than older brothers?" I complain to Sara.

"Well, we don't have an ice cream machine, so we don't have a choice," she replies. She's getting frustrated. I can tell by the way she's picking at the edge of her tunic.

David takes his last bite of Hot Pocket. "This sounds like a job for an engineer. Let me see what I can cook up." He raises an eyebrow at us. "*Cook up.* Get it?"

Sara groans.

I say, "David, no way. The last thing we need is you pulling apart another kitchen appliance and turning it into some robo chef."

From the family room, Mom calls, "Not another project! You've already made a real dog's dinner of the garage. And you

292

promised you'd finish the toaster." That cracks Mrs. Hameed up.

David starts up the family laptop. "Mom, I am trying to help my dear sister," he says, grinning at me and Sara with all his teeth showing.

"What's he going to find on the Internet?" Sara asks.

"Knowing my brother, probably some broken-down, ancient ice cream maker somebody's selling on a 'Please take my trash' app."

We go back to our notebook for more brainstorming. Suddenly, David stands up, closes the laptop, and says, "Where's Justin? It's brother-project time!"

"We get dibs on the kitchen," I say, just in case.

"You can have it," David says. "All I need is an empty pretzel jug and a big freezer bag."

"What are we making?" Justin asks David as he hops down the stairs. "Is it a robot?"

My brothers put on jackets and disappear into the garage with Robin trailing behind them.

"Is it this nutty at your house?" I whisper to Sara.

"Every Saturday," she says with a laugh. Sara peeks into the family room. "I'm glad we got our mothers together. Mama's only friends have been ladies from the mosque, or her catering clients. She's never had anyone in the neighborhood to hang out with."

"Same here," I say. "My mom used to work at a community theater. She liked the people there. But when Nan got sick and

293

she took a leave of absence, nobody from the theater ever called to check on her. She needed a real friend."

"I did too," Sara says as we get out ingredients for our ice cream recipe. "I needed a friend at school."

"And you picked me, because I'm an awesome cook."

Sara rolls her eyes. "Nope. I thought, *I feel sorry for that girl. She has no one to cook with.*"

"That too. But now . . ."

"Now we're just friends. And cooking partners."

"And recipe contest winners." A moment of doubt creeps in as I wonder how we're going to churn our ice cream. "Sara, for real. Do you think Halwa Cuppa Tea has a chance?"

"I hope so." She closes her eyes as if she's dreaming. "I can picture it. The two of us on TV, wearing Hameed's Kitchen aprons."

But without Mrs. Kluck's ice cream machine, that's never going to happen.

By the time we've steeped six tea bags in our custard, David, Justin, and Robin Hood tumble into the house in a blur of grease stains, sweat, and fur.

"Elizabeth! Sara!" Justin pants. His cheeks are rosy from the cold. "Wait till you see what we made."

David leans against a wall, arms crossed and relaxed, like he's super proud of himself. I should tell him that his puffy winter coat makes his legs look even more like toothpicks, but I restrain myself.

Mom, Mrs. Hameed, Sara, and I follow Justin to the garage with Robin Hood leading the way and David behind. There is Justin's bike, also known as Blue Thunder, with a plastic pretzel jar attached to the handlebars.

"Um . . ." I say.

"It's very . . ." Sara says.

Justin is about to explode. "It's an ice cream machine!" He jumps up and down.

I'm confused. "It's a bike with a pretzel jar stuck on the front."

"Ah," says David, "but it's not stuck." He points to the clear jug. "The jar has a spindle through the middle. It's resting gently on the front wheel. So—" He motions to Justin.

"So, when the wheel spins, the jar spins!" Justin says. Robin Hood barks.

Sara says, "I still don't get it."

But I do. I've watched enough videos of old hand-crank ice cream makers to see David's vision. "All we need is ice, and some salt to keep the temperature low."

David says, "Exactly. Put a bag full of liquid ice cream mixture into the jug, go for a ride, and in a few minutes . . ."

"Churned ice cream!" Sara says, beaming.

Now I'm jumping up and down. I throw my arms around my brother's puffy-jacketed middle. "I will never get mad at you for taking apart my old alarm clock again." I can't believe he did this for me and Sara. "David, you're brilliant!"

"Took you long enough to notice."

Mom and Mrs. Hameed go back to studying, but Sara and I put on our jackets. We carefully place the bag of liquid ice cream into the plastic jug. David packs in the ice. Pouring in salt to keep the ice cold is Justin's job—but it's so frigid today, I can't imagine anything melting. We all take turns riding Justin's bike around the block with the ice cream maker rolling on the front wheel. Justin's bike is too small for us, but no one cares.

My whole family helped me and Sara today, all of us together. I wish Dad had been here. I can picture him trying to ride Justin's bike with his long legs sticking out. I hope he gets a new job soon so he doesn't miss stuff like this.

When our hands are too cold to stay out a moment longer, the four of us go inside. It's time for a taste test.

I give a spoon to each person: Mrs. Hameed, Sara, Mom, David, Justin, and one for me. We dip our spoons into the freezer bag full of Earl Grey ice cream with halwa pieces.

"Mmm," David says.

"It's delicious, girls," Mrs. Hameed agrees.

"I've never tasted anything like it," Mom says. "The nuts and coconut complement that floral tea flavor."

"Don't tell them about the curdled milk," Sara fake-whispers in my ear.

Justin raises his hand, as if we're in school. "I like curdled milk."

"On what planet?" I ask.

He says, "On Planet Ice Cream." Everyone laughs.

"So, this is it?" I ask Sara.

"This is it." She takes another taste of the ice cream. "Our Secret Award-Winning Recipe. Halwa Cuppa Tea."

"Halwa Cuppa Tea," says Mom as we all clink spoons.

33

Sara

POPLAR SPRINGS MIDDLE is one mile from my house. Every inch of that mile is filled with Christmas lights hanging from trees, mailboxes, and houses. "Christmas is almost here," Baba informs us with a wry smile as he drives. "In case you forgot."

"How can we ever forget?" I grumble, but I don't really mean it. I love the way my neighbors celebrate their big holiday. It reminds me of Eid, how happy we all are to dress up, worship, and give gifts to mark the end of Ramadan.

It's weird coming to school at night. We pull into Mama's usual spot, and I scramble out before Baba even cuts the engine. I inhale a lungful of crisp air. It hasn't snowed yet in Maryland, but the temperature is close to freezing.

This is it, what Elizabeth and I have been working on for so long.

Baba carries big foil containers full of samples of Mama's most popular dishes. "What is this curry made of, rocks?" he asks.

"Think of Elizabeth's dad," I tell him severely. "He's gotta drag a ton of ice cream around."

Baba grunts, but he straightens up a little. I leave him behind and lead Mama to the entrance of the school, where my poster hangs by black rope, waving a gentle welcome in the cool night air. The colors are bright, and the faces in the middle glow from the light above our heads. "Ta-da!"

Mama turns to look at me with a huge smile. "It's absolutely stunning, jaanoo!" She's wearing a green-and-white silky shalwar kameez—the colors of the Pakistan flag—and a matching white hijab that makes her almost radiant.

I reach out to squeeze her hand. "Shukriya," I say. "Are you ready?"

We enter the school together, ignoring Baba's grunting behind us. The hallways are dimly lit, but I can still see the snowmen and reindeer in every class window. The teachers have been busy. We go into the gym, and my jaw drops. It's flooded with bright lights. Music streams through speakers above my head. Long tables line the walls, each representing a different country. There's Germany, with a towering pile of what looks like hot buns in straw baskets. There's Mexico, with a trio of students practicing mariachi. There's Poland, with a woman who looks like Mrs. Kluck's not-so-evil twin sister standing beside it, arms crossed over her chest. Toward the back of the room is a table for Haiti, where Ms. Saintima sits with a broad, welcoming smile. I wave at Micah, who is setting up a line of djembes for the percussion-group performance. It's all buzzing with activity and bursting with color.

"Finally! You guys are late!" Elizabeth rushes up to us, all smiles. She's wearing a plain black T-shirt over white capri pants, and a little hat that says PAKISTAN in green embroidery. She points to a table in the corner, covered in green cloth. "Our table's all set. Mom and Dad helped me."

"Sorry," I reply sheepishly. "It's called South Asian Time." She looks at me blankly, and I explain, "We always go late everywhere. It's almost a tradition."

"Mrs. Hameed, come see what we made!" A couple of girls from cooking club wave frantically to Mama. She hurries off to talk with them.

I look around. "Where are your mom and dad?"

Elizabeth points to a table nearby. "My dad couldn't come. My mom's at the England stall. Maddy and Steph are selling scones and jam, and I think my mother is literally going to polish them off singlehandedly."

Maddy and Stephanie are wearing identical white aprons with SUPPORT HOWARD COUNTY GENERAL NICU in neon green. Maddy waves. I remember Rabia's comment about forgiveness and plaster a polite smile on my face.

There's a movement near the gym entrance. Students flock around someone short and bald, dressed in a navy blue blazer that seems right out of a catalogue.

Elizabeth nudges me. "There's the judge."

I try not to stare. I've seen Chef Alfonso Morgan on television many times. Once my family went to his cookbook signing at the Curious Iguana bookstore in Frederick. Baba even shook the chef's hand. "*He's* going to judge our fusion ice cream?" I groan. "He's probably eaten every exotic ice cream known to mankind."

Elizabeth and I watch as Chef Morgan moves along with a wave of adoring fans to the back of the gym, where a few chairs are set up for teachers and guests.

"I'm sure he'll like our bike-churned ice cream," she finally says, but her voice is uncertain. "We should have brought the bike here so people could churn it themselves. How cool would that have been?"

"Totally. If Mr. Harrison would let us ride bikes in the hallway. Which would never happen."

Baba sets up the ice cream, and we get to work assembling. One scoop of Earl Grey mixed with chunks of halwa, a few pistachio pieces, with a sprinkle of coconut and chocolate flakes on top. Repeat countless times, until our hands ache. Pretty soon we have rows of plastic bowls of ice cream spread out on the table. A small sign says HALWA CUPPA TEA in neat letters. I've also printed out flyers with Mama's catering menu and prices. They sit in a neat pile ready to be handed out. My HAMEED'S KITCHEN logo is on the top of each flyer. I watch nervously to see if anyone notices.

A few students come up and we hand out samples. Before long, there's a line in front of our table. Mrs. Newman wanders over with a plate of rice in her hand. "Hello, girls." She smiles. "What do you have here?"

I give her a sample, then venture, "The poster looks nice outside, doesn't it?"

301

Mrs. Newman's smile broadens. "Definitely! I've been telling your dad you have a future as an illustrator."

I gulp. "Really? What did he say?"

"He just smiled."

I take that as a positive sign. Mrs. Newman walks away, muttering "Delicious" as she eats her ice cream.

There's a lull in hungry students, and I look up. The gym is full of kids and parents, plus most of our teachers. Mrs. Kluck and Mama are standing side by side near the Poland table, trying to chat. I can tell by Mama's rigid backbone that the conversation is uncomfortable, but at least they're talking.

Elizabeth wipes her hands with a towel and shivers. "Remind me never to serve this much ice cream without wearing gloves again."

"Remind me never to take part in food competitions again," I reply, eyeing the line in front of Maddy and Stephanie's table. It's about fifteen kids deep, and at least half of those kids are back for seconds.

Elizabeth waves away my concern. "So what? They made scones. Big deal."

"Wah!" Baba walks over with his mouth full and a plate of scones for both of us. "You girls have to try this. Mazedaar! It's out of this world."

I give him a dirty look, but we each take one scone anyway. We bite into them together, as if ingesting an enemy's secret poison. Baba's right. It's creamy raspberry mixed with a familiar taste I can't put my finger on. "Ginger?" I ask nobody in particular.

Elizabeth nods. "With a hint of cinnamon."

"Genius," I whisper.

Baba's already walking back to the England table. "I should get another one, for your mama," he tells us. "I don't think they will last long."

Elizabeth gives me an unnecessarily bright smile. "Forget the scones. Our ice cream is much more original."

"Uh-huh."

She smacks her forehead. "I totally forgot! Are you wearing it?"

I finger the zipper on my cardigan. It's maroon and very plain, worn over a faded pair of jeans as if tonight is an ordinary winter night. "I don't know . . ."

She sighs loudly. "Come on, don't be afraid! It's going to be fine."

"What's going to be fine?"

I whirl around. Mama is standing behind us, looking highly interested. Elizabeth pushes me forward. I glare at her, then pull the zipper open and face Mama. I'm wearing a gray T-shirt with the logo I designed hand-drawn in fabric marker. Front and center, it reads: HAMEED'S KITCHEN. I watch her carefully, one hand still gripping the zipper in case I need to pull it up quickly. Her face turns from blank to confused to stunned. I may stop breathing, but I'm not sure. One-Mississippi, two-Mississippi, three-Mississippi.

She smiles and squeals, "Sara, this is amazing! Did you design this?"

Elizabeth gives me an *I told you so* look. I nod quickly, not sure of what to say. "I thought you should have a logo to promote your business. Stephanie gave me the idea," I admit.

She leans closer and kisses me. "Is that what you were working on in your sketchbook?"

I nod, her kiss making me embarrassed but also weirdly happy. "It started as an art project, but it's something I think you can use."

Elizabeth adds, "Sara has lots of cool ideas for your business, Mrs. H. You should listen to her."

"I don't know what to say. You girls are always surprising me."

The microphone crackles to life above our heads. It's Principal Harrison. "Students, please get your entries ready for the first-ever Poplar Springs showcase! Our judges are Mrs. Kluckowski, myself, and the esteemed Chef Morgan from *Let's Get Cooking!*"

Everyone claps and cheers madly. I'm more nervous than excited as the judges come around to the tables, sampling foods and making notes on their clipboards with serious faces. Mama nods enthusiastically at all her girls, even Maddy and Stephanie. When the judges reach their table, they spend several minutes chewing and nodding.

Then they're at our table. Elizabeth makes fresh bowls of ice cream for them to try, taking care with the coconut and pistachio toppings.

The judges take dainty bites and jot down notes. Mrs. Kluck looks like she can't believe what she's eating. "This is actually very good," she tells me, as if I've committed a crime.

"Thank you," Elizabeth answers for both of us.

I peek at Chef Morgan's clipboard. His writing is atrocious. "Good effort," he tells me, and the trio moves to the next table.

Good effort? That's it? Who does he think he is? I suddenly feel hot. I look around for an escape route. Elizabeth's mom comes up to talk to her, and I slip away. I leave the gym with its bright lights and noise, and sit on the floor in the empty hallway.

"What are you doing out here?" It's Rabia, dressed in a purple puffy jacket, jeans, and a matching purple hijab. She unzips her jacket and sits down beside me, leaning her shoulder against mine.

I put my hand on my chest to stop my heart from racing. Rabia at Poplar Springs Middle is a sight I never thought I'd see. "I could ask you the same question."

"Your mama told my mama all about this brand-new ice cream you cooked up, so I convinced her to bring me. She's parking the car."

"It's no big deal."

She puts a hand on my knee. "You're always too modest."

305

"I don't think we're going to win. I wanted that TV spot. I was going to wear my Hameed's Kitchen shirt." I unzip my sweater again and show her the logo.

"Who cares? You tried your best." She looks around. "Where are your brothers? I haven't seen those munchkins in forever."

I shudder at the thought of Rafey and Tariq running loose in my school's hallway. "Elizabeth's older brother, David, is babysitting all three boys: the twins and Elizabeth's younger brother, too. They're going to make popcorn and watch super-hero movies."

She stands and pulls me up with her. "That reminds me. I'm starving."

We get back to the Pakistan table as Chef Morgan is announcing the winning recipe. I stand with Elizabeth on one side and Rabia on the other, holding hands like some sappy team on *America's Got Talent*. "After much deliberation, we have decided that the prize goes to Maddy Montgomery and Stephanie Tolleson for their Raspberry Ginger Scones!"

Everyone claps. I let go of Rabia and Elizabeth's hands and slowly applaud. Rabia reaches over and says, "I'm still proud of you," and I blink away sudden tears.

Maddy and Stephanie are screaming like lunatics, hands on their cheeks. They scramble to the podium and shake hands with the judges. Then the microphone bursts into life again. Chef Morgan looks straight at me and announces, "Also, we'd like to award honorable mention to Sara Hameed and Elizabeth

Shainmark, for the most inventive recipe. Your fusion ice cream has potential."

Elizabeth gasps and hugs me. Then Rabia hugs me too. I'm crushed between them and I can't breathe, but it's a good feeling.

"Thank you, Chef Morgan." Principal Harrison takes the microphone and looks around. "Time for some acknowledgments."

The entire gym groans.

He holds up his hand. "Thank you to the volunteers and teachers who worked so hard to make this event a success. And a special thank-you to parent Hina Hameed, who's taken charge of our afterschool cooking club and prepared our students for this showcase. I've had the pleasure of tasting some of Mrs. Hameed's cooking, and let me tell you, it's delicious!"

Mama is beaming so proudly, I think her jaw might break. I reach over and hug her. "He's right, Mama," I say. "You're an amazing cook. *Shaandaar!*"

She hugs me back, then faces the crowd of parents forming a line for samples of her food. "Take a flyer, please. My daughter designed it," she tells everyone.

Someone taps me on the shoulder. "Congrats." It's Maddy, with Stephanie standing behind her, all grins.

"Thank you," I reply, and the smile that comes to my lips surprises me. "Congrats to you and Stephanie, too."

I want to be mad at Miss Perfect, but I can't. She's nicer than I'd ever imagined she'd be. And an awesome baker.

307

Maddy bites her bottom lip. "Listen, I want to tell you I'm sorry about what I said at the mall. It was horrible of me."

I can't believe she's doing this now, in her moment of triumph. I look down at my palms, noticing the pattern of lines. "It's okay."

"My parents wouldn't come today," Maddy continues, her tone low. "They said our school shouldn't celebrate foreigners and their food."

I'm not sure why she's telling me this, but Stephanie's nodding along, so I say, "That's too bad. Foreign food can be pretty good."

She gives me a proud look. "That's exactly what I told them. We shouldn't judge food until we try it. Just because it's different doesn't mean it's less delicious. Same goes for people."

"You said that? To your dad?" Ever since Elizabeth told me Mr. Montgomery's nickname, I can't help but picture him as a truck with a narrow, expressionless grill plastered on its front. I'm amazed that Maddy stood up to him.

She nods. "He was pretty shocked."

I lean forward and touch her arm. "I forgive you."

She lets out a breath with a whoosh. "Can we be friends? I don't want to fight anymore."

I look up to see them all watching me, Mama, Baba, Elizabeth and her mother, even Rabia. Waiting for me to decide how I want to live the rest of sixth grade. Maybe all of middle school. "Yes, I think we can do that," I finally reply.

34

Elizabeth

OUR MOMS' CITIZENSHIP CEREMONY is on a school day, but we all get permission to go—David, me, and Justin, Sara, Tariq, and Rafey. It's the perfect opportunity for me to break out the red, white, and blue outfit I wore on Election Day. Sara is wearing jeans and a blue-and-white tunic with lace on the neckline. We make a big group at the local community college, all of us kids, Mr. Hameed, and Dad, who took a personal day off from work. Even Bubbe is here, wearing a navy-blue poncho and a red silk scarf.

We sit in the theater and wave small American flags. There are tons of other families who came to support their moms, dads, grandmas, brothers, and friends. Nearly fifty people become citizens. We all rise to say the Pledge of Allegiance together in one loud voice that swells and echoes around us. The judge tells us that the new citizens on the stage represent more than thirty nations. She reads the names of every single country. Sara and I cheer when the judge calls out "the United Kingdom" and again when she says "Pakistan."

"You are a mosaic of people from all around the world," the judge says. "You are adding color to that mosaic, sharing your traditions, your art, your food. Especially your food." Everyone in the audience laughs. "As you become U.S. citizens, don't lose who you are. Our differences are what make America great." There's lots of hugging and balloons and so many pictures! Some people cry. David records it all on Mom's phone so Aunt Louise can watch.

That night is our big party. Sara and I spend the afternoon with Bubbe in the kitchen. Mom and Mrs. Hameed are not allowed to help, since they are the guests of honor, but we give little jobs to Justin, Rafey, and Tariq—setting places at the table and mashing potatoes for samosas. Bubbe's going to supervise the frying.

"That was us, a few months ago," I tell Sara as we watch our brothers get a little too enthusiastic with the potato masher. "Do you still hate cooking?"

"Not as much," Sara admits. "I still don't like that our house always smells like onions and spices, or that Mama runs her catering business out of our kitchen." Sara chatters on, nothing like the unfriendly girl I met three months ago. "We have so many orders since the festival. I'm glad your mom is helping. Mama needs someone to keep track of everything so she can focus on cooking."

It's the perfect job for my mom. She set up spreadsheets and trackers, and even made Mrs. Hameed a shopping list so she simply checks off the items she needs to restock. It's only a few hours a week, but having a job makes Mom happy. And her pay, at least for now, is free dinners a few times a week. Even my brothers have to admit that Mrs. Hameed's food is better than Hot Pockets.

Sara says, "I can see how some people think that cooking is fun."

"Like when you get to make an ice cream machine out of a bicycle?"

"Or like making Mrs. Kluck's clumpy strawberry jam in FACS class," Sara teases. "That sounds super fun."

"Ugh! Don't remind me." When the second semester of sixth grade starts later this month, I'm taking FACS with the plaid tyrant. "Good old Mrs. Kluck," I say. "What if I sneak some ground coriander into my jam?"

Sara puts on her mock-serious face. The one that reminds me of Mrs. Hameed scolding our class. "You'd better be a model student," she warns me. "Mrs. Kluck will have her eye on you."

I wish Sara were taking FACS with me. I'm going to miss having her as my kitchen partner. But she got special permission to take an extra semester of art. Mrs. Newman is helping her put together a portfolio so she can apply to a summer art program. And Sara's been sharing her awesome design skills with our friends, like Stephanie, who begged Sara for a complete redo of her cupcake logo.

As I roll out dough, I run through the list of treats Sara and I are making for the party. Samosas and other finger foods, cupcakes frosted like flags, and of course our Halwa Cuppa Tea ice cream.

I wanted to invite the whole cooking club to the party, including Maddy and Steph, but Mom said the townhouse would have enough people in it without eight extra middle-schoolers piling into our kitchen. Plus, it's a school night.

I wouldn't have minded the crowd. I've figured out that I'm a lot like Bubbe. I love baking, and dressing in loud colors, and being at school, where there are tons of kids and there's always something going on. Sara is more like my mom, only instead of knitting when she gets overwhelmed, Sara has her sketchbook.

We have a surprise for Sara's mom tonight. Mom took me and Sara to the print shop and had food labels made that say HAMEED'S KITCHEN in brown swirls that begin as steam and transform into henna designs. We wrap the labels in a little box with a bow on top. Sara draws multicolored patterns on it. That girl will draw on anything.

Because they are the tallest, Dad and David hang red, white, and blue streamers all around the townhouse. It's like celebrating Fourth of July in January.

When we're done cooking and it's time to put out the food, Sara puts a hand on my arm. "I never thanked you." She says it so quietly, I lean over the tray of cookies I'm holding to hear her.

"Thanked me for what?"

She pulls at the sleeve of her tunic. "For being my friend."

"You did the same for me," I tell her.

312

I told Maddy that starting Poplar Springs Middle was tough for Sara, but the truth is, it was hard for me, too. I was so worried about Mom, and sad about losing Nan, that I didn't know who I wanted to be in middle school. Sara reminded me that I'm goofy and I love trying new things, especially in the kitchen. I needed Sara as much as she needed me.

I expect Sara to cringe, because I'm being totally sappy, but she nods. "I think you're right."

Then we walk out of the kitchen carrying trays of our families' favorite foods, ready to start the celebration.

Halwa Cuppa Tea

Earl Grey Tea Ice Cream with Chunks of Doodh Ka Halwa

There are two stages to Elizabeth and Sara's recipe: preparing the halwa and making the ice cream. Doodh Ka Halwa takes time to cook and set, so you may want to make it a day ahead. It will keep in the refrigerator for several days.

NOTE: This recipe requires the use of a stove and hot liquids. Make sure an adult is supervising, especially if you have not used a stove on your own before.

Doodh Ka Halwa

Halwa is a group of dense, sweet confections eaten in South Asia, the Middle East, and other parts of the world. There are several different types of halwa, such as carrot, lentil, or nut. A variety of bases are used to create halwa, such as semolina, milk, or butter. The base determines its consistency, which ranges from pudding to cake. This is a milk-based halwa. It will be the consistency of a thick porridge after heating, but once it's chilled for several hours, it will resemble a soft bar like a brownie.

COOKING TIME: 1–2 hours

CHILLING TIME: 4 hours +

SERVINGS: 2 cups

This makes more than you'll need for the ice cream recipe. Cut the leftover halwa into squares and enjoy!

INGREDIENTS:

1 tablespoon water, more as needed

1 teaspoon freshly squeezed lemon juice, more as needed

8 cups (2 quarts) whole milk

½ cup sugar, more depending on desired sweetness

2 tablespoons ghee (clarified butter), plus more for greasing pan

½ teaspoon ground cardamom

½ cup unsweetened shredded coconut

½ cup pistachios, finely chopped

PREPARATION:

1. Grease a 13x9-inch (3 quart) brownie pan with ghee and set aside.

2. Combine water and lemon juice and set aside.

3. Pour the milk into a large saucepan, keeping in mind it will bubble up the side. The wider your pan, the shorter the cooking time will be. Bring the milk to a boil over medium-high heat, stirring constantly with a wooden spoon to keep it from burning, until it is reduced by half, approximately 30

minutes. Adjust the heat as needed to keep the milk from boiling over.

4. Stir the water and lemon juice into the milk until the mixture starts to curdle (it will form soft solids on your spoon). If it doesn't curdle, add more water and lemon juice until you see curds. Continue stirring over medium-low heat until the mixture is the consistency of soft scrambled eggs, about 25 to 30 minutes.

5. A few tablespoons at a time, stir in the sugar. Add the ghee and cardamom. Turn the heat down to low, and stir until the mixture comes away from the side of the pan. Remove from the heat and mix in the coconut and pistachios.

6. Transfer the mixture into the prepared brownie pan. Using a spatula, press the halwa flat. Cover and chill it in the refrigerator for at least 4 hours, and up to overnight. Cut the halwa into gumdrop-size chunks and refrigerate until ready to use.

Earl Grey Ice Cream

NOTE: You can make Earl Grey ice cream using any vanilla ice cream recipe. Simply steep Earl Grey tea bags in the milk or cream until the tea flavor is to your liking.

COOKING TIME: 30 minutes
CHILLING TIME: 1 hour
SERVINGS: About 8 half cups

INGREDIENTS:

2 cups whole milk

½ cup heavy cream

7 Earl Grey tea bags

5 egg yolks

⅓ cup honey or ½ cup sugar

¼ teaspoon vanilla extract

1 cup Doodh Ka Halwa chunks (page 315)

SPECIAL TOOLS:

Ice cream maker

PREPARATION:

1. Pour the milk and cream into a large saucepan. Stirring constantly so it doesn't burn, bring the milk mixture to a boil over medium-high heat.

2. Remove the saucepan from the heat and place the Earl Grey tea bags in the milk mixture. Cover and steep the tea for 5 minutes. Remove the tea bags and discard them.

3. In a medium bowl, whisk together the egg yolks and honey or sugar.

4. The next step is called *tempering*. This is a method used to combine the heated milk with the egg mixture to make a custard—without scrambling the eggs! Slowly add a small amount of the hot milk, about ¼ cup, to the eggs, whisking gently. Once the milk is incorporated, add another ¼ cup of

milk to the eggs. When at least half of the milk has been added to the eggs, pour the custard back into the saucepan.

5. Add the vanilla.

6. Over medium heat, stir constantly without letting the mixture boil, until the custard passes the spoon test: Dip a spoon into the hot liquid. Using a fingertip, carefully draw a line across the back of the spoon. If the line through the custard stays, it is ready.

7. Take the saucepan off the heat and let it cool.

8. When the custard is at room temperature, place it in the refrigerator to chill for at least an hour before churning.

CHURNING:

1. Using the chilled custard, follow the instructions on your ice cream maker. When the ice cream has thickened to milkshake consistency, stir in the halwa chunks. Continue to churn until the ice cream is semi-solid.

2. Enjoy right away or freeze until the ice cream is firm enough to scoop.

For additional recipes, please visit
www.saadiafaruqi.com **or** www.laurashovan.com.

Authors' Notes & Acknowledgments

Laura Shovan

This book began with a question: What does it mean to be an American when your parent is not one?

Growing up, I often felt the way many bicultural children do. The mannerisms, habits, love of tea and *Doctor Who* I'd picked up from my British family made me a bit of an oddball in New Jersey. Yet, I wasn't quite at home in England either, where my brothers and I were jokingly referred to as *Yanks*.

I began to form an answer to the question of my Americanness when my wonderful agent, Stephen Barbara, suggested writing a collaborative novel. (Thanks, as always, for the great advice, Stephen!) Right away I knew which author I'd reach out to—my friend Saadia Faruqi, whose work as a writer and interfaith activist I admired.

It is my great good luck that Saadia accepted the invitation to write this book together. The candid conversations we had about race, immigration, food, mental health, and families are woven into Sara and Elizabeth's story. Without Saadia's encouragement, I would have been less brave about examining my own life as the child of an immigrant. Saadia's agent, Kari Sutherland, gave us wonderful early feedback on each draft.

There are commonalities among first generation Americans, but our experiences differ widely depending on our culture of origin, legal status in this country, and whether we are refugees or chose to start a new life in the United States. I interviewed many new citizens and first generation "kids" for *A Place at the Table*. Liz Dunster, Marc Liu, Samantha M. Clark, Christina Soontornvat, and Laura Yoo's insights and openness enriched this story.

Huge thanks to Nikki McGowan and the young chefs at Dunloggin Middle School's cooking club. It was informative and fun to sit in on your class. Plus, I got to eat homemade spaetzle.

I am indebted to several readers for their feedback. To the ladies of the MG All Stars critique group—Margaret Dilloway, Karina Glaser, Leah Henderson, Janet Sumner Johnson, Casey Lyall, Ki-Wing Merlin, Timanda Wertz—I know you have my back. Thanks to the following authors and educators for their reads on specific content: Carole Lindstrom, Naomi Milliner, and Aliza Werner.

Our editor, Jennifer Greene, has loved this novel and trusted me and Saadia to do our best with it all along. That has been a real gift. We appreciate you, Jennifer. Thanks to the entire team at Clarion Books especially Anne Hoppe, Amanda

322

Acevedo, and Samantha Brown for making us feel like part of the HMH family.

This book is about family, and I couldn't have written it without mine. My brothers Rex and Jason Dickson continue to be important people in my life. Special thanks to Jay for reading drafts of all my books. My parents, Franklyn and Pauline Dickson, have been stalwart supporters of my writing since I was small. It was my mother who taught me that making art is a necessary part of life, and for that I am forever grateful.

Saadia Faruqi

This book has been a labor of love for me. One doesn't easily begin an endeavor that will showcase the ugly side of immigrant and first-generation life. A big thank-you to my partner in crime Laura Shovan for encouraging those stories and feelings, for those long conversations and shared experiences. I thought the end product would only be a book, but it resulted in an amazing friendship as well.

If we're being honest, when Laura first approached me with the idea for a dual narrative immigrant friendship story, I didn't think it would make for a great book. Who wants to read about the everyday trials and tribulations of newcomers to the U.S.? In my own culture, we tend to gloss over the challenges first generation kids face because they are so lucky to be here. Their lives are seen as blessed due to the sacrifices of their parents and grandparents. If they talk about their challenges—what kids say to them at school or how they feel disconnected from their own culture—they are called ungrateful. But at the same time, these were issues I realized my own children dealt with every day. So I decided to take a leap of faith and write about that.

There's a lot of food in this book, but in case anyone is wondering, I am not a cook. I do love biryani like Sara does, but I cannot make it. Thank you to all the immigrant Pakistani women who cater for people like me. This book is a love letter to Pakistani food.

Overall, this book has been such a tremendous team effort, and a big thank-you goes to our agents Kari Sutherland and Stephen Barbara for guiding us so gently and happily through the process. There were a lot of cooks in this kitchen but we didn't spoil the food, I think. I'm grateful to our editor Jennifer Greene and the entire HMH/Clarion team especially Amanda Acevedo and Sammy Brown, who've been so supportive throughout. A big thank-you to our cover illustrator Anoosha Syed and designer Sharismar Rodriguez, who have brought so many themes in the book to gorgeous light through their art. And of course, thank you to the many writing friends who critiqued our pages and gave incredibly helpful feedback. This book is the result of so much hard work by so many people.

Thank you to my family—Nasir, Mubashir, and Mariam—

who take up the responsibility of our everyday affairs while I hide in my office to write. I can see how proud you are of me, and I never want to let you down. Thank you to Ammi for always being encouraging and excited about my work and shouting it from the rooftops. Finally, thank you to my extended desi family who never once asked why I'm a writer instead of a doctor.